Around the Horn

By

Peter Barbour

Bloomington, IN  Milton Keynes, UK

authorHOUSE™

AuthorHouse™
1663 Liberty Drive, Suite 200
Bloomington, IN 47403
www.authorhouse.com
Phone: 1-800-839-8640

AuthorHouse™ UK Ltd.
500 Avebury Boulevard
Central Milton Keynes, MK9 2BE
www.authorhouse.co.uk
Phone: 08001974150

First published by AuthorHouse   3/9/2006

ISBN: 1-4259-1168-4 (sc)
ISBN: 1-4259-1167-6 (dj)

Library of Congress Control Number: 2006900035

Printed in the United States of America
Bloomington, Indiana

This book is printed on acid-free paper.

Contact: Peter Barbour
at pbnam@aol.com

For all of their love and support

I dedicate this novel to my parents

AROUND THE HORN

CHAPTER ONE

My name is Mickey Charles. I recently turned fifty-three, and noticed that middle age had a firm grip on me. The ridiculous emotion of losing something beyond my control, a condition one can hardly escape like hair falling out in the shower, had become a daily entertainment. Watching these changes as I aged, made it clear why I sometimes dreamt up fantasies to face reality. I recently became a bachelor again, and found myself in a restless state of mind that was void of peace. To get over my emotional doldrums, I tried to find sanctuary through my work.

For the past twenty-five years, I lived in the Hollywood Hills working as a 'Hyphenate'. That is, I was a Producer-Writer-Editor, and like a chameleon, I changed into that part of myself that was best suited for the moment. But, this time around, I was suffering from a broken bond with a woman that I had expected to be with for the rest of my life. I was lost, and no amount of work was going to do the trick. So, I chose to take a sabbatical in Austin. My timing couldn't have been better as I learned soon after my arrival that my old friends and classmates would be celebrating our thirty-fifth high school reunion at a local party house that evening.

Every time I returned to the home of my childhood, memories flooded my brain like a Hill Country rain overflowing the creeks of Central Texas. I grew up in Austin, and out of childhood and adolescence. I was fond of the

1

old Austin, the one we enjoyed as a small town; the one we thought would never change. Unfortunately, we witnessed it succumb to personal greed and corporate cultivation, the victim of those who explored, exploited and exploded. Despite the seemingly uncontrollable growth of my hometown, and the urban problems that accompanied such phenomena, I still found solace in my old neighborhood of Tarrytown, which it seemed had stayed the same. I was free to wander there, free to relive my memories, and this brought my restless mind a little peace.

As I sat rocking on the back deck of my parent's townhouse, I took a deep breath and my senses filled with the distant, familiar childhood scent of spring. I smelled the freshly cut grass, the wildflowers in full bloom, and looking down, I saw memories from my youth reflected in the sliver of water that was the creek. Soon after I left Austin in the Seventies, my folks moved a few blocks away from my boyhood home, to a new street cut through the woods behind our former house. They moved into a more manageable townhouse free of the toil associated with the large home and the expansive yard where I spent my formative years. This new vantage point was near my most prized possession as a child: The Clearing.

It was in the woods of Tarrytown where the seeds of my forest of imagination were sown, took root, and grew like the aging oak trees off of my parents' back porch. Sitting on their deck, I soaked in the early morning sun streaking through the leaves of the oaks and elms, and I easily recalled my experiences in the woods of my youth. So many restless days were spent as cowboys and Indians, exploring and rock collecting, playing strip poker with neighborhood kids, cooking hot dogs on the barbecue pit of our hidden fort, and dreaming of what we might become. Mostly, I recalled the laughter with my friends while we passed through another day of childhood, free as we were of adult responsibilities.

I descended the outside stairs and opened a door that led beneath the house. A smile emerged, for the storage room contained items from my youth such as the extra-long single bed and small pine desk that I used until I graduated from Austin High. I also saw memorabilia of my brothers' past. My mother's attempt, I assumed, to hold on to the great feelings we had as a family sharing love, friends, and good times.

In summer, if we weren't water skiing or tubing on the lake, my brothers and our friends were usually playing a game we called "cork ball" in our front yard. It was an ingenious game invented by an unknown kid whose combined passions for elementary school playground bombardment and America's pastime came together in one brilliant moment. The game used the rules of baseball with one critical exception: You could throw at, and hit the runner to get him out. We taped a whiffle ball to cover the holes so it became a "corked" ball, and using an oversized soft plastic bat we could hit it a surprising distance. However, because the ball was taped, and correspondingly heavier, it stung like a wasp when it blasted bare skin. We used to play almost every afternoon until the multitude of fireflies lit the landscape in the warm evening air.

Local neighborhood girls occasionally visited and we retired to our backyard where we listened to the music of Little Richard, Buddy Holly, or Chubby Checker. Their magical sounds blasted from our first hi-fi speakers that were perched in the playroom's open second story window. We spent more hours than I could count learning to twist or jerk in the process of discovering rhythm.

The autumn brought the urge for football in our yard, or across the street at my friend Jack's larger more perfect Pop Warner-sized backyard. From two-on-two to five-on-five, we could play for hours without a break. And, talk about your beautiful weather. From late September through Thanksgiving in the Texas Hill Country, the weather is just short of perfection.

As autumn turned into winter, my daily desires fell to the two loves of my early life: basketball and movies. Our neighbors' paddle tennis court, which had a wooden backboard and hoop at one end, became my playground as I spent hours trying to copy the moves of Sam Jones, Cousy, Russell, or one of my other heroes of the hard court. I remember the alarm inside my head going off a little before seven a.m. every weekend. I would leap from bed already in my sweatpants, throw on a T-shirt, grab my basketball, and run out to practice dribbling between my legs. As an adult looking back, I'm amazed at the patience of our neighbors and my parents, who allowed me to awaken them so early every Saturday and Sunday while I worked on my dream.

Sometimes those weekends were too cold to play outside, which led me to discover the movies. Sitting in the dark Paramount Theater on Congress Avenue, I was able to lose myself among characters of the late Fifties and early Sixties. Unknown to me at the time, my childhood dream of making a last second basket at the buzzer would be replaced by an adult nightmare of trying to complete a film the day before its release date.

Finally, every spring, came the smell of cut grass, the crack of the bat, the smooth sailing curve ball just out of range for my friends, the cotton candy, and the pretty girls in the stands. My third childhood love had to be baseball. Our national pastime, a metaphor for life and my industry of filmmaking, where an individual can shine independently of others but, eventually, is only as successful as the collaborators or teammates he or she works with every day.

I continued to rummage around the room, looking for memories, when I opened the aging desk drawer. To my delight, I spotted my commemorative 1962 World Series cap. I flipped it over and on the underside of the bill was an autograph from my hero, Mickey Mantle. Reflecting on the moment he signed it produced a smile, goose bumps, and a shiver.

I set aside the cap and picked up my seventh grade junior high school yearbook. Flipping to the back I saw hand-written notes from classmates wishing me the best of luck in the summer:

To MC…You're the best. Just the best. Hope to see you this
    summer.

Stay cool. Love, Becky.

To The Mick…This was really a great, great, great, great
    year.

Let's hope next year tops it, what do you say? See ya on the
    lake. Danny.

Dear Mickey… 2 good 2 be 4 gotten. Love, Amy.

What a hoot junior high was. It's hard to imagine a better time in my life. You see, I was at the top of my game; my glory years came earlier for me than for other hopeful athletes. In seventh grade I could out pitch my peers in baseball, and could dribble, pass, and shoot better than all of them in basketball, excepting my aforementioned friend, Jack, who lived across the street. Jack developed early, and in my defense, it's unfair to compare me to someone who was taller than our first grade teacher.

Underneath the yearbook, I saw a three-ring notebook and opened it to reveal assigned writings from my earliest years. The first paper I picked up was entitled "THE COMMERCE COMET, A STUDY IN COURAGE," a story I wrote about my hero when I was twelve years old. I was proud to see I had gotten an "A."

I was born when Mickey Charles Mantle was a rookie. My father's name was Russell Charles, and he was a huge Yankee fan. After some insistence, I guess my mother thought it would be all right to give me the moniker of my Dad's favorite ballplayer, since my two older brothers, David and Larry, were named for a Biblical figure and a family member on her side.

Opening the second drawer of the desk, I found a photograph of my 1962 Little League All-Star team. Picking it up, I glanced at the guys with whom I spent most of my youth. There's Danny, still my closest friend among the group. I still see him from time to time; he's a doctor for the San Diego Chargers, so we get together every once and awhile on the West Coast. Next to Danny is Jack, who at age twelve, looked almost six-feet tall, and towered over the rest of us. Jack was a great all around athlete when he was young. He lettered in four sports in high school, but I'm sure he would have shined in baseball, if he had not been distracted by the fact he was so good at all of the others. Next to Jack was Stan, my first friend in Austin. I met him a month after my father died and we had moved to Austin from the small south Texas village of Pleasanton. Stan took over his father's paint and lacquer company in his twenties and expanded it to locations in several other cities. He lived around the corner from me and I bet we played as much one-on-one basketball as any other two boys in the country. The next in line is Dave; his father Judge Looney was one of the coaches in our league. Dave was the second fastest All-Star and had a sixth sense when it came to base running. In fact, I heard he's still running, but then that's another story and one I'm afraid the old Judge wouldn't want to hear. On the other side of Dave Looney was William, a guy that everyone called Billy. Billy recently retired from his job with the State of Texas General Land Office where he worked as a geologist. I seem to remember Billy hitting .530 as a twelve-year-old, which normally would have won a batting crown. The only reason he didn't win it was the boy next to him in the picture, my first black friend, Willie. I lost touch with Willie and don't know what became of him, but he was a great ball player and had all the tools.

After placing the photograph on the desk, I saw my old baseball glove on the floor in the corner of the room. I picked it up and immediately headed for the woods like I was a kid again. Walking down the rocky creek bed with the small trickle of water here and there, I listened to the gray squirrels playing tag in the trees high above me. I was looking for a particular spot that led down the hidden trail to The Clearing. Everything looked different with time, but suddenly I recognized the old oak stump that I positioned to block the entrance to my secret place. Climbing up from the creek, I grabbed the stump and pulled myself up to what used to be my secret trail, completely grown over with weeds. Using my mitt as protection from the poison ivy, I slowly proceeded a few yards toward my destination.

When I was ten years old, I took my family's ax and pruning shears and cleared an area seventy-five feet long and five feet wide. At the far end of what I had named The Clearing, stood an ancient oak I called the "Catcher." Still nailed to the Catcher was my old target, an aluminum trash can lid with a carpet attached to its exposed side. It sits roughly in the strike zone, two feet from the ground at the bottom, and rises to a twelve-year-old's armpit at the top. A few feet in front of me was a small mound I had fashioned out of gravel and sand. I noticed the ground had cracked and weeds camouflaged it, but in the center of the mound, I still saw my rubber. Utilizing my grandfather's workshop, my brother and I built the pitching rubber from a two by four, which I half-buried at the proper elevation on the mound. It was positioned the precise Little League distance from my Catcher, and was secured with cement and mud.

As a kid I remember using a basket of baseballs. I threw diligently to my Catcher until I had thrown eighty pitches, testing new ones or just trying to perfect the curve. I originally hung netting around the tree, so errant pitches wouldn't disappear into the brush. It took me many years as a batboy to collect the dozens of old balls I found. They were precious like Easter eggs, and I remember many sojourns outside the Little League fence in the weeds and woods searching for the forgotten balls. I never wanted to lose even one.

Standing on my old mound with my adult size gave me the sensation of being a giant. I picked up a rock about the size of a baseball and tossed it up and down with my right hand. I toed the old rubber like I did in yesteryear. I concentrated on the weathered target. Slowly starting my windup, I pivoted and kicked my leg toward an imaginary left field and let the rock go in a blistering arch toward my Catcher. I followed the rock's trajectory over the weed-covered path and I was transported back to my childhood.

****

The ball hit the carpeted lid with a thud, dead solid center. Standing at the other end of The Clearing, I was a twelve-year-old dreamer reaching down toward my basket of balls next to the freshly raked pitching mound. Searching for an optimum ball, I rattled off an imitation of long time New York Yankee announcer, Mel Allen.

"Whitey Ford has worked a full-count on Orlando Cepeda, three balls, two strikes, two outs. The tying run, Willie Mays, is on second and the winning run, Willie McCovey, takes a large lead off of first. The crowd's going crazy. It's the bottom of the ninth in the seventh game of the World Series with the Yankees leading one to nothing on Mickey Mantle's towering home run in the top of the inning. Until Mays' two-out double and an intentional walk to McCovey, Whitey had given up only one hit and set down twenty-four of twenty-six batters faced."

Satisfied I had selected the optimum ball, I approached the mound. Leaning down and picking up the resin bag, I shook it a few times loosely in my right hand. Stepping up to the mound, I focused on the target nailed to the oak tree, all the while continuing my announcer-like diatribe, "All of the pressure in the world is riding on the able, strong arm of the southpaw Ford. Hold on to your hats, folks, this is going to be an historic moment in the annals of this, the oldest and greatest American game."

Even though I was right handed, I always pretended to be my favorite pitcher, the great lefty on the Yankees. I eyed the target and nodded at the sign from my Catcher. I toed the mound, started into the windup, cocked my arm behind my ear, and broke one off of the shoulder of the imaginary Cepeda. As the ball broke down at a radical forty-five degree angle, it landed with a thud in the bottom left corner of the target. I jumped into the air, screaming, "That's it, folks! The Yankees have won the World Series! The Yankees have won the World Series! The Yankees have won the World Series!"

Running toward my Catcher, and I jumped up and hugged the old oak, digging my cleats into the bark for a foothold. The act was reminiscent of Yogi Berra's leap onto Don Larsen six years before, after the improbable, yet most famous World Series event ever: The perfect game. After the excitement of the moment, I looked around inside the netting and spotted about forty baseballs. Some of them were torn on the laces and a couple of balls had horsehide flaps where the stitches had broken. However, a little sorting produced some lively, newer balls, found on my most recent escapade into the woods outside Bishop Field.

I picked up the balls and focused on a task I had to perform before I went home to do my homework. Every day I stayed until I threw three strikes in a row. I had learned that skill test from my basketball practices with the church team the year before. As our coach, the pastor told us we could go home after we made five consecutive free throws. It struck me as good practice for whatever sports I eventually pursued. The coach always said, "Repeating skills leads to confidence. You always want to go on your way feeling confident about yourself."

I toed the rubber, started my windup, and released the first pitch, which hit the target. A second pitch launched and thudded into the orange-carpeted lid nailed to the Catcher. One more strike to go. I eyed the target, concentrating, and focusing like a pitching machine. I took a deep breath and fluidly rocked my arms. Bringing them together over my head, I lifted the left leg high. Then, pivoting on my right foot, my eye never left the target as I cocked my right hand behind my ear and pushed off hard and launched the ball toward the Catcher. It flew directly at the target as a flash of motion exploded into the netting in the shape of a kid. The streaking youngster tripped into the net, stumbled across the plate, and was struck in the temple with the ball.

I saw his body fall limp into the netting at the other end of The Clearing. He fell in a frighteningly similar manner as a man who got shot by a rifle.

"Oh my God, I killed him," I thought out loud as I ran for the motionless body beside my Catcher.

Surprisingly, I discovered an unconscious black boy about my own age. The victim wore a Giants cap, a dark T-shirt, torn cut-off jeans, and sneakers. I knelt down beside the seemingly slain kid, looked up at the heavens, and screamed, "No! Please, no! I didn't mean it!"

The boy regained consciousness with a growling moan. As his hand reached for the already forming growth above his right eye, he spied me kneeling over him. I was gasping for breath. I didn't understand or even think about it at the moment, but it was one of my first bouts with adrenaline. "Are you all right?" I asked, trying to catch my breath. "I never saw you."

After a moment or two more of moaning, he looked up to me with no small amount of irritation, and said, "Is that all you got? My mama could throw harder than that."

I was speechless. Then he tilted his head back and let go a very restrained belly laugh. This move, however, must have resulted in a flash of pain exploding in his head, because he raised his hand to his swelling bump and stopped laughing immediately.

I helped him sit up and braced him against my Catcher. I looked close at the rising bulge on his forehead. "I'm sorry. You have a whopper on your head."

"I'm gonna have a hell of a bump, ain't I?" he said as he looked around The Clearing.

"What were you running from?" I asked innocently.

The kid stuck his chest out, "What makes you think I was runnin' *from* something? Because I'm a Negro, is that it? All you rich white boys, y'all are all alike."

Stunned by the answer, I sat back from my hurting victim. "Whoa there, hoss. I didn't mean anything. I just wondered why you were running."

"I like to run," he said.

"You're kidding."

9

"It's something no one can keep me from doing. And here in the woods, usually no one sees me, so no one messes with me. Until today," he said, rubbing the bump on his head.

"I'm sorry. Maybe you need to see a doctor?"

The boy responded immediately, "No. Just help me up. I'll be okay."

I gently grabbed his arm and pulled him up to his feet. He looked around gesturing at the surroundings, "What is this place?"

"What does it look like?" I responded indignantly.

The kid picked up a baseball and checked out its scuffmarks. Then he turned and quizzically peered at the tree with the carpeted target. He turned to me while pointing, and said, "Well, I guess this is supposed to be a catcher and that pile over there looks like a mound about Little League distance from the plate. That probably makes you a pitcher and I suppose your pop built this so you could chase his big dreams."

"My daddy's dead," I said simply.

"I'm sorry. I didn't --" he started.

"He died when I was four. A long time ago, before I moved here."

The kid gestured toward the mound and spoke with genuine awe, "So, you did all of this?"

"One of my older brothers helped me with the mound, but I made the clearing," I said with a sense of accomplishment. "I blocked the trail that leads here and my brother had to swear on my father's grave he would never tell anyone about it. And, now, so will you."

"Say what?" he questioned.

"You have to swear with a blood oath."

"No blood sucking is going on around this boy. Anyway, why would I wanna tell anyone about this place?"

"Are you kidding? There're some kids out there who would like nothing more than to destroy all of this -- just for the fun of it. So, I can't take the chance. At least not until the season starts."

"Season?" he asked.

"Little League. Next month."

"Oh."

I reached into my pocket and brought out a small penknife. The kid took a step back like he was going to bolt.

"Hey, it doesn't hurt," I urged. "You can do it yourself. Just prick the end of your finger like this. It's no big deal, and that way I can be sure. It'll make us brothers."

I stuck my index finger with the penknife and squeezed it for a drop of blood. I then handed him the knife.

"Okay, now it's your turn. Then we touch fingers and silently swear on the soul of our favorite ball player. That's all there is to it."

The boy followed my lead, and the next thing I knew, he punctured his finger and pressed it up to mine. We closed our eyes and silently swore to our baseball Gods.

Taking my hand away and opening my eyes, I said, "Now we're blood brothers, which is nearly the same as kin. We are sworn to secrecy and loyalty. Okay?"

Wiping the blood from his finger on his shirt, the kid stuck his hand toward me and said, "Since, we're brothers an' all, you might as well know my name. I'm Willie. Willie Veils."

"I'm Mickey Charles," I said as I shook his hand. "Nice to meet you, Willie."

"I never had a blood brother before," he said, rubbing his swollen head again, "but this ain't any different than with my real brothers. I'm always gettin' hit in the head."

"You have older brothers, too. Mine love to pick at me, you know, rough me up. I guess they think it makes me tough."

Willie laughed, "Heck, mine enjoy the whippings. They love seeing me cry. But, I always got even on the sandlot."

"How old are you?" I asked.

"Eleven. But, I'll be twelve next week."

"I just turned twelve. Do you play Little League?" I asked.

"No, not Little League exactly. We got a team, well, nine players with no uniforms. Sometimes we travel to East Austin and play against local teams over there."

Clarksville, I thought -- he must live in Clarksville.

CHAPTER TWO

After reconstruction in Texas and other Southern states, their cities grew in population. As they did, white populations usually expanded in three directions while the Black/Latino populations would grow in one. In some cases this wasn't true. Some Hispanic or Black populations were too large to corral, as in San Antonio and Houston. In most of the smaller Southern cities or towns, the Black and Hispanic sections were located in the least desirable, most depressed area. The larger, growing white populations were 'protected' by centralized laws that kept the minorities in their place. The other side of the tracks, across the river, the East Side, South Side or any other particular demarcation were designed to limit access for what some misguided souls looked on as inferior parts of humanity.

These locally degrading decisions isolating the races were collectively known as the "Jim Crow laws," named after a black character in a popular folk song from the 1830's. The Jim Crow period, not a result of emancipation as much as reconstruction, dominated life in the South. Decades before civil rights pioneer, Rosa Parks, took her famous seat on the bus, a Creole named Homer Plessy sat himself down in a "WHITES ONLY" rail car in Louisiana on a hot day in 1896, and indefatigably challenged the local laws segregating people in public places. The resulting Supreme Court decision in the case "*Plessy vs. Ferguson*" was to do the ultimate injustice: ruling "separate but equal." Unfortunately, it led to sixty more years of legal decisions in reality, creating separate but never-to-be-equal status for minorities in the South. From decisions like Plessy and others, towns and cities in the South prospered and continued to expand in a segregated manner as set forth by tradition and prejudice which was passed on from generation to generation.

One of the exceptions I learned about in my early years was right in my own hometown of Austin. After the Civil War, the ex-slaves from former Governor Pease's plantation were given land by their ex-owner in a way of keeping them nearby for future paying labor. The freed people formed a black community on the property containing rolling hills and streams, and set up residences on the bluffs overlooking the Colorado River valley. The area was a fertile, green, vital land just right for the pickings of these newly freed laborers and farmers. Forming a new village named Clarksville created all on their own, those former slaves thrived, grew, and always tried to remain independent of nearby Austin.

As the capital city began to grow, East Avenue became the demarcation line -- though it remained unspoken -- to the west of which Negroes and Mexicans were not allowed to purchase land. Austin, it seemed, grew at amazing speeds in its infancy. The first capital of the State, a compressed village, was contained within the limits of East to West Avenues and the Colorado River to Fifteenth Street, just beyond the Capitol building. During the early 1900's and after, Austin grew into a town and soon it started to encroach and engulf the small black community to its West on the bluff overlooking the verdant river valley. After WWII, the town became a city and while it continued to grow it discovered the rolling hills along the Colorado River west of the Negro hamlet of Clarksville to be the most desirable for expansion. Eventually the little village was completely surrounded by the white enclave known as West Austin. Yet, the citizens of Clarksville had to endure several hardships over the years in their fight to keep Austin from devouring their home and forcing them to resettle with their "kind" in East Austin.

Keeping with the Jim Crow policies of its day, early 20th century Austin, through acts of its City Council, deprived the Clarksville residents of city services like schools, street repair, garbage collection, and normal maintenance. However, the small nucleus of survivors from the founding forefathers, after Juneteenth, refused to be driven away from their families' lands. Clarksville survived and after the Supreme Court's decision in 1954's *Brown vs. Board of Education* reversed the half-century old "Plessy" ruling, Austin's city management relented and provided services once again. So by 1962, things were ripe for further changes.

"You live in Clarksville," I stated to Willie as if he didn't know it.

"All my life," he replied.

"My brothers drove me by it on the way to the Babe Ruth Field down by the railroad station. Never knew anyone from Clarksville before. Do you come over here a lot?"

"Over here?" Willie said, looking me up and down. "You mean to rich white Tarrytown?"

"No, actually, I just meant these woods."

"Oh. My mama is a maid at the big pink house up on that hill over there a ways. Sometimes, she brings me to work with her so I can run in these woods down to the lake and take a swim in the lagoon beyond Taylor's slough."

"Did you know that all that Taylor's slough land is owned by our Vice President's wife?"

"Lady Bird," he said with a smile. "I heard that. But, then she's never there to ask her permission and there ain't no houses around, so I just take the chance."

After I finished laughing, I decided to change the subject back to one of my favorites. "So Willie, who is your baseball God?"

"Say what?"

"You know," I said, showing him my bloodstained finger.

"If I tell, does that mean I break our deal?" Willie queried.

"No, no. We're blood brothers, now. We can't hide anything from each other, that's against the rules," I said, actually making it up as I went along.

"Well, then my favorite is number 24, the captain of the San Francisco Giants, the best center--" he started.

Interrupting, I spurted out, "Willie Mays, the 'Say Hey Kid', right?"

"Right on," Willie said with authority. "But, his teammates never call him that, they call him Buck."

"I saw him play at Candlestick Park last summer," I boasted.

"In San Francisco -- really, Mickey?" He asked with a spark in his eye.

"My grandparents took me to the Grand Canyon and Yosemite National Park, which was really neat. Then we drove to San Francisco and saw the Giants play the Dodgers."

"You don't know what I would give to see Willie Mays play live," Willie stated.

"Maybe someday you'll get the chance. Especially, now that there's going be a National League team in Houston."

"Oh yeah, the Colt 45's. But then, it's Houston," Willie stated a little dejectedly. "My Pop said they probably wouldn't let us in to see 'em play."

Not getting what Willie really meant, I said, "Mays was something to watch. He made a basket catch in deep center and threw out the runner trying to go from second to third to end the eighth. Then, he led off the bottom of the ninth with a home run that won the game."

Willie seemed to be forgetting the bump on his head because he excitedly engaged the conversation about his favorite player.

"He's so clutch. He hit four homers in one game, last year. Remember that?"

"Sure, I do," I said. "I think only Lou Gehrig, Gil Hodges and Rocky Colavito had done that before."

"Let me guess who your favorite player is?" he asked.

"Okay, go for it."

"Give me a couple of hints." Willie winked.

"When he was a teenage phenom he was known as the Commerce Comet."

"I got nothing," Willie said.

"Okay, well, he almost had his leg amputated after a football injury in high school because he developed a bone disease called osteomyelitis. And, since he's been in the major leagues, he's had about ten operations." Looking at Willie's blank stare, I continued, "The greatest switch-hitter of all time, number 7--"

"Oh, oh, I know, it's Mickey Mantle. It's Mickey Mantle, right?" Willie asked.

15

"Right on," I said with a sly smile.

"I didn't know he almost had his leg cut off," Willie said.

"If penicillin hadn't been invented a few months before his injury, he would have lost the leg to infection. I wrote a paper on him this year in class," I proudly declared. "I'm kind of an authority on the subject."

Willie smiled, "Sounds like it. You know, if Mantle hadn't gotten injured last year, he might have broken the Babe's record instead of Maris."

"That's what I think, too," I said. Then, there was a moment or two of silence before I asked, "How's your head?"

"It's feeling better but I'm going to have a hell of a bruise."

"You mean, you people bruise?" I asked innocently.

Willie shook his head at me and said, "Of course we bruise. But, it's one of our strengths. We just don't show 'em."

"You feeling good enough for a swim?" I asked.

Willie instantly forgot everything and replied, "Sure."

I dropped my glove and jumped toward the trail, throwing a comment over my shoulder, "Race you there."

I was off. I started to hear some protests behind me, but I knew not to look back. I was afraid I had bitten off more than I could chew.

I always thought there were three types of speed when referring to an athlete. First, there's normal speed, sort of the average of the slower runners, people who earn their profession from other means than the quickness of their feet. These tend to be the power hitters and most catchers in baseball, or large offensive linemen in football. All of which are people I would not tell to their face that they are slow, so I call their speed normal. Next on the evolutionary ladder is what I call the burners. These are extremely fast human beings. On a hit to the alleys the burners are standing on third when the normals are just sliding into second or retreating to first. And then, there are the extraordinary talented individuals I classify as the jets. They just seem to make everything around them look like it's a special effect in the movies where the people in their background move in super-slow motion. When a jet is running full tilt boogie, you can only accept the majesty of their talent in total awe.

As I dashed down the trail toward Taylor's slough, I learned that day I was among the normal. Not that I ever thought I was a burner, but fairly early in the race, thinking that I had a pretty good lead, I had my first close up experience with a jet. He was a blur, a mass of motion sucking up air. Willie passed me like I was on a Sunday morning jog. As I observed his elbows and ankles driving through the whirlwind of dust he kicked up, a smile came to my face, for I was witnessing speed I had not known existed, and it was exhilarating. When I arrived seriously out of breath at the entrance to the hidden lagoon on the edge of Lake Austin, Willie had already stripped down to his cut-offs and was frolicking in the water.

Spotting me panting with hands on knees, Willie shouted out, "You call that runnin'?"

We both started laughing before our delight in the moment was rudely and abruptly interrupted by the violation of a scream from a brute.

"What you doin' swimmin' in my lagoon, Nigger?" yelled the suddenly appearing Noah Parkes, the oversized moronic bully who ruled the West Austin Lake neighborhoods.

I had always avoided Noah in the past. He was fourteen years old but the idiot had been held back two years in his early grades, so this year he ended up in my class at Casis Elementary School. Noah Parkes was as large as Jack and much more ominous. My older brother stood up to him a long time ago on my behalf, and on that day Noah had backed off. But it was pretty easy to figure out the dimwitted bully wasn't about to drop his grudge.

Without thinking, I found myself yelling back at the hate, screaming out, "That's not fair, Noah! He has just as much right to swim in this lake as you!"

Unfortunately, Noah Parkes was only two quick steps and a roundhouse away from my chin.

"This is none of your damn nigger-loving business, Charles--" he yelled. I didn't hear anything else before I hit the ground and slipped into unconsciousness.

When I opened my eyes, tears seemed to flow like a flooding river after the levy broke. My jaw ached with a kind of pain I could only associate with a horrible trip to the dentist. I glanced around and noticed Willie and Noah

17

Parkes were gone. Over by the bushes, I spotted the Giant's cap, dark T-shirt, and sneakers in the same pile where Willie had discarded them before his plunge into the lake. God, I thought, I hope that Neanderthal idiot didn't drown my newfound jet.

Not knowing how long I had been out added to the overall shock and uneasiness I was registering with each shooting pain in my swollen, throbbing jaw. However, I had to know if Willie was okay. With that thought foremost in my mind, I pulled myself up to my feet, picked up Willie's clothes, and started walking up the trail that ran through Taylor's slough. I was on a mission to find the pink house on the hill above The Clearing where Willie said his mother was a maid. I had to find out if he had survived the onslaught of Noah Parkes.

There weren't a lot of pink houses in Austin in 1962, so it wasn't hard to find. As I walked up the driveway toward the carport entrance to the beautifully landscaped house, I felt a little anxiety. Not from the pain in my jaw, though it still persisted, but rather from worrying about the welfare of my new friend. With a little trepidation I knocked on the door. After a moment, a middle-aged, average sized black woman opened it with a quizzical look on her face.

Before I could say anything, she said, "You must be Mickey. Oh, my Lord, son, lookey what that boy did to you. You get your self in here, young man, and let me get some ice for that face of yourn."

I entered and the lady closed the door behind me but that didn't begin to shut her up as she ranted, "Willie ran in here a minute ago with a story of the Devil's own. I just didn't want to believe such a thing. My Lord, if we don't have 'nough troubles in this world already without bigger peoples taking advantage of the smaller or less fortunate ones."

During her tirade we had a short walk down a hallway before we came to a huge wood framed kitchen that had an island counter with chairs all around. At one end of the island sat Willie in his cut-offs.

"Willie, thank God, you're okay!" I said as I ran over and started to hug him.

He pulled away, half-sobbing, "Stay away from me, man. I don't deserve no attention. I ran away."

18

"You ran away?" I said, not questioning but rather admonishing him with admiration, "You mean, you got away -- from Noah."

"That boy is plumb crazy. After he knocked you out with one hell of a punch, he turned to me and said he was gonna drown me, throw me in Taylor's slough, and let the Johnson family find the body. So, I wasn't about to let him catch hold of my butt. Had to swim out the other side of the lagoon and run most of the way down to Windsor Road before he ran out of wind and stopped chasing me. All the time, I was thinking what my kinfolk had told me about running in West Austin outside Clarksville. That scared me into running faster. I was explaining it all to Mama. We were gonna come back for you – honest we was."

I was happy to see him alive. That's all I was thinking. I really don't know what I was going to say. Willie's Mama pressed something moist and soft to my swollen jaw and said, "Hold this poultice right here in place while I set you straight. Willie's speaking the truth son -- he was gonna take me back there to find you. Now, don't you speak -- just keep this on that jaw of yours and you'll be chewin' the pig by dinnertime. Ol' Teresa gonna look after you 'cause you looked after my Willie."

Out of nowhere the lady threw back her shoulders and head and let go the biggest of belly laughs, wiping at tears in her eyes. I looked over at Willie, but he shrugged his shoulders at me, indicating he had no idea what his mother thought was so funny. She was still chuckling as she grabbed a bag of ice on the counter and held it up to Willie's forehead. Catching her breath, she said, "I heard how you two met. Knowing each other is proving to be damaging to your health."

About thirty minutes later, I was still holding Teresa Veils' poultice in place and continuing to listen to her almost relentless, machine-gun like monologue on several subjects. Some of which were of the utmost interest to Willie's Mama like the case of her nephew, Don Baylor, the future MVP of the American League's California Angels. Don was seventeen years old at the time and he was the star of the Austin High School squad that my two older brothers played on. Don's high school career was already legendary before his senior year at AHS, so it wasn't unusual to see several pro scouts at an Austin High game when he played. However, as Teresa explained, Don would be even better, but he couldn't play organized baseball until he was fourteen years old.

"Why is that?" I asked genuinely interested.

"Why? He lived in Clarksville son. There's no Negroes allowed to play in West Austin Little League or Babe Ruth league. No written rules against it, just those unspoken ones. The only exception was when Don tore up the Pony League in South Austin when he was fourteen, and the powers that be had to have him play in the West Austin Optimists' Babe Ruth league the next year."

Suddenly, I had a great idea. I turned to Willie and said, "You ought to come to our Little League try-outs next week at Bishop Field."

"You crazy," Willie responded, "they ain't gonna let a colored boy play in your league."

"It's like your Mama says, there are no rules against it. You just have to live within the borders of Lamar, 35th Street and the lake and, as far as I know, Clarksville is right dab in the middle of it all. Heck, you probably live closer to the park than I do."

"What do you think, Mama?" Willie asked.

"Well--" Teresa started.

"What's to think about?" I interrupted. "I never saw anyone our age as fast as you. Coach Travis always says when he makes us run wind sprints at the end of every practice, 'Speed wins games, boys'. You are bound to be picked, even if you can't hit."

"I don't know," said Teresa. "The world moves in mysterious ways, Mickey. Sometimes, there's no explainin' it. If Willie were to try such a thing, he could get hurt. Oh not physically, I don't think, but the taunts could scar his mind."

"Mama, I want to do it," Willie stated emphatically.

"You sure, Son? There's gonna be a lot of pressure. And, a lot of people not wanting you to make it."

"I'm sure. I want to play organized ball, Mama. I always have, but I never thought I could."

"All right, Son, if that's what you want, your father and I will support the decision," Teresa said proudly. She turned to me, "Now Mickey, when did you say those try-outs were gonna be held?"

CHAPTER THREE

At the end of winding, rolling Enfield Road is the Tom Miller Dam that creates Lake Austin out of the Colorado River. Next to the dam is the office building for the Lower Colorado River Authority, known locally as the LCRA, a holdover from a WPA project from depression days. The LCRA built the dam and continued to maintain and manage the electricity it generated. Across the way from their offices was the parking lot for employees and behind it was the Yard, which housed all the various equipment necessary for the spread of electricity throughout the area.

For the kids of West Austin Little League, the Yard was nothing more than a nuisance. This was due in part to a series of factors. First, in the early fifties, when the West Austin Optimists Association was looking for a place to build their Little League field, they made a deal with the LCRA for a patch of land by the Yard which would be leased at a rate of one dollar per year. Second, the field was constructed at an angle to best keep the blinding sunlight out of the batters' eyes during the planned late afternoon games. Third, the Yard was surrounded by a mean-looking barbed wire fence and patrolled by two large black Dobermans. So, all those foul balls to the right side of the field could easily drift over the protected fence of the Yard and be lost forever. Many fearless players would approach the gates to the Yard only to be driven away by a snarling attack from one of the previously hidden guard dogs. The worst of all days was the annual try-outs when kids from ages 9 to 12 auditioned their talents for the managers and coaches of the four-team league. I should know, because for the second year in a row I would pitch to the prospective ballplayers, most of which have very limited skills, resulting in many a weak foul ball being deposited into the Yard.

On a crisp, beautiful, spring Saturday afternoon I was alternating the pitching chores for the try-outs with a fellow twelve-year-old teammate Bob, a Jewish friend who lived just around the corner from me. He was my only Jewish friend, I suppose, because I never met any others. But, to my sensibilities he seemed just like me. I didn't see the big deal since Bob and his kind worshiped the same God. So what, they didn't think he had a Son who walked on the earth. They thought He was still coming. I wasn't sure which was true, for at twelve it all seemed so mysterious. All I knew was Bob was a good, true friend who was one hell of a pitcher.

During the agonizing process of pitching to the neophytes, Bob and I managed to make it through the misery of the nine-year-olds, the sweating angst of those ten and the nervousness of the slightly uncoordinated eleven-year-olds that were trying to make the league for the third time. We weren't throwing hard, just meat right down the middle and no curves. Each batter got ten pitches to hit but most only made contact with half, if that many. Then they were asked to bunt and run down the base path where the league's statistician, Matilda Potts, stood with a stopwatch recording the various times it took the youngsters to reach first.

Matilda, known to all as Tildy, was a widow with no children who had 'adopted' the West Austin Little League, which played just across Enfield Road from her sprawling, ranch style home. Tildy had volunteered to help a few years back and now she practically ran the show. She organized the try-outs, scheduled the season, and kept the myriad of statistics on the players that she recorded during her attendance at every game. Tildy was indispensable and greatly admired. The parents, players, and coaches all loved her.

While each kid took his turn at bat, the four managers would walk around with their clipboards watching various players and making notes, occasionally stopping to ask questions of one of the unknown applicants to get a better indication of their character. In the outfield, assistant coaches would hit fly balls to the eager participants wearing paper numbers pinned to their backs. Between pitches to the batters, the coaches hit grounders to players at short and second, who in turn tried to throw to Jack who had volunteered to play first for the exercises. It was kind of funny, but the massive, muscle-bound Jack made the youngsters trying-out look like *kidgets*. He was wearing an old sweat soaked Seven Up cap representing the team that he, Stan, and Dave Looney had played on for the past three years. Bob and I were on Rylanders and Seven Up was our most feared opponent, however, our heads were covered with the All-Star caps we proudly earned the year before.

The day was wearing on and all went pretty much as expected until it was Willie's turn to bat. Bob had finished pitching to the fifth twelve-year-old attempting to impress some manager enough to get one of only four spots available. My manager, Travis, went over to the dugout and motioned inside for the previously unseen Willie to come take his cuts. Tildy thought it might be best to keep Willie out of view of the parents who had kids trying out until the last moment. I guess she thought if they brought out the Negro before everyone had a chance to show their stuff, there might have been trouble. As Willie grabbed a couple of bats and swung them to get loose, I thought I heard rising murmurs from the stands. Before anyone screamed out, I shouted from the mound loud enough for all to hear.

"All right, Willie. I'm all warmed up. No more soft stuff. I'm coming after ya'."

Willie tipped his hat toward me in the way of thanks for associating with him at all and whispered with quiet determination, "Bring it on."

He approached the batter's box and suddenly all of the managers, coaches, parents, and players stopped everything and focused on this four-foot-ten-inch black kid as he reached down and rubbed some dirt on his hands. Jack walked over to the mound and said, "This the boy you were telling me about?" To my nod, he said, "Well, let's see what ol' Blacky can do."

Willie stepped up and took his stance. I studied it. It was slightly open, his bat was sort of cocked a little, and he looked confident. I wound up and threw a semi-fastball that Willie swung at, and connected solidly, hitting a screaming line drive directly back through the middle sending the three of us tumbling away from its flight.

Jack said, "Whoa! That was close. I'm out of here." He headed for the dugout to get a safer perspective.

Bob grabbed a ball off the ground and tossed it to me saying, "He's very good. I'm gonna shag from a little further back." He picked up three or four balls and took up a position by second base.

The second pitch was a little inside but Willie just stepped toward left and blasted a shot down the line that hit the fence in the air 186 feet away, denting the Louis Shanks advertising sign. I turned to Bob who only smiled and nodded his head as he threw me another ball. I let up a little on the next pitch and kind of threw a floater that Willie double clutched a Texas leaguer into right center. On the fourth pitch, I reached back for a little more heat and found the outside lower corner of the strike zone until Willie sent the offering screaming down the first base line. Travis whistled to get my attention and gave me the signal for the curve ball. So, the next pitch I threw was a slow curve starting at Willie's left shoulder, I broke it across the plate where it made contact with his bat and arched up high and far coming to rest in the woods behind the left centerfield fence. I watched Willie, expecting to see him gloating from the homer, but I saw just the opposite. He had the look of a bulldog, his dark brown eyes glazed with determination and his body language depicting the ultimate competitor. To my amazement, on the next pitch, I got him to chase a curve in the dirt, which he missed dramatically. Willie backed out and tipped his hat toward me, and then he reentered the batting box. The last four fastballs I threw him were all cleanly hit into gaps around the field. I was impressed. I hadn't thrown my hardest or my best stuff, but that didn't matter, for I knew nothing much would ever faze this kid. He was a natural ballplayer.

"Nice hitting," I shouted. "Now, lay one down and show 'em your speed."

A grin came to Willie's lips, but I think I was the only one who saw it as I wound up and pitched. Willie drag bunted down the third base line and seemingly was out of the batter's box at full speed before the ball hit the ground. He crossed first a few seconds later as the ball stopped rolling half way down the base path. Tildy looked at her stopwatch, then at Willie, and then she walked over to the managers and the coaches and showed them Willie's time. Some dropped their jaws, but most just shook their heads.

I walked over to Willie who was standing along the right field line and shook his hand, "Welcome to the league brother. You are too much!"

Willie broke into a big grin, "That was really fun, Mickey! But, I'll be ready for that drop curve of yours next time we face each other."

Jack and Bob suddenly showed up. I introduced them to Willie and then patting him on the shoulder, I said, "Guess he kind of showed us what he had."

Jack reached out his hand to Willie's, "I got to shake your hand. That was some show."

Bob was next to jut forward a hand and blurted out, "Dang! Good hitting!"

"Well, Mick," Jack said to me as he rubbed his hands together and winked, "it looks like our All-Star team just got its lead-off hitter."

Bob turned to me and said, "Hey, Mickey, Rylanders has a twelve-year-old opening don't we, because of Rudy leaving?"

"That's true Bob," said Travis, as he suddenly appeared. "But unfortunately, we pick second."

Travis extended his hand toward Willie, "And I'm afraid this gifted player is going to be the first pick. Willie, you can really hit and run. It's going to be a pleasure watching you play in our league."

"Thank you, Mr. Bowie," Willie said.

"Son, you can call me Travis, or you can call me Coach, but no one around here gets away with calling me Mr. Bowie. You got it?"

"Yes sir, Coach," Willie snapped back.

Tildy approached, stopwatch in her left hand and wrapped her right arm around Willie hugging him close to her body. "You are a cheetah! Look at his time boys," Tildy said as she shoved the timing instrument in our faces with her free arm. "In all my days, only one other person ever timed out under 3.5 seconds and that was Mickey's older brother Larry, who ran a 3.42, three or four years ago. Anyway, shine the light on this, y'all. Look at that time. This boy here's a cheetah."

We stared at the watch that revealed 3.11. It was a moment of synchronicity as the three of us opened our mouths and collectively uttered the most serious of appraisals, "Wow."

Tildy produced a sheet of paper and handed it to Willie. She said, "Willie, this form has to be filled out by your parents. It gives us information for our directory. Also, we'll need a medical history from your doctor." She produced another paper and handed it to Willie. "It's all written out for you and your parents right here. These are the basic rules to get you officially registered in the league. But don't you worry son, this ain't no red tape. You'll be spending your afternoons right here. And God Bless you for that. God Bless you all, boys." With that, she took hold of Travis' arm and started to lead him off. As they walked away, she said, "Now, Travis, we got to get across the street and start making our draft. We had a pretty good overall bunch today, don't you think. Yes, indeedy, a pretty good overall bunch."

The tryouts were over. The kids turned in their numbers and found their parents waiting for them by the gates. Each received a hug, kiss, or slap on the back and words of encouragement from their proud mamas and papas. As some of the cars were starting to pull out of the parking lot, we were still hanging out on the field. Bob turned to Willie and asked, "Are your parents picking you up?"

"No, they both work on Saturdays. I'm on my own."

"Well, then," Jack responded. "I'm hungry. Let's go to Dale Bakers."

Open pit barbecue is practically considered an art form in the Hill Country region of Central Texas. With Austin as the epicenter, the ultimate connoisseur can travel no less than sixty minutes in any direction and find a kind of earth-rattling, smoked heaven on a bun with a side dish of beans, potato salad, and cole slaw. Every town in the area has the "World's Best" open pit barbecue restaurant. Usually known for smoked beef brisket, spare ribs, beef ribs, turkey sausage, and the like, but each is unique in its own way. Open pit barbecue is nothing more than parts of the cow seasoned with a "rub" made of salt, pepper, cayenne, some vinegar, and an amount of secret ingredients that don't really matter much but are a little bit different in each spot, cooked over a fire from whatever wood of local origin is nearby. The main thing that separates Hill Country BBQ from other notable restaurants in the country is the strongly held local opinion that beef barbecues better than pork. And to most people the best part of the barbecued beef is in the brisket form.

Austin had a brisket making barbecue institution that was my favorite, known as Dale Bakers, named logically after its owner. Across Lake Austin Boulevard from the 12th hole at Muny, the city owned golf course, just down the road from the Tom Miller Dam and Bishop Field, sat the West Austin eatery famous not only for its brisket, but it's paprika spiced potato salad, special cole slaw, hot links, its catering, and its owner. Dale was not a tall man but he was rather heavy. Maybe this was because he kept sampling from his own menu. During the summer months, Dale served as an umpire at Bishop Field and his restaurant always hosted the awards dinner at the end of the season, so the Little Leaguers always admired and respected him.

With Willie sitting on the handlebars of my three-speed Schwinn, I pedaled up to the parking lot of Dale Bakers after Jack and Bob had entered the restaurant. Before I could follow them inside, Willie held me up and said quietly, "Can't we sit out back?"

It didn't matter to me that Willie was afraid or felt he wasn't allowed. From what, in my naiveté, I had no idea, but somehow I was sensitive enough to his uneasiness that I capitulated and walked with Willie to the back outdoor section of the restaurant where we ordered our Dr Pepper's. Through the back outdoor wire mesh, we saw Jack and Bob inside taking their sandwiches and sitting at a table with all the condiments before they realized we weren't joining them. Grabbing their plates they exited the building and joined us at the picnic tables overlooking the lake behind the restaurant.

Between swallows of his huge sliced beef brisket sandwich, Jack asked Willie, "I understand you're related to Don and Doug Baylor?"

"They're my second cousins," Willie responded.

Jack said, "Well, they're good people. I played football at a camp with Doug. And Don may be the best athlete ever at Austin High. Hell, he was All-District football on offense and defense and would've won the state's shot put and discus last year if hc hadn't been playing basketball and baseball."

Willie replied, "He is good at a lot of things, but he thinks one of his teammates may be a better baseball player at this age -- some boy named Covert."

"My brothers think they'll both be pros someday," I added. "But, if I only had one pick, I still think I'd take Baylor."

The other three nodded in agreement as Jack, who had just gulped his sandwich and slugged down the last of his Dr Pepper, let go a belch which pretty much summed up the fact it was time for everyone to leave. Jack and Bob said their good-byes and added congratulations to Willie. Then they got on their bikes and pedaled west along Lake Austin Boulevard directly into the setting sun. Willie eyed my handlebars once again, saying, "Really Mickey, I can walk. It ain't that far and you don't want go that direction, anyways."

"Oh, get on. It's not that far out of my way so what the heck. Come on!"

Willie stepped up into place and we rode off. After a mile, we passed O. Henry Junior High School, which even though Willie and I went to separate elementary schools, we would both attend in the fall when we got to seventh grade. A mile farther on we crossed under the Missouri Pacific railroad tracks and took a right to enter the outskirts of Clarksville. Willie was leaning back toward me, indicating which way to go, when we left the asphalt pavement that, up to that moment, I had known as the only street surface in the world. As we rode down what appeared to be a trail, the sand-pitted rough and rocky road in Willie's neighborhood of Clarksville, I soon learned the norm here was not what it was for those of us in Tarrytown.

Bouncing along on the handlebars, Willie shouted, "Hey, Mickey, try to miss the boulders."

"I'm trying the best I can. What happened to these roads, Willie?"

"Say what?"

"The roads! Where's the pavement?"

"Dunno. This is how it is in Clarksville. Always has been."

It was my first experience with the less fortunate. The houses we passed were what may be best described as small, dilapidated wooden structures, not houses like on the streets of Tarrytown a few short blocks away. I didn't really know what I was feeling, but there was suddenly something in the pit of my stomach, in the middle of my gut. An ache, a slowly pressurized pain that seemed to come out of nowhere and probably wouldn't go away until I could understand the reason for my discomfort.

After a few turns, Willie pointed at a little yellow house, which was better kept than most of the previous ones we had passed along the way. He said, "This is it, right here."

I turned into his driveway and locked the brakes bringing the bike to a sudden stop, and sending Willie flying off the front end. I was attempting to make him tumble, but of course with his athleticism and balance, he landed on the balls of his feet, performed a graceful 360, and tipped his cap to me.

"Thanks for the ride, Mickey," he said and headed for the screen door off the driveway. Before he got there he stopped and looked back at me. "You know how to get out of here? I wouldn't want you to get lost in my 'hood'."

"Just gonna backtrack. I shouldn't have any problem. See you later, Willie," I waved and started to pedal away.

"Hey, Mickey," Willie yelled as I was leaving his driveway. I stopped and looked back. "I really want to thank you for all of your help. I won't let you down?"

"Say what?" I said.

Willie and I smiled at each other. We didn't know it for sure, but we could definitely sense that this was the beginning of something great.

CHAPTER FOUR

Ms. Vance, my sixth grade teacher, was droning on about city manager run governments versus mayor run councils or some such thing. I couldn't really tell you. For on that beautiful spring morning at Casis Elementary School, I was drifting as I often did in classes. My eyes would have direct contact with the teacher following her every move. This would mask the fact that I was paying the least amount of attention to her as possible as I daydreamed about the most current crisis in my life. I never got caught because I was very good at drifting.

That particular day my thoughts were focused on 'Kitty,' known to all others as Jill, except to me. I used the nickname I gave her when we were nine -- the time I first went to her house on Forest Trail and observed her cat's new litter of kittens. Kitty, who sat across the room by the door, was my first crush and it was just beginning to happen. It came out of nowhere the day before -- I had known her since first grade -- but suddenly sitting there that day, I couldn't think of anything else but presenting my bracelet to Kitty so that we could go steady. I wanted to do it before I lost the nerve. I figured recess on the playground may be as good a time as ever, but that was two hours away. How was I ever going to make it that long?

When you're twelve years old, time is a totally misunderstood concept. You think it should serve you, instead of you having to wait on it. Children are impatient from the fact that time is, to them, elusive. The sad sideline to this thought is, as one ages and begins to comprehend the sense of time, it never really becomes a friend. Patience comes with this understanding and from the experience of learning how to wait, but then so do wrinkles, gray hair, baldness, sagging parts of the body, and all other physical attributes to which time is not kind.

When I was twelve this sort of understanding had not entered my young mindset. Yet for me, other things were starting to surface. And I was beginning to notice them. In fact, that very morning in music class my voice shrieked a few times when I tried to hit the high notes. That was odd.

I had awakened with the thought of asking Kitty to go steady. This was because the night before I was talking on the phone with our mutual friend, Deborah, and she said Jill was just waiting for me to ask her. For some reason, hearing this made me break into a cold sweat, and the shakes. It was a miracle that I survived the previous sleepless night. It was horrifying, this feeling I was experiencing, but I was determined to survive it. While I was ignoring Ms. Vance's dull verbosity, I was trying to work up the inner courage to follow through with the act. The previous Christmas my grandmother had given me a silver wrist bracelet with my name engraved in flowing letters. It was very dear to me and I had always worn it proudly. However, that morning, I had wrapped it in a handkerchief with a hand-written note that posed the poetic question asking if Kitty would be my girl.

"Mickey!" I seemed to hear calling me, from a tunnel far away and echoing off the walls of rock across a lake. "Mickey, Mickey!" the voice reverberated. I was kind of mad it was interrupting my drifting, when I was suddenly brought back to reality by a chalkboard eraser banging off my forehead.

I looked up at Ms. Vance, who had thrown the perfect strike from the front of the room. She was known to do that when a student of hers fell asleep. But, in my six years of classroom experience, I had never been caught drifting. This whole girl thing could be driving me crazy, I thought, as I tried to regain my composure.

"I'm sorry, Ms. Vance, what was that you said, I didn't quite hear it all?"

Ms. Vance, to my twelve-year-old sentiments, seemed a rather tall, dark-haired ogre of a lady who probably never had a boyfriend in her entire life.

That fact alone was kind of scary, but she also had a temper to beat the band and obviously a very deadly accurate right arm. She approached me as I was trying to clear the cobwebs of my confusion.

"Mr. Charles," she said, "I simply asked if you were Mayor, would you give all of the power in the city to Ms. Kitty?"

I shook my head. "What?" I thought, as I was really confused, and a little upset, by the fact my deepest thoughts had been so rudely interrupted by this mountain of ugliness standing before me. I had to revert to my own safety valve, the often used and effective little white lie.

I grabbed at my stomach and feigned a pain, saying, "I'm not feeling very well, Ms. Vance. I'm sorry. It's my gut. I need to use the restroom right away. You wouldn't want to be responsible for me losing my eggs and bacon right here in front of the whole class."

"We'll just see about that, Mr. Charles," she said, not amused in the least. "Bathroom privilege denied. Do the circle."

"But, Ms. Vance--" I started to argue.

"Charles!" she said in a loud, stern voice. I released the grip on my stomach for I knew she wasn't playing along. The teacher didn't have to speak again, either. She just pointed at the chalkboard on the back wall. I stood up and approached it, and then grabbing a stick of chalk I drew a rather uneven circle about five inches in diameter. After setting down the chalk, I placed my nose directly in its center and stood erect with my back to the class as I heard some snickering here and there behind me.

All teachers' procedures on disciplining students were very different. Usually the consequences came as a reflection of the personality of the individual who was dolling out the punishment. I had seen all kinds, like the borderline child molesters serving as macho shop teachers, who loved to give "licks," which meant paddling the behinds of their miscreants with two by fours of their own design. Or the gung-ho PE coaches who made their transgressors, mostly those suspected of being "different," endure endless running until the student's tongue had turned a funny shade of pale. There were, of course, the English teachers who thought that endless writing on the chalkboard, with the proper grammar quoting the righteousness of their judgments, would undo the wrong from one's misplaced pranks. Ms. Vance, in her singular semi-wickedness, thought up the circle.

After getting over the initial embarrassment of being caught at anything which might bring the teacher's punishment, I actually didn't mind quiet time in the circle, for I could then drift without the worry of the ridiculous, constant, unwanted interruptions. My mind went back to thoughts of what was the utmost importance -- the rest of my day. If all went well, as I rode my Schwinn to my first practice with Rylanders at Bishop Field, I would know I was in a relationship with the most popular girl in the school. How great would that be, I thought. Then, the school's fire bell rang, interrupting yet another great drift.

I was the Fire Chief, which was a position akin to President of the Class, since it was the highest democratically selected position in the sixth grade. During a fire drill at Casis, I'm afraid to say, my duties were rather elementary. Each class had its fireguards who wrangled the boys and girls into a single file and led them out of the room and onto the playground, where the Fire Captains of each grade took control and insured order. The Fire Wardens from the fifth grade had the responsibility of making sure the gym and cafeteria were free of students and employees. Inside the main school building it was the responsibility of the Fire Chief and the Assistant Fire Chief, always sixth graders, to make sure the halls, libraries and labs were all empty. Then, they met at the administration corridor and jointly reported to the Principal -- a cigar-chomping Mr. Robbins -- that indeed the drill had gone as planned and the students were all safe.

Now, the timing of unknown events sometimes brings strangeness to ordinary proceedings, throwing off the natural elemental process of fate and destiny. On that spring day, when the only thing riding on my mind besides baseball, was talking to Kitty, I had the chance of a lifetime when the fire bell rang. You see, Kitty was the Assistant Fire Chief and we were about to roam the halls together -- alone. Now I would see if I had what my older brothers called "gonads," which I assumed was a reference to courage.

After we had performed our duties, Kitty and I reported to Mr. Robbins that everything was A-OK. He looked at his stopwatch and smiled, taking out a cigar. He lit it as we stood there a little uncomfortably and finally he said, "Give them a couple of minutes before you bring 'em in."

The final duty we had on a fire drill was to ring the bell three times as an 'all clear' signaling the students to return to their respective classrooms. Kitty and I walked out of Mr. Robbins office that day and slowly sauntered down the hallway toward the fire bell. She had never looked lovelier -- which understandably caused me to lose the ability to speak as I looked at Kitty, smiling at me. My right hand was in my pocket clutching the handkerchief with the poem and bracelet. Kitty was just waiting to receive it, yet my jaws were locked, frozen like a stone in the Petrified Forest. Kitty seemed to sense my uneasiness, I guess, because she just reached out and gently took my left hand and walked with me to the end of the corridor. After a bit of silence, she reached up and rang the bell with three quick thrusts, never taking her eyes from mine. I felt a quiver rush through my entire body. I didn't know why. Maybe I sensed her disgust in my failure to make the commitment -- a situation that would unfortunately haunt me my whole life.

When Kitty and I returned to our class, she took her seat by the door while I walked over to mine by the window. As I took my seat across from Deborah, she looked at me as if to say, "Well?" I shrugged my shoulders and she rolled her eyes. To Deborah's disdain, I mouthed the words, "At recess, I swear."

Unfortunately, I wouldn't get the chance. For when the bell rang for recess that day, I happened to be standing in the circle, to which Ms. Vance had returned me after she discovered me sitting at my desk after the fire drill. When the bell rang for recess, I naturally stepped away from the circle and started to go put on my sneakers stored below my desk. Unexpectedly, I heard Ms. Vance's shrill voice, "Mr. Charles! Where do you think you are going? Get back to the circle until you are released. Thank you very much."

It was Ms. Vance's unwritten rule that once you had been sentenced to the circle, the minimum time served should be no less than twenty minutes. Since the fire drill had come only a few seconds after I had been sentenced, I had to finish my time. As the class headed out for the playground, I gave a last shrug to Deborah and returned to the circle.

After I thought all of the kids had left the room, I suddenly felt a massive presence behind me. Noah Parkes whispered in my ear, "Better watch your back, nigger-lover."

An instant shiver rushed down my spine. I braced for the inevitable punch, slap, or kick, but it failed to follow. Instead, he laughed derisively in my ear and then left me alone in the room. I had the uneven feeling that trouble was not only brewing but also impending as long as the 'Neanderthal' Parkes was in my neighborhood.

During the recess I had a lot of time to myself for thought. It had been four days, though it felt like two weeks, since Willie had stunned the tryouts with his performance. As expected, he was notified the next day he had been selected first, to play on the team that had come in dead last the previous two years – City National, for which my friends Danny and Billy had shined as their only stars. With Willie batting in front of them, I thought they could contend for the championship, along with my team Rylanders and the favorites, Seven Up, led by the home run-hitting trio of Jack, Stan, and Dave Looney. The fourth team was Louis Shanks and they had a few good ball players and a helluva institution as a Manager. This year's battle was looming as one of the brightest in the history of the West Austin Little League.

I was really looking forward to our first practice at four o'clock that afternoon. I had been preparing for weeks. When I wasn't spending time in The Clearing, I had been throwing and running with my brother who was trying to get into baseball shape for his upcoming high school season. I treated this time as my own spring training before practice started in earnest.

Otherwise, all I had left to do was this excruciatingly difficult task of asking my first girl to go steady. Dang it, I thought, I'll just pass the handkerchief to Deborah and ask her to relay it to Kitty and let the poem speak for itself. Let's see-- what did the poem say? Oh, yeah it goes:

> Complete is each day when I see your shining face
> For you heat me up like fire because you are so pretty
> So from the bottom of my heart I am asking if in your grace
> Ms. Kitty would you allow me the pleasure of going steady.
>   Mickey Charles

Longfellow probably smiled, but at least he didn't turn over in his grave like Shelley or Keats, but heck, I was a passionate twelve-year-old blinded by the simple sight of a young pretty, popular girl. At least now I had my plan. As soon as recess ended and I got my nose off of that darn blackboard, I'd ask Deborah for the assist. Perfect -- I thought -- nothing could go wrong now.

There are times in life when you have trouble getting out from under the insecurity of doubt or fear or troubles. It's like you have lassoed a black cloud filled with all your flaws and it continues to follow you dumping its negativity on your slumping shoulders. For kids, this time is short-lived but anxiety filled. As I was about to learn, this can lead to some very embarrassing moments.

I was again sitting across from Deborah after recess and had mouthed the words of my plan. She nodded saying she would pass my "love" package on to Jill in the private hiding place in the girls' restroom. Ms. Vance was now rattling on about the United Nations. She was challenging its effectiveness in lieu of the Cold War making the veto from either side of the Iron Curtain an impasse to any serious edicts from the organization, which might lead to world peace and international cooperation among nations. But at the time, I couldn't have cared less. When Ms. Vance turned to the chalkboard behind her and started to write, I began to pass the handkerchief holding the bracelet and my poetic request across the desk toward Deborah. Just as her hand touched mine, we heard Ms. Vance, "Mr. Charles, Ms. Thorne. Bring whatever that is up here and share it with class, won't you."

That was a very long slow walk for the two of us. As our stern-faced teacher took the handkerchief from Deborah and started to open it, I felt my face catch on fire. I started breaking out in a sweat and my body began to shake. Though it was unlikely, I was hoping no one would notice.

Ms. Vance took the bracelet and glanced at it, then the note, and said, "Mr. Charles, I see you're a poet. Why don't you share your talent with the whole class?" She handed me the note.

I glanced over to where Jill was sitting and hoped against hope that no one knew that Kitty was what I secretly called her. I cleared my throat, but my mouth was bone-dry, and though I had always been an accomplished public speaker, this was not to be my shining hour.

Holding the paper in my trembling hands, I pretended to read the poem. Actually I was reciting from memory, my eyes closed so as to not make contact with any fellow student. When I finished, every kid in the room was laughing except for Deborah, Kitty, Ms. Vance, and me. To escape the ridicule, I felt like digging a hole through the world to China. Just as I thought my heart couldn't pound any harder, it did when I saw Kitty stand up and walk toward me. She held out her hands toward mine and said, "Thank you, Mickey. I would love to go steady with you." She reached up and kissed me flat on the lips. The laughter in the background changed to whoops, whistles, and applause.

Ms. Vance had had enough. She told the class to read the chapter on the Security Council and marched the three of us off to the Principal. But, you know, I didn't really care. Because, now I had a girlfriend, my black cloud had blown away, and baseball season was about to begin.

CHAPTER FIVE

The unmistakable smell of the Hill Country spring was in the air and the beautiful state wildflower, the bluebonnet, lined the streets while I rode my bike toward Bishop Field. I was pedaling to my first day of practice with Rylanders, named after a local supermarket "dynasty" of two stores in West Austin that sponsored the team. The sponsors covered the cost of the uniforms and got to place an advertising sign free-of-charge on the outfield fence. This did not mean they had any say over the league, the team, or any player for that matter. But, without such benefactors, the league might have died in its infancy. The players and their parents of West Austin Little League held in the highest esteem these pillars of retail that championed their endeavor. Our parents only shopped for their groceries at Rylanders or bought furniture at Louis Shanks. And, though we drank Dr Pepper mostly, we still drank Seven Up, which was bottled at Mr. Sawyer's factory located by the river. None of us had bank accounts yet, so City National didn't make a lot of sense to the nine to twelve-year-old set, but I guess it worked for the parents because the local Tarrytown financial institution had been a sponsor from the start, just like the other three.

Our aforementioned manager, Travis, was legendary in local baseball lore for his unique accomplishments during an All-American college career at the University of Texas, where he had been given the nickname "Rabbit." He earned the moniker for his play in centerfield, roaming "Billy Goat Hill" at the classic Clark Field on the UT campus. The field had a natural structural obstacle, a limestone cliff that rose out of the outfield reaching a height of 14 feet in dead center. The wall of rock was only 340 feet from the plate and the outfield fence was 400 feet away, so there was a plateau on which the ball could land and most players could scurry for a rare inside the park home run. However, when the Rabbit was in center and a ball was launched up on top of Billy Goat Hill, the next thing you knew, the ball was being thrown to third base in an attempt to nail a runner trying to stretch the massive blast to three bases. There was a myth going around the state he never discounted or denied that he even caught a ball on top of Billy Goat Hill for a putout. If it was true, I always thought Travis should have been called the "Jackalope" instead of the Rabbit.

Travis' assistant was Robert Towery, who we called Coach T. He had been a teammate of Travis at the University of Texas where he was All-Southwest Conference as a second baseman. Coach T had been like a second father to me and I fondly remember his smiling demeanor and confident approach to life. He used to always tell us that we had a path to follow in life and, if we didn't stray off the path, then with hard work and dedication we could accomplish anything, and fully realize the satisfaction of our goals and dreams.

Skidding to a stop on the gravel parking lot beside the field, I placed my right leg on the ground, hopped off my Schwinn, and grabbed my glove, all in the same motion. I scissor-kicked my way over the four-foot chain link fence running down the left field line of Bishop Field. The smell of freshly cut grass filled my nostrils as I set down my glove and started to stretch my legs and arms. It was a smell that years later would still bring a smile to my face and flood my mind with memories of playing baseball. No one else on my team had arrived yet, and I liked it that way. First one on the field so I could stretch out in earnest before my buddies appeared and gabbed while they "acted" like they were warming up.

After a while, Travis pulled up in the old Ford station wagon. I jumped the fence and grabbed the bat bag as he handed it to me from his trunk. Suddenly, cars were appearing one after another and fellow teammates were jumping out and joining us on the field. Coach T arrived and pulled out four boxes of brand new baseballs purchased that day at Rooster Andrews.

It was the only sporting goods store people used in West Austin because Rooster offered the league discounts on equipment. The league made him an 'Honorary' sponsor, and for this, he had a free sign on the center field fence to advertise his establishment.

The sixteen players on Rylanders were a mix of five twelve-year-olds, four eleven, four ten, and three nine-year-olds. Lined up in two rows, eight of us paired up with another eight and threw balls back and forth warming up our young arms. Travis and Coach T stood over to the side sharing jokes and stories for about ten minutes before they clapped their hands and whistled, calling us to gather around home plate.

"Everyone take a seat on the ground here," Travis said and we all obliged sitting on the grass in front of the batter's box. "Now, Coach T and I would like to welcome all of you back who played last year. We had a good run, just came up a few bases short. Hopefully, with our four new players, we can overcome that hurdle this year. Could all of you new fellas, please stand up?"

Three young-looking nine-year-olds -- who it seemed could have passed for brothers, all with blond hair -- stood up along with a rather rotund, round-faced youngster. I had seen him in the halls this year, but I didn't know him because he was in Ms. Caldwell's class with Danny, Jack and Stan across the hall from Ms. Vance's. Travis gestured toward the three younger ones and said, "Guys, this is Randy, Glen, and Randy."

One of the boys tipped his hat, another sort of weakly waved at everyone while the third just burst out saying, "Howdy everybody, I'm Glen Farley. I play second base."

I glanced over at our eleven-year-old second baseman, Marky, who smiled and called out, "Welcome to the bench, rook." We all laughed.

Travis held up his hand, "All right, fellas. Glen here has a little bit of enthusiasm and it wouldn't hurt the rest of you to catch some of that fire. Now, y'all sit down. Um -- two Randy's -- let's see what we can do about that." He pointed at one and said, "This fella's last name is unpronounceable so we'll call him Randy." He pointed at the third kid, the one who had waved weakly at us and ask, "And, what is your last name again, son?"

"Fitzgeraldston, sir," the boy said quietly.

41

"Well, I must say that is a mouthful as well -- we'll just call you Fitz. Is that all right with you?"

The boy smiled, "Yeah, that's fine." He seemed to relax a little now that he had a nickname. It made him feel a part of the team. Travis had a way of making his players feel comfortable with who they were and bringing out the talent they had lurking within.

He turned to the chunky boy and placed his arm on his shoulder, "Now I know y'all are wondering how we're going to replace Rudy Stearns who moved to Corpus with his family and left us a hole at first base. Well, here's my plan. This is Don Brandt. His family relocated here from Waco and we are pretty darn lucky to get him. He had to miss the tryouts because he had his tonsils out that day, but the coaches of the four teams gave him his own workout. Believe me boys, Don is going to more than replace Rudy. He was an All-Star in his Little League last year. And after seeing him hit, I'm betting he might win the home run title this year and help us win a championship. Now, since Don is a catcher with a very strong arm, I'm going to ask Dean, our catcher last year, to play first base. What do say, Dean, you game?"

Dean was kind of slow of foot and of mouth. He never really moved at a pace that was normal, always a step or two behind the crowd and moments behind getting a joke. He drove me nuts as a catcher, so I was thrilled with the news. He kind of stammered a little before saying, "uh, but, um, uh...wh, wha, what will my Daddy think? He wants me to be a catcher, like he was."

Travis took a moment, and then said gently, "Well, Dean, if necessary I'll have a talk with your father. You know, son, there aren't very many left-handed catchers, but there's a lot of left-handed first basemen. And, nothing against you Dean, but once your Dad, who was a very good catcher in his day, sees the talents of the Waco kid here, I bet he'd agree with the move. Besides, you would rather be in the starting line-up than backing up, wouldn't you?"

"Well, I -- I guess." He said and added, "I, I'll -- try whatever you think, T. T. Tr. Travis, you're th--th--the coach."

"Well, that's the spirit, Dean boy!" Travis said as he leaned down and patted him on the shoulder. "And we're going to give you some extra training so you'll be real comfortable over at first. Okay, all of you back from last year, when you're not fielding, running, or hitting, I want you all to introduce yourselves to the new boys and make them feel at home. Remember, we're a team, not sixteen individuals. Okay, everybody give me three."

We leapt to our feet and ran down the first base line and out into the outfield on the first of three laps around the park. There was always a lot of running during the first couple of weeks of practice. We usually ran three to start off and five when we were done, and no telling how many during practice from punishment for fielding, hitting, or mental mistakes. As we were jogging in centerfield, I moseyed over and ran next to our new catcher. I stuck my hand out, "Hey, I'm Mickey. Welcome."

Don shook it and said, "Thanks. What do you play?"

"One of the pitchers. Bob and I alternate at third and the mound," I said as we continued our laps. "You were an All-Star as an eleven-year-old. What did you hit last year?"

"I hit .385 with six homers," he said simply.

I pumped my fist in the air as I rounded the corner and headed toward home, "Yes!"

When the laps were completed we spent an hour on situational fielding. Starting with nine position players in the field, the other seven ran the bases while the coaches set up various situations that came up in real games. We practiced the cut-off throws, backing up the other players, learning all the moves in each of the game situations. If you missed a cut-off or made some mental error, Travis would yell out, "Give me one." You would drop your glove and take a lap while your backup replaced you in the field. When you finished you became a runner with the others. Travis and Coach T would stop from time to time to counsel a base runner or fielder after a mistake, always trying to remain constructive in their teachings.

Next was batting practice with Coach T throwing easy, no junk. Each player took his turn taking swings until Travis had seen enough and asked them to lay one down and run to first. The three nine-year-olds were first, hitting mostly weak grounders that died before they reached the dirt in the infield. Then all of the others took their turn, until Travis finally called Bob, Don, and me in from the field to take our turns.

I was not a great hitter. To tell you the truth, knowing how hard it was to have control over my own pitches, I was always a little wary of being hit by others, especially those who threw harder than me. I tended to step in the bucket and it caused me to swing off-balance. Determined not to step down the left field line, I made the mistake of over-correcting and moved both feet resembling a Mexican jumping bean in the batter's box. It was something I needed Travis to help me correct. However, when it came to hitting, I was certain he thought I was a lost cause. Because after five swings -- I had hit three out of the infield, but two were lazy fly balls -- he said, "That's enough, Mick, lay one down."

"Come on Travis, just a few more." I pleaded.

"I'll make you a deal," Travis said. "I'll have Coach T throw you one more and if you hit it you get another one and another one, but when you miss you'll owe me two -- deal?"

"You got it." I said, and dug in determined to impress.

Coach T threw the first one high and tight and I missed it by a mile. I threw down my bat in disgust and started the first of my two laps. While I was running in the outfield, Don took his cuts and showered the fences with line drives. I found I had to keep my eye on him even while I was running out by the fence. Just as I finished my second lap, Don let go three mighty swings, sending balls out of the park, landing in the trees behind the left center field fence. When he tried to bunt however, he missed the ball as badly as I did on my last swing. Coach T smiled and said, "Go ahead and run. We're not having you bunt, anyway." Don set down his bat and jogged down the base bath like he was on a home run trot. Travis yelled out, "Got to hustle a little, Don. Give me one."

Wind sprints were next. We lined up along first base and sprinted back and forth down the base path while Travis shouted out encouraging slogans like, "Speed wins games" and "Strong legs beats eggs". We never knew what the latter one really meant, but he loved to say it. Another one he tried that day was, "You can run into problems or run out of trouble, you just got to use your head." Travis was always preaching about the mental part of baseball.

He used to quote Yogi and shout out, "Baseball is ninety percent mental, the other half is physical." When we finished the wind sprints, all sixteen of us were bent over gasping for air, some on all fours. Don, the overweight new kid, was rolling around on the ground like a wounded seal. I went over to him to see if he was all right and between groans he said, "I haven't run this much in my whole life."

"It kind of shows." I couldn't resist the jab. "We only do this for the first couple of weeks. After that, it's a gravy train."

Following another groan, and he rolled over and mumbled, "A couple of weeks. Oh-h-h-h no."

Travis gathered us around first base and he went over the rules of base running as we all started to get our wind back. We all knew the rules, of course, so I guess it was for the new players, but they would likely never get on base anyway, so really all he was doing was giving us a little rest before we had to run some more.

All in all, the first practice went pretty well. We had a good team, if Dean could adjust and make some plays for us at first, then we were going to be all right. I was jazzed and couldn't wait for the season to begin, but I knew I had a month before that would happen. A whole month, I thought, as I finished the last of my five laps at the end of practice. A month seemed like forever.

CHAPTER SIX

On Sunday between September and May, everyone in West Austin was operating on the same schedule. That is, everyone I knew. In the mornings, they were all going to various churches around the city. Some of my friends and their families went all the way downtown to the Episcopal or Catholic cathedrals, and others traveled over to University Presbyterian on the "drag" by the University of Texas campus. Some in Tarrytown might stay in the area and attend the Methodist and Baptist churches on Exposition Boulevard. My family went to the Church of the Good Shepherd, an Episcopal variety of worship, also located on Exposition.

Good Shepherd offered several Sunday services that people could attend for their weekly obligatory service to the Lord. Early birds could receive the spiritual worm at 7 a.m. from assistant Pastor John Logan. Thank God for Mr. Logan, for without him our church would never have entered a basketball team in the city leagues, where I received valuable early experience in the sport in which I would later excel. There was a 9:15 a.m. service, where after twenty minutes of singing hymns, reciting the various old creeds and prayers passed down from the Apostles, and hearing some announcements, the kids and teenagers went next door to the parish house for Sunday School. Every once in awhile a few of us would skip class and go across the street to Tarrytown Pharmacy, sit down at the counter, read the latest Superman comic book, and drink milk shakes.

There was an 11 a.m. service, where everyone in the congregation stayed and listened to the sermon for the day. I could barely stand our Pastor, Mr. Braxten, who had an astoundingly amazing talent to bore. He would drone on in a low, constant monotone that was hypnotically annoying. I used to think if he would bottle it he could make huge sums marketing his speech as a sleep aid -- his sermons were always interminable. I probably heard three or four when I was twelve, but I couldn't focus enough to drift like I did at Casis, so usually within three minutes I was fast asleep, snoring quietly beside my agitated older brothers.

My friend Danny, who I mentioned would be playing with Willie in our upcoming Little League battles, was my mate on Sundays. His family never missed a 9:15 service that I can remember, and on that April 1962 Sunday, after the first week of baseball practice, we knew we had too much to talk about to attend Sunday school. So while fidgeting and yawning during the obligatory twenty minutes of church services with Mr. Boring Braxten, Danny and I gave each other the thumbs up signal indicating we were to meet at the pharmacy for shakes and team comparisons.

Danny was already sitting at the counter when I got there and had ordered us both a shake. The pharmacist, Mr. Weedbern, set them on the counter just as I sat down.

"Thanks, Mr. Weedbern," I said as I spun around on my circular stool. He only grunted and walked away.

Danny looked up from the Austin American-Statesman sports section and said, "Maris hit two yesterday and Mickey hit one. They're at it again and the Yanks are dominating."

"But, Whitey's arm is hurting. Terry better have a good year to make up for it," I declared, grabbing my shake as I scooped some whipped cream off the top with a long spoon and popped it into my mouth in one swift motion.

"They have that fast rookie too, remember?"

"Jim Bouton," I said. "Yeah, he's really good. Bouton shut out the Senators the other day on seven hits in his first game, but he had seven walks. Ralph Houk said he almost pulled him and sent him back to the minors 'cause his first nine pitches missed the strike zone. One more ball and Houk was going to give the rook the hook."

"Houk's a lout. I miss ol' Casey," Danny grinned.

"Poor Case, he's managing the Mets after all those championships with the Bronx Bombers."

We were experts on the Yankees because they were our team. The Colt 45's in Houston and the Texas Rangers in Arlington hadn't been in existence before 1962 and fan loyalties in the major leagues usually depended upon which team's broadcast your radio could receive. Due to the hills around Austin, we only got static from the St. Louis broadcasts that people only forty-five miles to the north, in Salado, received clearly. Danny and I became Yankee fans because they played frequently on the Game of the Week broadcast on television for several years. Plus, they generally won the World Series, and it was always easier on the soul to follow a winner.

"What do you think of Willie?" I asked, changing the subject as I took another revolution on the stool.

"Oh, you were right, Mick. He's great! And, you ought to see him run!" Danny exclaimed.

"I have."

"We're going to win it all," Danny said excitedly. "Willie's going to lead us to the Promised Land."

"You're dreaming! Who do ya'll have for pitching? You can't win it all without three good pitchers, and what, all you have is Roberts," I said emphatically. "And he's got control problems."

"Did you ever see Willie pitch?" Danny asked gently as he grinned at me.

"What? He pitches, too. He never told me that. Figures," I said rather dejectedly. "Is he a good pitcher, oh don't answer, I'm sure he's good."

"He's great. Reminds me of Larry Peoples -- speed wise," Danny said nonchalantly, holding back his glee at the information, knowing it was turning my stomach.

"That fast, huh? Wow. But did he have any control?"

"Don't know yet. Just saw him throw a few. Coach Dale didn't want to press any of our pitchers too much the first day," Danny said as he slurped the end of his shake. "But, he did hit three home runs in batting practice. I tell ya, Mickster, we're gonna compete."

"I got to admit, Louis Shanks may have the cellar all to themselves this year. But, we'll have to wait and see before we start talking a championship for City National. Come on! Seven Up has got some big hitters and big throwers, and you know, we're in fine shape with Fish, Bob, and me -- three 'A' pitchers," I said rather proudly.

"I hit four homers in batting practice," Danny said, preferring to ignore my predictions. "I think I'm going to have a great year."

"Probably. But, your team will still need some more pitching," I said as the capper before changing the subject once again. "Are you coming today?"

"Of course. What time?" he asked.

"Two. At Westenfield," I said as I pushed myself away from the counter and walked over to the comic book section to browse.

"All right," Danny said as he started for the front door. "See ya there."

"Later Alligator," I threw out over my shoulder as he disappeared.

Sunday afternoons, from the fall until opening day of the baseball season, were spent playing touch football at one of the many playground parks dotting the area. Westenfield Park was located on the outskirts of Tarrytown, just across the Missouri Pacific railway tracks from Clarksville. The park had a swimming pool, two cement tennis courts, and a full-length-concrete basketball court. There was a big stone carousel, a couple of large slides, a jungle gym, seesaw and swings for the youngsters. Behind all of this, next to the railroad tracks, was the softball field that would double as our sandlot football arena for that Sunday.

While pedaling toward Westenfield, I decided to ride by Willie's and see if he wanted to join us for a game. He didn't have a phone, but he told me once I could call the Clarksville Baptist Church and they would get him a message. But, I didn't have time for all that and I knew where he lived.

Working my way through Clarksville's rocky streets reminded me of Combat, one of my favorite TV shows, where army squadrons had to constantly negotiate mine fields. I was concerned about hitting a pothole and getting a flat, when suddenly some projectile struck my right arm above the

49

elbow. The force of the blow and the surprise of the moment almost knocked me off my bike. I skidded to a stop and looked back at a couple of young black boys. They were tossing rocks in the air and laughing menacingly, almost daring me to come their way. I rubbed at my arm where the small rock had hit me.

"Hey, why did you do that?" I yelled at them.

"You ain't s'posed to be here," one of them said threateningly. "What you doin' in these parts, whitey?"

I chose to ignore them and got on my bike to pedal away as one of them called after me.

"Where you going, yellow white boy? You come back here."

But I kept pedaling and immediately a couple of rocks landed on both sides of the bike just barely missing me. I didn't look back, and turned left onto what I hoped was Willie's street. I was relieved to see his driveway and rode up to the side of the yellow-painted wooden house. I looked back down the street. The kids had not followed, but I suspected I would run into them again on the way back to Westenfield Park. I was sure hoping Willie would be with me. I checked my arm. There was a small abrasion and it stung a little, but I suspected there was no major damage.

I knocked on the outside screen door. The door opened and standing on the other side of the screen was a tall, slender, unkempt black man who I suspected must be Willie's father.

"Hello, sir," I said with the utmost respect. "I was wondering if Willie might want to come play football over at Westenfield?"

I think the man was stunned to see and hear a white boy standing right in front of him at his very door in Clarksville. He looked me up and down, twisting a toothpick between his teeth. I assumed he had just eaten, or maybe I was interrupting his lunch. I didn't really feel a sense of welcome generating from his demeanor and waited for a response for I don't know how long before finally hearing Willie's mother, Teresa, in the background.

"For cryin' out loud, who is it, Walter?" she yelled from inside.

"Dunno. I may be secin' thangs. Some white boy's a standin' here," he said indifferently.

"It must be Mickey. Let the boy in for Christ's sakes." Then she screamed out, "Willie! Get your business done in there, son. Your little friend's here."

Suddenly, Teresa appeared over the shoulder of Willie's father, who had one hand on his hip. Teresa stuck a rolling pin in the triangle between his arm and his body and pushed the screen door open.

"Oh, I'm so glad you came by, Mickey. This here stump of a log is Willie's papa, Walter. He don't say much," Teresa said, as I stepped up into the house and extended my hand toward the man.

"Mickey Charles. It's nice to meet you sir," I said.

"I don't mind talkin'," he said as he shook my hand. "And I have thangs to say. It's kind of hard to get in a word around here, is all. You must be the boy that talked my Willie into playing organized baseball with those white boys across the tracks?"

"Uh, well, I only --"

Teresa didn't give me the chance to respond.

"Walter Henry Veils," she barked, "you know very well who this is. What you doing? Trying to give the boy a hard time? This boy here is good peoples and they're not 'nough of his kind around no more. So you behave, and show your son's friend some respect."

He kind of smiled at me and winked. Then he said, "See what I mean about getting' a word in 'round here." He chuckled and sat down at the kitchen table behind him.

I looked up to see Willie enter the kitchen, "What's up, Mick."

"You want to play some touch football over at Westenfield?" I asked.

"Right on!" he answered enthusiastically. "Are there any stickers? Can I play barefoot?"

"No stickers that I know of," I said.

"William Abraham Veils, you go put on your sneakers, young man," Teresa piped in. "No boy of mine runs around Tarrytown in his bare feet."

Willie ran off to get his shoes. Teresa turned to me and said, "Mickey, we gonna barbecue some spare ribs this afternoon. Maybe you can come back and share 'em. Any of your little friends are welcome to join us."

"Why thank you, Ms. Veils. That's right nice of you," I said, with a degree of concern that my grammar was slipping into a version of Clarksville speak.

"Mickey! I don't want to tell ya' again, son. The name's Teresa. All righty?" She demanded. Then she pointed at her husband saying, "And that lump of lard, you call Walter, but he'll pretty much answer to anything. Don't ya darlin'?"

Walter chose to ignore Teresa's rhetorical question. He was working the end of his toothpick with the utmost concentration. Willie showed up with his sneakers tied together and wrapped them around his neck. He kissed his mother on the cheek and threw his arm around my shoulder saying, "Are ya ready to go, my blood brother?"

"Let's roll," I said and followed Willie out the screen door. I stopped and turned to his father. "Mist--um, Walter, it was nice meeting you, sir."

He took his toothpick and pointed it at me, saying, "The pleasure was all mine, son, all mine," and he broke out into a belly laugh. I was beginning to observe a similar family trait.

Teresa came to the screen door as we reached the bike and yelled, "Remember those spare ribs, boys, Walter's gonna have 'em ready 'bout five."

We waved. Willie took his position on the handlebars and we started off. I was a little disappointed when I took the first turn and the two nasty rock-throwers were gone. I kind of grinned because I actually wanted to run into the rock-throwing brats, and I wondered why. I guess I wanted to prove to them that I belonged.

The rest of the kids playing touch football that day were already warming up when Willie and I arrived at Westenfield Park. There was Danny, Jack, Stan, Bob, and Fish, my other Rylanders' pitching mates, and Dave Looney, who, before I knew Willie, had been the fastest burner among us. Perfect, I thought, after giving the crowd a quick count. With Willie and me, it'll make an even four a side. I liked four on four more than five, six or seven on a side, because you had a larger spread on the field and usually scored a lot more touchdowns, which is what it's all about in sandlot. We made Danny and Bob captains, since they played the most at quarterback, and they chose up teams. Danny won the toss and with the first pick took Willie, so Bob took Jack. Then Bob got the first second pick and took Dave Looney. Danny looked at me and said, "I'll take Fish". I shot him the bird. He smiled. They flipped again for who gets the first pick of the last two, between Stan and me. Bob won and took Stan. Danny laughed and said, "We' re stuck with Charles again."

"For that -- I'm starting at quarterback," I shot back indignantly.

"Until the first interception, it's all yours," Danny replied gallantly.

Two hours later I was still throwing for our team, which had a one touchdown lead as we were closing in on the ultimate goal of becoming Sunday champs. The first to score ten touchdowns won automatically, and up to this point, I had been having a career sandlot football day. I was in a zone. With Willie and Fish's speed, and Danny's height, I seemed to be throwing to wide-open receivers all day. Nine touchdowns and no interceptions, and in my mind, Johnny U couldn't have done better.

We were about to receive our kickoff after their eighth score, when I noticed three girls sitting on the swings. They turned out to be Kitty and her friends Robyn Sage and Trudy Prentice. Even before we had gone steady, Kitty had a habit of showing up late on Sundays because she lived right down the street. Usually, I would spend a few minutes talking to her and her friends after our games. But now, since we were going steady, I was feeling a little different, almost like I was embarrassed she was here, and worried about what the other guys would say. Maybe my friends would taunt me, or make fun of me in some way. Nevertheless, the game continued.

We took the kickoff back to about midfield. I called a criss-cross for Fish and Danny and a stop and go for Willie. I felt like finishing our opponents off fast. I don't know if I was trying to impress my girlfriend, or simply wanted to end the game and disappear. Danny snapped me the ball and I faked a quick button-hook to Willie and then, as he streaked past Dave Looney, who had struggled to guard the jet all day, I glanced Kitty's way before I let go a mighty throw. Unfortunately, I had gripped the ball a little too tightly and it floated up and into the wind like a wimpy shuttlecock coming to rest in Dave Looney's intercepting arms. Willie was twenty yards downfield on his pattern, so even he couldn't catch Looney as he streaked for their goal. I was the only chance. I had an angle until the move Looney put on me at the sidelines made me think my legs were made of rubber. I rolled on the ground as he scored the tying touchdown. I looked up to Kitty who, I thought, looked embarrassed by my play and when I saw her turn away to her friends, I thought the worst. She was probably whispering her displeasure in my performance and wanted to break up immediately after the game. Willie brought me back to the moment.

"Man, Mick, what's up with that throw," he said. "Tryin' to impress the women folk over there?"

As he helped me up, I nodded my head and stated, "You know, I just learned a little lesson about concentration."

"Nice pass, butthead," Danny growled as he ran by me. "You center the rest of the game -- I'm taking over." He was fired up. It was the first time today he would play the position for which he was born, and would have probably made a career of, if it hadn't been for the serious knee injuries he incurred later during high school. But this day, due to a little kismet maybe, Danny wouldn't get his chance to shine at quarterback.

I glanced over at Kitty as the other team was kicking off and then I shook my head as if to wash away the images like an etch-a-sketch. I looked up to see the ball practically on my face. I barely caught it with my fingernails and took four quick steps to my left before pivoting and throwing a lateral across the field to Willie who was set up behind the blocking wall of Danny and Fish. It was a play I had set up in an earlier huddle in case I ever received a kick, and this was the first time we got to use it. Willie streaked down the far sideline behind a couple of tidy blocks by his teammates and the victory was ours. I turned to get the satisfaction of my new girl's attention, but my bubble burst as I saw Kitty wasn't even watching. She and her friends were laughing on the swings.

Both teams shook hands and patted one another on the back after the game. Danny and Jack made a point of inviting Willie to play with us any Sunday. Willie then chose the moment to invite all of them to come over to his house for spare ribs that his daddy was barbecuing. I looked at my friends, who all seemed a little uncomfortable, looking down, adjusting their caps, and tying their shoes before finally Fish said, "Thanks for the invite, but my parents are expecting me for an early dinner."

"Yeah, me too," mumbled Jack and several others simultaneously.

Dave Looney blurted out what the others were maybe thinking when he said, "Hell, man, I ain't getting' caught dead in Clarksville." With that, he waved at the rest of us and walked away.

Danny patted Willie on the shoulder and said, "I'll take a rain check, it's my younger brother's birthday. I have to go home for his party."

Everyone said good-byes and started to walk away leaving Willie and me alone. I pointed over at the girls and said, "Before we go, I want you meet somebody."

I put my hand on his shoulder and walked with Willie toward the swings. Kitty saw us approaching and jumped out of her moving swing and landed softly in the sand, which prompted her other two friends to stop swinging. As we got nearer, I noticed them exchanging concerned glances and whispers, but didn't think anything about it at the time. Later, I would understand. Kitty took a couple of quick steps and jumped into my arms, hugging me. She said, "Nice lateral."

I broke the hug and held her at arms length, "You saw that!" I said surprised.

"Yeah, it was great. Made up for that wounded duck you threw a few minutes before."

One thing that attracted me to Kitty was her knowledge of sports, especially football. Her dad, a renowned local artist, had always drawn the caricatures on the covers of programs for Texas Longhorn home football games. Because her father drew the cover, from an early age, Kitty would study the program information, and developed into a sports trivia whiz. Unlike many females of the day, she learned about the various sports and could communicate on an almost equal level with the boys. Kitty turned and checked out Willie standing a few feet away and asked, "Who's this?"

"This is Willie Veils," I explained. "He's from Clarksville. Willie, this is Jill. But, I call her Kitty. We're going steady."

Willie shook Kitty's hand and said, "Mickey hadn't told me how pretty his girl was. It's nice to meet you Jill, really nice to meet you." Then he playfully slugged me on the shoulder and said, "You dog."

I had no idea what that meant and neither did Kitty, who chose to change the subject when she said, "Willie, I would like you to meet --" but then she stopped as she began to introduce her two friends on the swings. To her surprise, they were walking down the road away from the park and already out of earshot.

"Um, that's strange. I guess they had to go," Kitty said with a little disappointment in her voice. "Mickey, I forgot to tell you, Robyn's mother is throwing a party for her birthday on Thursday around their pool, and they'll be dancing and serving food and stuff, but no swimming. There's something wrong with their pool. So you can go, right? It's Thursday after school at four o'clock at Robyn's house. You know where that is? It's on Spring Lane behind Tarrytown Methodist Church?"

"I know where Robyn lives," was all I could offer as I kind of wished my Rylanders' practices were Thursday instead of Wednesday. I nodded uncertainly. I guess I was going to the party.

"Okay, great. I'll see you in class tomorrow." She leaned over and kissed me on the cheek and turned to Willie, "It was nice to meet you, Willie. I hope to see you again someday."

"Oh, you'll see a lot of Willie," I said.

"Oh," Kitty tilted her head. "Why is that?"

"He's playing with us at Bishop. He made Danny's team and he's really good."

Kitty smiled. "Well, a Negro in our Little League. I have to shake the hand of the Jackie Robinson of West Austin."

Willie took her hand, shook it and said, "He and Willie Mays are my heroes."

"Good ones to have," she declared as she turned and skipped away, shouting back over her shoulder, "See y'all later."

"This Negro," chimed Willie, "has got some ribs if you be interested, master Mickey."

It was my turn to punch his shoulder as I said, "Stop it or I'll start calling you Little Black Sambo."

"You know better. Let's go eat some ribs."

56

As I pedaled away from Westenfield with Willie sitting in his usual position, I felt like I had been involved in an extremely profound sandlot football game. I'm not sure if it was because of my performance in front of Kitty or the fact Willie had played with us for the first time.

Unknown to us, we had innocently started a backlash among some parents in Tarrytown. It was beyond my comprehension that one of our weekly Sunday rituals would lead to a number of unfortunate, silent years between the oldest of West Austin families, some who even attended the same churches.

CHAPTER SEVEN

Due to the presence of Trudy Prentice at our Sunday touch football game, repercussions, retaliations, and scandals reverberated throughout the stuffier confines of Tarrytown for the next couple of days. Her father, Mr. Prentice, a firewood supplier, was a rude, overweight slob of a man who ran a cedar chopper operation west of Austin. He was a full-fledged, card-carrying member of the John Birch Society; a conservative organization aimed at keeping the status quo Jim Crow realities in place. He came from an old area family, a descendent of some of the original followers of Stephen F. Austin who settled along the Colorado River at Waterloo Bend. Because of this history and his lack of real education, he held onto his old-line thinking. He was still fuming from being forced to accept that Negroes were being allowed to attend O. Henry Junior High School with his oldest daughter. Among his efforts to impede progress had been the formation of a committee that attempted to circumvent the *Brown vs. Board of Education* decision in front of the City of Austin School Board. He was unsuccessful in that sinister campaign, but he did find he had many allies to his twisted, antiquated ways of thinking. The thought of his daughter sharing the same West Austin playground with a Colored was quite revolting to the misguided Mr. Prentice and he couldn't leave well enough alone. The stink he started that Sunday evening with calls to his allies, then Kitty's father and my mother, and parents of some of the others, was a weak attempt to keep the walls of demarcation from tumbling like those of Jericho.

Mr. Prentice, who had two daughters and no sons, had never been involved with the West Austin Little League and was apparently unaware of Willie's participation, or surely we would have had a disturbance before this time. Each of the parents contacted were caught totally unaware when they answered their telephones that Sunday evening to the screams of Mr. Prentice's veiled threats and sincere warnings about an intolerable situation developing in Tarrytown. In his racist opinion, if "one nigger child" was allowed to integrate the playgrounds in his neighborhood, then by this summer there would "surely be darkies swimming in the pool" at Westenfield Park with his daughters, and he wasn't about to let that happen. He knew how the "dominoes would tumble" and soon he might have a "Niggard" family wanting to reside on his street, and in his mind, this would ultimately lead to violence -- which for him, was the only way of keeping the white wash of his neighborhood intact. While Mr. Prentice was setting his prejudiced tumbleweed in motion -- to eliminate the decay of West Austin civilization -- I was devouring some of the most delicious, greasy spareribs alongside Willie at his family's backyard in Clarksville. We were sitting around an old weathered picnic table beside the large stone barbecue pit Walter had built, eating the spareribs, drinking Dr Peppers, and sampling some of Teresa's mouth-watering homemade potato salad and cornbread.

There wasn't a lot of conversation as we all worked toward the bone of the matter. After finishing my second plate, I noticed the time was getting on and I would be expected at home for my own dinner in less than an hour. I was always hungry when there was food in sight, so I knew I wouldn't really have a problem forcing myself to have another meal with my own family when I returned home. I made my apologies for eating and pedaling, but the Veils seemed to understand my predicament. Teresa offered me portions of everything to take home, but I declined with the exception of a few bones for my dog. I wrapped them up in a brown bag and secured them under the bike strap and off I rode toward my next meal.

I had a good time at Willie's and learned several more items of interest about his family. Willie originally had two older brothers, but the oldest one was killed crossing the railroad tracks when Willie was ten. The tragedy "united the neighborhood, which healed some old scars and provided some good from the horrifying and tragic event." Teresa, even though it was years later, still wiped a tear from her eye as she related the story. Walter, as it turned out, worked for the Texas Transportation Department in the division charged with maintaining state highways and airport runways. Sometimes his work took him away from Clarksville for a couple of weeks at a time. More recently he had to travel to towns like Marshall, Tyler, Paris, and Athens, up in the northeast part of the state for his work detail. Teresa worked six days a week for two gentlemen, Bruce and Fletcher, who were interior decorators and lived together in that large pink house on the hill where I met her. I think I remember my mom talking about Bruce and Fletcher. I thought about asking her if they might be the same ones when I got home for dinner. I learned Walter and Teresa were, unfortunately, not going to be able to watch their son play Little League ball because of their full work schedules. The only day we didn't have games at Bishop Field was Sunday, their only day off. That's too bad. I can't imagine my Mother ever missing a game.

Pedaling down Windsor Road, I knew I still had one obstacle to avoid if I wished to make it home in time for my second feeding in an hour. Brutus, a massive, black, slobbering beast of a dog that lived at the corner house patrolled the entrance to my neighborhood. This was long before leash laws in Austin and everyone's animals were free to roam the neighborhoods. If I wasn't in such a hurry, I would have pedaled around to the other entrance about eight blocks away but today I would have to shoot the gauntlet. Besides, I thought, having to pedal for your life to get past the ferocious beast was nothing more than a pay back for the many times my dog, Napoleon, had stopped Brutus' owner's car in the middle of the street in front of my house.

Napoleon had a singular gift among fellow dogs for chasing cars that bordered on perfection. He would hear the engines before the car was in sight, so no matter what the speed, Napoleon would take up his position in the center of street blocking its right of way. Ultimately, when the car came to a stop in front of our bold, but somewhat tunnel-visioned boxer, he would attack by biting the front bumper of the auto repeatedly, until we could persuade the driver to floor the car and move on down the road. When the driver would finally obey, Napoleon would do a side step under the lurching car and before you knew it, he was racing on the curb alongside the vehicle as it motored away.

There was the one dark but hilarious time when my mom and I decided to test our speedy boxer to see how fast he could run. She backed out of the driveway and then well down the street, while Napoleon attacked the bumper, we reversed to our starting position for the dash. My mother pressed the pedal to the metal and we were off. I kept both eyes on the dog while she kept one eye on the road and the other on the speedometer. As she called out, "10, 15, 20", he was running full speed, barking, and looking directly at our car while avoiding all bushes, curbs and trees along the way. Mom yelled out "23, 27, 30", to which I screamed, "Stop!" for I couldn't believe what I had witnessed. As he reached his cruising speed of about 29 or 30, Napoleon had jumped a bush he caught sight of in his peripheral vision, but he apparently missed seeing the gas lamp which rose out of the center of the vegetation. The pole supporting the lamp looked a bit like a cartoon when it took the shape of my dog's head upon impact. When we stopped, I explained what happened, but Napoleon was nowhere to be seen. We drove back to find the dog lying by the back door with both paws over his nose, still somewhat dazed. We checked him out and found that nothing was broken, which seemed miraculous considering the impact I had witnessed. My mother thought this would finally break Napoleon of his nasty neighborhood habit. Nothing doing -- for on our very next trip, as we started the car to leave, Napoleon rose to face another challenge and chased us to the end of the street.

My focus tightened as I neared ground zero on my bike. I rounded the corner with a head of steam as I saw Brutus on his haunches ready to pounce into action. I pedaled for my life as the dog began to race down his yard on an angle to cut me off before I passed. Utilizing a move similar to the one Dave Looney had schooled me on in our football game earlier, I avoided the oncoming charge of the animal and actually left Brutus sliding on his stomach across the pavement after his legs came out from under him.

I was home free. What a day, I thought. What a great day!

I turned into my driveway and rode in between my brother's souped-up hotrods. Anchoring my bike against a tree, I was startled when Napoleon jumped up and placed his paws in the center of my back, knocking me to the ground. I grabbed the brown bag and opened it, saying, "Here, look what I got for you, Napy." I gave the dog the rib bones and then ran toward the carport door directly off our kitchen. I think I was even whistling when I opened the door to our house.

My day immediately changed, as my Mom met me face to face in the entrance demanding to know where I had been.

"At Westenfield, playing football," I responded.

"I heard your game has been over for a couple of hours. So, I repeat, where have you been?" she asked. She could be very demanding, but when she was, my mother always had a pretty good reason. I mean, I hadn't mentioned the two hours at Willie's barbeque because I thought she would be really mad if I spoiled her time-consuming efforts in the kitchen.

Attempting to step around her, she blocked the way, "What?" I said. "Let me by."

"First, young man, you have some explaining to do. Where have you been? Tell me now!"

"I was at Willie's house. His mom invited me over for some ribs and I couldn't turn her down. But, I didn't eat a lot, I promise. I'm still hungry. What are we having for dinner?"

My mom chose to ignore me and just stared, saying "You rode your bike into Clarksville by yourself. What were you thinking? You trying to get yourself killed!"

"What? I've done it before. It's not that bad," I said. "The roads sort of suck."

Bam! She hit me upside the head with an open right hand. "Don't you go speaking like some degenerate. I don't know about you spending time with that boy. Nothing good can come of it."

"But --" I started, forgetting she hated that word.

"Don't you 'but' me Mickey Charles! I don't want to hear anything out of you right now. You march your self down the hall and do your homework."

I paused at the door on the way out of the room, still in full wonder about why she was flipping out. "What about dinner?" I asked quietly.

"Dinner is ruined. Do you want to know why?" she said as she moved toward the center of the kitchen and sat on a tall stool. To my shrug, she said, "Well, I'll tell you. For the past hour and a half I have been talking to one after another of your young friends' confused, concerned, angry, and extremely upset mothers and fathers."

"Why?" I asked. "What happened that was so bad?"

"You don't know?" she said flabbergasted.

"How could I know, I told you, I was at Willie's since we played football. I don't know what happened!" I exclaimed.

"Willie happened! You happened! Get it! You and Willie, this whole thing is what happened! Do you understand?" She was whispering a scream, all the while trying to contain her discomfort with the whole subject.

"No! I don't understand! What's wrong with this planet?" I asked.

"What's that supposed to mean young man?" she asked.

"You know, why's everything got to be so crazy. People don't see people as just people. They got to see them as aliens or something. It's just crazy!" I screamed out, holding back tears.

"Mickey, it's not crazy, it's the way things are," she said.

"Well, the way things are really suck." I dashed off to my room and slammed the door behind me.

When you're twelve, you never get the last word. I knew that, but I needed a minute or so to collect my thoughts. What had we done except play touch football with a Negro. Oh my God, what a transgression. Come on -- get real. My mother's got to be with me on this one. I can't always be on the wrong side, can I? Sooner or later, I'm bound to get something right. She must be upset because all of these calls ruined dinner. But, come on, we only played touch football.

"Mickey," my Mom said, knocking on my door. "Honey, I'm coming in."

"It's open," I said.

"Let's talk son. I don't want to let this thing fester. We need to discuss it plainly, without getting all upset with each other. We'll work through this together and come up with a plan. What do you say?"

"We were just playing touch football. What's the crime and why is everybody so upset?"

"This here Mr. Prentice is sort of an extremist," she started, but I interrupted.

"Trudy Prentice's dad started this ruckus! Why? What's going on?" I was on the verge of tears from the confusion.

"Evidently she came back from the park and told her father about seeing you and Willie walking arm and arm, and he went berserk. I don't know how to explain it all. I mean what you're doing probably isn't wrong, but to people like Mr. Prentice it is. He was raised under a different set of rules. That doesn't make what he believes right, but it's all he knows. And though time changes, sometimes people don't. And, I guess that's where we run into problems."

"What do you think about all of this?" I asked

"Me? Well, I don't think we need to push anything on other people, Mickey. We got along this well so far, why upset the apple cart. Maybe next time you have Willie join your game, you go play at House Park where no locals will see you," she said, referring to the high school football field downtown.

"You mean, you think what I did was wrong?"

"It's a choice I wish you hadn't made. Let's leave it at that," my mother replied.

"Well, Willie is my friend. You ought to see the way his family took me in and shared their spare ribs and all. I want to return the favor and have Willie over next week for steaks."

"Oh, I don't know, Mickey. We've got some concerns about doing something like that right now. Let's give it a little time. Maybe later, we'll take Willie somewhere, okay, Hon?" my mom stroked my hair. I knew that was a sign the conversation was about to end. We didn't have a lot of physical touching in my family, so when it happened there was usually a reason. The

64

stroke of the hair was a way of offering the peace pipe. It meant for the time being, the discussion was over.

She kissed me on the forehead, left me to my thoughts, and closed the door behind her. I fell back on my bed, stared at the ceiling, and couldn't help mumbling to myself.

"It was only a touch football game for Christ's sake!"

CHAPTER EIGHT

The next morning I entered the sunroom of our house, where my family usually shared a large breakfast, our favorite sections of the paper and upbeat conversation about the day ahead. I discovered the mood was somber, to say the least. My oldest brother, David, was missing, probably still producing Z's in his bedroom. He was a senior in high school and had special privileges. My other brother, Larry, a sophomore, was devouring the sports page. He looked up and whispered to me, "Smooth move, Junior."

My stepfather looked up from his crossword puzzle and winked at me. I could hear my mother in the kitchen and I guess she heard me because she called out, "Mickey, is that you? Come in here, son."

"Yes, ma'am," I said and headed into the kitchen.

My mom looked up from the range where she was frying some eggs and did a double take. She asked, "Why on earth are you already dressed?"

I usually ate breakfast in my pajamas and then showered and dressed, but only after checking the Yankees' morning box score. Today, I just didn't feel like being held under the microscope of breakfast scrutiny.

"I'm sorry," I said. "I guess I forgot to tell you there's a pre-school meeting of the Chess Club and I'm already late. I'll have to skip breakfast this morning."

My mother probably knew when I was using the little white lie, but she hardly ever called me on it. "All right. Go make sure your oldest brother's out of bed before you leave."

I started out of the kitchen but she stopped me, saying, "And, Mickey --"

"Yes."

"It's best for all if you keep quiet at school about all this Willie business. Just let it lie. Don't force the issue. It will be forgotten in a few days. Okay?"

"Okay," I said, as if I wasn't going to talk to everybody about it, I still had to appease my mom.

I made sure David was out bed before I left our house. I exited through the front door so I wouldn't have to walk past the rest of the family in the sunroom. Of course, with no Chess Club meeting to attend, I headed for The Clearing to give myself some quiet time to think. I needed to figure out what to say to Kitty and my friends. I'm sure some of them really caught hell and I guess it was my fault, even though, I kept repeating to myself -- all we did was play touch football.

I reclined on the pitcher's mound in The Clearing and looked up at the billowy clouds blowing by on the southeasterly winds. I fantasized about catching one of the floaters and taking a trip. It would take me somewhere far away from here, where maybe everyone would get along and we wouldn't need parents or teachers or preachers to tell us their own versions of what was right and wrong.

I decided to head off Kitty at the pass. Knowing her mother always dropped her off at the back entrance to the school, I was hiding there when their car pulled up. After Kitty's mom was out of sight, I stepped out from behind an oak and yelled for Kitty to join me. We started down a trail that took us around to the playground.

"Are you all right, Mickey?" she said concerned.

"I guess. Did your parents yell at you?"

"Oh, no," Kitty said. "Mother thought it was a big fuss over nothing. When she told my father, he called Trudy's dad a 'Bircher'."

"Why did Trudy start all of this?" I asked.

"I'm sorry I asked her to come down to the park," she said. "I'm sure she thought telling her father about Willie was the right thing to do."

"What did Willie ever do to her?" I asked.

67

"It's not just Willie for them, it's the whole Colored race. My parents called them bigots and Daddy said they'd never change. He said to tell you this is a free country for all, no matter what some idiots think."

"Oh, God," I said as I sighed mightily.

She reached over and hooked my arm with hers and we walked down the trail to the playground. We strolled toward our classroom across the softball field. Just as we reached the door, Kitty said, "I liked Willie."

"I do too."

"The kids say he can really play baseball."

"Willie," I confirmed, "could be the best we ever had."

"That's pretty neat," Kitty said, then she kissed me on the cheek. "See ya' at lunch."

She went inside our classroom and I waited a few minutes before following. One thing was for sure: since she mentioned lunch, I remembered I skipped breakfast and I was really hungry.

The cafeteria at Casis Elementary also served as the auditorium for special events, lectures, PTA meetings, and student election speeches. For the past three years, I spoke from the stage at the far end of the cafeteria when I ran for the various fire office positions. It's kind of hard to believe I won with slogans like: "Don't be a hick, vote for Mick" or "If it's a fire you need to lick, then vote for Mick". My particular favorite was "Don't be picky, vote for Mickey," which I had printed on my buttons.

At the near end of the hall was the kitchen and cafeteria serving line. After receiving the meat, vegetable, potato, roll, milk and a slice of pie or some Jell-O, you paid twenty-five cents to the lady at the end of the counter for a very nutritious meal. That day I doubled up on a couple of items. After paying forty-five cents, I carried my tray to our class table and found an empty seat alongside Kitty and Deborah. At lunch, you still had to eat with your own class, but after you finished, your teacher could excuse you to mingle with the other students. I ploughed through my meal so I could finally get to talk to the other kids who had played touch football the day before, at Westenfield Park.

After swallowing the last of my pie, Ms. Vance excused me and I found the others at a table by the stage. I waved and sat down.

"Howdy, y'all. Can you believe this mess? So give me the bad news."

Fish raised his hand saying, "My parents blew a lid and grounded me for a month. When they found out Willie was playing in our league this year, they threatened to pull me out. It's crazy. I like Willie. My parents just don't get it."

"How about y'all?" I asked the others.

"We're okay," Jack said. "My folks were fine. They blew it off. What did the General do?" Some of my friends playfully referred to my mother as the "General" -- I guess for her dictatorial manner.

"It ruined her dinner," I said. "She was mad as a hornet. She thought I caused this by pushing Willie to play. None of us have a problem with Willie, right?"

"None of us do," Danny confided. "But, Dave's mother kept him out of school today. He called and asked me to get his assignments. Said his mother went berserk and yelled her head off."

"Maybe, I should drop by after school," I stated. "And, try to smooth things out."

Jack said, "I think you've done enough."

"What's that mean?" I asked.

"It's just, well -- I'm afraid if you go roughing feathers, Mrs. Looney won't allow Dave to play with Seven Up this year."

"You're crazy. Judge Looney is your coach," I replied.

"They're getting a divorce," Jack stated. "The Judge moved to the Westgate apartments."

"I didn't know," I said.

"Nobody did. Dave's gonna live with his mother. And, you know how crazy she can get."

"What a mess," I mumbled.

Danny put his hand on my shoulder and said, "It'll be okay. It was just a touch football game."

"Exactly!" I said, and shook my head.

The school bell rang ending our lunch period and as we were walking out of the cafeteria, Danny asked, "Who you pitching against us Saturday?"

"Do we play City National opening day?" I asked.

"Correct-oh-moondo. So, come on, who's pitching?" he asked.

"I don't know. Travis hasn't made up his mind."

"Who ever it is, we'll be ready," Danny said.

"Opening day," I exclaimed. "I can't wait."

We walked down the hall along with the other sixth graders. Our stomachs were full, our minds somewhat bewildered, but our expectations remained very high. And after a little discussion about baseball, I was almost beginning to feel normal. Then I saw Kitty talking with Robyn down the hall, heading back to our classrooms. This reminded me of the upcoming party. I turned to Danny and asked, "Are you going to Robyn's party on Thursday?"

"Yeah. My mother's making me go."

"Thank God!" I exclaimed. "I'll have someone to talk to -- I was afraid it would all be dorks."

We reached our respective classrooms across the hall from one another at the end of our wing. Danny saluted me and said, "See ya later, alligator."

"In a while, crocodile," I replied and then walked directly into Ms. Vance standing at the entrance to our room. "I'm sorry, Ms. Vance, I didn't see you there."

"Mr. Charles, you must watch where you are going or you'll never know where you have been," she said sternly.

"Yes, ma'am, I'll remember that," I said as I slinked into our classroom.

After another period of drifting through Ms. Vance's droning about grammar, the day-ending bell finally rang. I walked home through the woods and between neighbors' houses until I arrived at our backyard. Napoleon had been sleeping by the backdoor until he heard my footsteps and bounded out to greet me. He loved to run about three-quarter speed and leap up squarely planting his front paws right into your chest. If you weren't braced for the force, he would knock you over and start licking your face. I dropped my books and hugged my dog, saying, "Hi there, Napy. How you doing, buddy?" As an answer, he wagged his stub of a tail and bounced around like the puppy he was several years before.

I glanced up at our second story playroom window and an idea came to me. If I didn't want to humiliate myself in public by dancing at Robyn's party, then I'd better practice. I opened the back door, entered our sunroom, and called for Napoleon to come with me. I left my books on the table and we raced up the stairs to the playroom.

It was a special place. We had a pool table that we could cover with a ping-pong table. When I was younger, on a particularly boring rainy day my brother, Larry, and I created a game we called Gnip-Gnop (ping-pong backward), in which we utilized the walls, windows, and ceiling to play our game that was a combination of racquetball and Ping-Pong. If it was raining outside, we could spend hours playing our Gnip-Gnop tournaments.

The playroom had two sets of bunk beds for sleepovers, or for guests from out of town. In the corner by the window was my first hi-fi, a Zenith Fidelity Record Player. It had been a present from Santa the previous Christmas and replaced an even older model my brothers had used for years. Our record collection was pathetic, to say the least, made up of about fifteen 45's. I started to flip through the selections looking for a slow record in which to practice dancing. There was "The Peppermint Twist" by Joey Dee and the Starlighters, "Runaround Sue" and "The Wanderer" by Dion, and one of my favorites, James Darren's "Goodbye Cruel World," which I picked out and placed on the player. It's not a song to dance to, but I thought while I searched for the right record, I could sing along with this one. I placed the needle on the record and it scratched to a start. When the song reached its famous chorus, I was down on one knee with an imaginary microphone singing along:

Well, the joke's on me, I'm off to join the circus
Oh, Mr. Barnum, save a place for me
Shoot me out of a cannon, I don't care
Let the people point at me and stare
I'll tell the world that woman, wherever she may be
That mean, fickle woman made a cryin' clown outta me.

Suddenly, Napoleon barked and attacked, knocking me over like a bowling pin. I don't think he appreciated my voice cracking when I tried to sustain a long note.

"Uncle," I said to the playfully mauling Napoleon. "All right, I'll stop singing. Let me up."

71

Napoleon jumped onto one of the bunk beds, barked a couple of times, and wagged his tail. I guess he felt that I was going to live up to my bargain. I jumped up and returned to the stack of records and continued flipping: "Twist and Shout" by the Isley Brothers, "The Twist" and "Twist Again" by Chubby Checker, "Twistin' the Night Away" by Sam Cooke -- the Twist was obviously huge in 1962.

Almost anyone could do the Twist, I thought; it didn't really take much skill. What I needed was a slow song to practice my box step. I flipped to the back to see some slower selections: The Four Seasons' "Big Girls Don't Cry," "The Night has a 1000 Eyes" by Bobby Vee, and the one I was looking for all along, which of course was the last one in the pile, "I Left My Heart in San Francisco" by Tony Bennett.

I took the record out of its cover and placed it on the turntable, on top of the other 45's already sitting there. I gently placed the needle on the spinning record. I extended one arm in the air like it was holding Kitty's hand and placed my other arm around her imaginary waist, holding her at a respectable distance.

As Tony sang, I awkwardly tried to move with the rhythm of the song. It was amazing how I could excel in golf, tennis, swimming, water skiing, and participate in all of the major sports, but simply placing one foot behind the other, in time to slow music, completely baffled me. I would be in high school before I was ever comfortable slow dancing and that was due to completely other reasons than improved rhythm.

As the song was nearing completion, Napoleon decided to become a critic again and barked at me to stop the box step exhibition. I laughed and grabbed my boxer and wrestled him to the ground. "I bet you're hungry, aren't you, Napy," I said. His ears went erect and he leapt for the stairs in one quick motion. I turned off the hi-fi and sighed, saying aloud to myself, "I guess I'm a cooked goose."

Thursday afternoon arrived and I walked up the steps of the Sage's house and rang their doorbell. The maid opened the door and I was ushered through the house to the outside deck surrounding a kidney-shaped swimming pool. Mr. and Mrs. Sage introduced themselves and I thanked them for having me. They pointed to the refreshments and goodies laid out on a spread in one corner of the deck and told me to make myself at home and have a good time. I looked around the back yard to see the boys on one side of the pool and all of the girls on the other. I surveyed the group of boys, looking for Danny. Unfortunately, he wasn't there. I didn't see any friends, only acquaintances from school, and most of them, sorry to say, looked like dorks. In a social environment that could even make a cool customer feel the heat, these kids looked completely cooked. This relaxed me a little, for I suddenly realized I couldn't possibly be the worst dancer at the party. I made eye contact with Kitty across the pool where she was chatting away with three friends. She waved and blew a kiss that I feigned to duck. She laughed and excused herself from her mates, walked around the pool, and met me by the refreshment table. I was a little self-conscious since we were the only boy and girl together, but Kitty put me at ease immediately saying, "I want you to know, the only dancing I'll require is one slow dance and the Twist contest, which I expect to win. The prize is really neat."

"What is it?" I asked.

"For the boy," she said, "it's a full collection of Chubby Checker's singles."

"Figures it would be the one thing I already have."

"The girl wins a twenty dollar gift certificate at Scarborough's Department Store. There's a purse, belt, and shoe combination I saw there last week that I must own. So, we're going to win, okay?"

"Let me get this straight. If we win, I get about two dollars worth of 45's I already own, and you get a twenty-dollar gift certificate at Scarborough's. How's that fair?" I asked.

"The Sage's didn't have any boys and the party is really for Robyn and her deserving friends, like moi." She pointed at her chin.

"I see," I said, defeated.

Suddenly, two hands covered my eyes from behind. I heard Kitty giggling and someone "shushing".

A high-pitched, fake voice screeched, "Guess who?"

"Some jerk who thinks he can hit my curve ball," I said, knowing it had to be Danny.

He dropped his hands from my face and I turned to look at him. "If we could bet on baseball," he said, "I'd bet you five dollars I hit your curve this Saturday."

Kitty lit up, saying, "Your season starts this Saturday? Mickey, why didn't you tell me?"

"I thought you knew."

We were interrupted by Mrs. Sage who announced they were going to start playing music and expected everyone to participate in the first dance, which would be a warm-up for the Twist contest to follow. Boys and girls were slow to pair off as the Little Eva's "The Loco-Motion" reverberated around the spacious backyard from the stereo speakers sitting on the diving board. Danny took Kitty's hand and started for the area designated as the dance floor before I grabbed his shoulder, saying "Whoa, there hoss! Where ya' headed?"

Danny feigned shock, said, "Oh, so sorry, Kemo Sabe," and bowed out of the way. I took Kitty's hand and we walked onto the dance floor. To see the twenty or so couples gyrating to the beat of their own drummer, out of time with Little Eva's lyrics explaining how to dance the Loco-Motion, was quite a sight.

> *Everybody's doin' a brand-new dance, now (Come*
> *on baby, do the Loco-motion)*
> *I know you'll get to like it if you give it a chance*
> *now (Come on baby, do the Loco-motion)*
> *My little baby sister can do it with me;*
> *It's easier than learning your A-B-C's,*
> *So come on, come on, do the Loco-motion with me.*
> *You gotta swing your hips, now.*
> *Come on, baby. Jump up. Jump back.*
> *Well, now, I think you've got the knack.*

There were no American Bandstand dancers in our crowd, only dual left-footers constantly out of step, stumbling over each other. Mrs. Sage was on the verge of hysterics while she watched Mr. Sage interweaving through the dancers with an 8-mm film camera recording the event for Robyn's posterity. While Kitty seemed to be close to the beat as she bounced, I bopped up and down at various speeds, sometimes bending my knees and looking a bit like a whooping crane with two broken ankles. I don't think it was what Little Eva described as "a little bit of rhythm and lot of soul".

The "Great Twist Contest" came next as Mr. Sage proclaimed it. As judges in the first round, his wife and he would select three couples to perform in the second round finals. All of the kids eliminated from the competition in the qualifying round would vote for the finalists. He asked all the boys and girls to pair up for the first song. Everyone was expecting one of Chubby's records like "The Twist" or its sequel, "Twist Again". However, Chubby had a new one that had just come out called, "Slow Twistin'" which Mr. Sage chose for round number one. A good thing about the Twist is that if you are coordinated at all, you can't look too bad as long as you can approximate the beat of the song. "Slow Twistin," however, proved to be a twist on the Twist. Moves we normally performed at the speed of sound, were done in slow motion.

Somehow, Kitty and I made do with the slow rhythm and managed a few new moves along the way while trying to keep our balance at such a pace. At the end of the song, we were still on the dance floor. One of the other two couples making the finals was Danny and his much shorter partner, Melissa. This was the Twist, though, where a height irregularity was not a setback, even though Melissa was a full foot and a half shorter than her partner. The third couple included the birthday girl, Robyn, who was partnered with a shorter partner as well, redheaded Rudy Robie, the president of the Slide Rule Club. The slide rule, a pre-calculator mathematical tool, was not real easy to operate properly and, therefore, the Slide Rule Club only had three members. So you can imagine the type of kid Rudy was -- a dork bordering on a loser. Little did we know at the time, he would enjoy a very successful business and engineering career, and would end up among the four hundred richest Texans.

Mr. Sage chose my favorite Twist song for the final, Joey Dee and the Starlighters' "The Peppermint Twist", which reached number one briefly the year before when the dance was the absolute craze. I had Twisted to that record for hours in our playroom at home. I whispered to Kitty, "This'll be a piece of cake, Kitty. Piece of cake."

"Concentrate, Mickey. We have to win."

The music started and, at first, the three Twisting couples were a little tentative with our moves, like we were waiting for direction from the song itself:

Well they've got a new dance and it goes like this
(Bop shoo-op, a bop bop shoo-op)
Yeah the name of the dance is Peppermint Twist
(Bop shoo-op, a bop bop shoo-op)
Well you like it like this, the Peppermint Twist

It goes round and round, up and down, round and round, up
and down
Round and round and a up and down
And a one two three kick, one two three jump

We were all involved one hundred percent now, following the chorus's directions jumping, kicking, and screaming. Out of the corner of my eye, I saw Danny lift Melissa into the air and slide her through his legs grabbing her on the other side. Dang, I thought, where did he learn that move? As I was spinning and doing my famous knee-bend maneuver simultaneously with Kitty, I noticed Robyn lifting Rudy and tossing him away from her body releasing the redheaded kid like a spinning top. When Rudy landed he did a split, then slowly rose, Twisting as he did. Oh My God, I thought, I better think of something fast!

Well meet me baby down at 45th street
Where the Peppermint Twisters meet
And you'll learn to do this, the Peppermint Twist

It's alright, all night, it's alright
It's okay, all day, it's okay
You'll learn to do this, the Peppermint Twist Yeah, yeah
It goes round and round, up and down, round and round, up
and down
Round and round and a up and down
And a one two three kick, one two three jump

Kitty and I finished with the famous patty cake Twist-a-rama move we copied from participants on the American Bandstand where we were spinning, jumping, patting hands, and Twisting, all at the same time. We were proud of our efforts and hugged each other in congratulations as the song ended. Mr. and Mrs. Sage led the applause from all of the partygoers. I noticed Rudy's freckled face's color now matched his hair; and he was out of breath from probably the most activity he had experienced in the last six months. Mr. Sage approached the couples on the dance floor and stood behind each one separately, holding his hand up for applause from the audience -- as a way of voting for the champion. It was a landslide. We never had a chance. Neither did Danny and Melissa. The champions were crowned -- the birthday girl and the president of the Slide Rule Club. Kitty was a little beside herself, but only for a moment, before she joined me in congratulating the winning couple. After Rudy received the four set Chubby Checker's collection of singles, he had to excuse himself and rush off to the bathroom. The poor kid had no wind from the lack of physical activity in his life -- as he was always inside reading or working in a lab his parents made him. I guess he had also been doing some private Twisting practice because he wasn't bad at all. This may have been that seminal moment providing the inspiration for that little invention he would come up with while he was still a teenager -- The Stair Buddy -- an indoor exercise machine that made him his first ten million.

As Robyn received the gift certificate from her dad, I turned to Kitty and whispered, "Sorry."

She shrugged saying, "We tried our best. They were better." We walked toward the refreshment stand and when we were out of earshot of the others, Kitty whispered, "We never had a chance. The fix was in." We laughed it off and filled our glasses with some punch. Kitty turned to me and held up her glass for a toast, "In honor of opening day, let's toast to Rylanders."

As we touched glasses, I felt a twinge of foresight, where I saw myself on the mound tipping my hat to a cheering audience.

CHAPTER NINE

The groundskeeper of Bishop Field, Mr. Ed Knebel, was a short, stocky, hunch-backed fifty-year-old man who looked at least seventy. He constantly had a cigarette dangling from his mouth as he clipped, mowed, or silted our field of dreams. He was an artist in his own way, and the patrons of West Austin Little League were extremely happy to have him. At 7 a.m. on that first Saturday in May, Mr. Knebel -- as everyone called him -- was putting the final touches on his masterpiece of a miniaturized ballpark. He had groomed the outfield, swept the infield, trimmed the foul lines and even polished the brass plaques that honored several past winners of special commendations that hung above the concession stand windows. By 9 a.m. he had finished preparing everything except for the fresh chalk for the batter's box and the foul lines. He always held off chalking for last because he avoided a mess that way; he demanded tidiness -- at least, until the arrival of the first players. Mr. Knebel went to his storage shed, which was tucked underneath the right field scoreboard, where his nephew worked during the game, and retrieved a wooden contraption containing screws and latches. He brought it to the home plate area and began to expand and spread out the individual boards until it resembled a pattern for dressmaking on a large scale. It actually was the outline for the two batter's boxes and the catcher's box. He laid it down and traced its perimeter with the lime-chalk dispenser that sort of spits the white powder out of a metal tube in a three-inch wide stripe. After this was completed, he removed the wood and folded it up. He then took a roll of

78

twine and tied one end to the right field foul pole. He unwound it down the line to home plate where he attached it in the proper spot to trace the foul line with the chalk dispenser. This done, he repeated the process on the left field side and *voila!* -- Bishop Field was ready for the 1962 opening day ceremonies and doubleheader.

Baseball was not actually invented by Abner Doubleday at Cooperstown like some myths would have you believe. In fact, I don't know if Abner Doubleday provided anything for the sport except maybe a field on which to play the game. Anyway, that was in 1839, about two hundred years after the American Colonials had brought over the game from England. It was called Rounders then, but all of the basic rules were the same. You used a bat and a ball, which in Rounders, like in our cork ball games, you got the runner out by hitting them with a thrown ball. This was called soaking or plugging the runner. This might be seen as evidence that Doubleday didn't invent the game, because in his version you soaked the runner as in Rounders. It wasn't until 1854 that rules required force-outs at all bases, and in non-force situations, tagging the runners instead of plugging them. Also, Abner isn't really the father of American organized baseball, because that honor falls to Alexander Cartwright. Mr. Cartwright, a Manhattan sports enthusiast and ballplayer, formed the Knickerbocker Base Ball Club of New York in 1845 and he wrote and published a set of rules, which along with amendments in 1848 and 1854, largely make up the game we know today.

It then took the bloodiest period in our history to spread the game across a reunited nation creating the national pastime. During the Civil War, New Yorkers brought baseball to their regiments. Confederate prisoners and soldiers from all over witnessed the game played in the open fields during R&R breaks from the fighting. It caught on like wildfire and spread among the troops as fast as the death and destruction. A few years after the end of the great battle to end slavery, organized baseball was being played in every state in the union. Professional baseball was soon to follow.

Only four years after the assassination of the Great Emancipator, the first professional baseball team was formed in Cincinnati, Ohio. It was called the Cincinnati Red Stockings and by 1876 they had been joined by seven other professional teams, creating the National League. As the century turned, eight more teams initiated the American League and the first World Series was played in 1903 between the winners of the two Major Leagues. Baseball became a game of grand scale with large stadiums built to house the huge fan bases who followed superstar ballplayers like Cy Young, Honus Wagner, Walter Johnson, Ty Cobb, Rogers Hornsby, Christy Mathewson, Shoeless Joe Jackson, and Babe Ruth. The peerless House That Ruth Built -- Yankee Stadium in the Bronx, New York City -- was completed in 1923 and topped all others to become the Taj Mahal of baseball arenas.

However, because of this grandness of scale, baseball was not accessible for participation by youngsters. In 1938, Carl E. Stotz, a friend and pallbearer to the great Cy Young, was playing catch with his two nephews, Jimmy and Major Gehron, when he accidentally stubbed his toe on an old lilac stump rising out of his backyard. He limped over to the stoop at the back of the house, telling the two youngsters to keep playing catch while he rested his aching foot. Watching his sister's sons throw a ball back and forth in the field in West Williamsport, Pennsylvania, Carl suddenly had a divine vision. He imagined his nephews, in uniforms, playing a game of smaller dimensions than those played at adult levels. He called the boys over and asked if they would like to play on a field with bats and gloves and other equipment, including uniforms with umpires calling the games, just like in the Big Leagues. The two were overcome with excitement from the idea, and thus Little League Baseball was conceived.

Ten years later a newsreel showed the national championship of ninety-four organized leagues. Viewed across North America, the newsreel promoted the new game for kids and the Little Leagues expanded exponentially. By 1951, when our West Austin league joined the national organization, it had grown to 800 programs in the United States and Canada. In 1962, there were 6,000 leagues around the world and 30,000 teams with nine to twelve-year-olds playing a man's game in the comfy confines of places like Ed Knebel's Bishop Field.

Tildy Potts had hosted her fair share of opening ceremonies and she was beginning to get the knack for the process. Each year, the bunting and banners increased in number and color. The public address system was replaced with newer technology as it slowly became available on the market.

She always improved something in the concession stand, creating new snacks for the various parent-volunteers to prepare. The semi-circular bunting made of crushed paper, striped in red, white, and blue paint, adorned fences running down the foul lines. Banners stretched from the awning above the scorer's table to the ends of the grandstands.

About ten minutes before noon, the parking lot had long been filled and cars were parked down both sides of Enfield Road for a quarter-mile in each direction. The families and friends of the players were packed into the grandstands and standing down both sidelines. Many fans had a Polaroid or a film camera to record events of the special day, and players and managers in their brand-new uniforms posed for team pictures in the outfield in front of banners displaying the sponsor's logos. After the photos, the teams gathered along each sideline awaiting introductions. Tildy strode to a microphone by the pitcher's mound, to rousing applause and hoots from the crowd.

She grabbed the microphone and flipped it on. Feedback screeched out of the speakers.

"Whoa," Tildy said. "Don't you just hate that?"

Everybody laughed and adjusted themselves for her introductory thoughts. Tildy continued, "Welcome everyone, to the 1962 West Austin Optimists' Little League opening day ceremonies. My name, for those who don't know, is Matilda Potts. I am the chairman of the board, and today we welcome all newcomers to the league. We hope all of you are able to benefit as much as those who came before you, from what we believe is a prime entertainment and athletic activity. This very morning from the White House, President John F. Kennedy declared the start of National Little League Week. In his declaration, he stated that this sport provided the boys of today with a building block for a moral and healthy approach toward life. He said the competition will strengthen all of our players mentally and physically. In the understanding and importance of teamwork and sportsmanship, our President said that by competing in Little League programs like ours, young boys are improving their chances to succeed at their goals in life. So boys, as I introduce each of you today, I want you to hold your head up high, trot down the side lines to home plate, and tip your hat to the those gathered to honor you. I want you all to know you are playing not only for yourselves, but for your community, and your participation in this game, and especially West Austin Little League, is our reward."

When the applause from the crowd stopped, Tildy introduced the manager, coaches, and players of Louis Shanks. Each member ran down the foul line to home plate, tipped his hat to the grandstands, and joined his team at a predetermined spot in the infield where they would sit for the remaining ceremonies. Then came Seven Up, Louis Shanks' opponent in the second game of our opening day doubleheader. Rylanders was introduced next, and then City National.

Trudy introduced the City National players in alphabetical order, so Willie Veils was announced last. Up till then, the applause had been relatively constant with periodic whoops and hollers for kids who had a lot of family in the stands. However, as Willie ran down the base path, the level of applause fell off to a polite, but suspiciously muted level. As he tipped his cap and joined his teammates, he never flinched or demonstrated any emotion at the crowd's display. Willie just focused on his teammates as they encouraged him by slapping him on the back or the rear end. Having made their supportive gestures in front of the crowd, they took their positions on the infield grass with the other teams.

Suddenly, there was a commotion down the left field line. We all turned to see what was happening and saw a lady struggling to hold back an agitated man from coming through a gate and onto the field. They were gripped in a muffled argument and the players were all buzzing. Something big was happening. I was sitting with my teammates, fixed on the troubled couple, when I heard one of our nine-year-olds, Glen Farley, mutter, "Oh, no!"

"What is it, Glen?" I asked.

"My father," Glen whispered.

"That's your father?"

He nodded, "and my mother."

At that moment, Glen's father tore his arm away from the grasp of his wife, moved away from the gate, and jumped the fence. He marched like a man on a mission, directly toward our team.

Travis stepped forward to intervene if he could. "Mr. Farley," he said, "can we help you?

"Mr. Bowie," he said with semi-contained anger, "your team and this league will have to go on without the services of my son."

"What's the problem, Mr. Farley?" Travis asked.

"The problem is sitting right over there," he said, pointing rudely at Willie.

Travis looked at Willie, wincing because he couldn't spare Willie this embarrassment. The crowd hushed and I'm sure most of them could feel the tension and hear pieces of the conversation. Someone from the stands obviously did, and shouted, "Get off the field, Roger!"

Mr. Farley turned and glared at the stands like an intimidating guard dog. Travis placed an arm on his shoulder, "Now, Mr. Farley. They're just boys. Trying to get along with each other. We're just playing a game here. Having some fun. I'm not sure this is the right time for this."

Mr. Farley pulled away from Travis and scanned the huddled faces for his son, who was hiding behind me at the back of our team.

"Glen Farley, get your butt over here, now!"

Glen looked around me at his angry father, summoned his courage, and yelled, "Please, father. I want to stay with my friends."

"You are not going to play in this league. We'll find you another league, where certain principles will be followed."

"But, father," Glen pleaded. "I like --"

"Shut up! Don't back talk me, boy," he growled as he suddenly maneuvered his way through my teammates. He pushed me aside, grabbed Glen's uniform at the collar, and dragged him toward the fence as Glen tried desperately to stand up. Glen burst into tears and there was an audible gasp from the grandstands. Mr. Farley picked up his horrified son, stood him on his two feet like a chess piece, and led him by the hand through the gate and out to their car, where he pushed the distraught youngster into the back seat. He screamed at his wife to get in the car, which she did, reluctantly, after a last glance back at the stunned crowd. Mr. Farley started the car and drove away in a cloud of dust.

For a moment or two, everyone in attendance was absolutely stunned to silence. Then, growing murmurs and whispers started to rise from people in the grandstands. Tildy looked around as if in shock and clearly didn't know what to say next. Travis noticed the uneasiness and approached her at the microphone.

"Tildy, could I say a few words?" he asked.

She stepped away from the microphone and my manager cleared his throat and addressed the grandstands. "Ladies and Gentleman, what we just witnessed here, was very sad in my opinion. I'm sorry it happened. I'm sorry for Willie. And I'm especially sorry for young Glen. We're going to miss him on our team. He had a wonderful kind of spirit that had a great influence on his teammates. I sincerely hope his father reconsiders, though it's his right to pull his son out. But I guarantee, the game will go on. And, this boy over here," he pointed at Willie, "is going to play in this league. He has earned the right and deserves to be here as much as any of these other boys. It's only right and that's the way we agreed to run this league."

There was some light applause from the grandstands, but Travis quieted them by holding up his hand. He said, "If there are any others who can't tolerate this situation, then I suggest you speak up now, so then we can get on with the business of kids having fun and playing baseball."

Everyone looked around. No one spoke, until a man down the right field line, yelled out, "Willard Montgomery, come over here, son! We're not playing either."

Willard Montgomery, a ten-year-old on Louis Shanks stood up. With slumping shoulders, he walked over to his waiting father, who quietly escorted him toward their car. Travis looked around, "Anyone else?" No one moved or said a word. "Okay, then, Mrs. Potts, I suggest we continue."

I looked over at Willie and as we made eye contact, we both shook our heads in unison at the silliness we were witnessing. We liked what Travis said, but we hated the fact that he had to say it.

"Thank you, Travis," Tildy said. "I, too, am sorry we had this interruption. Let's proceed," she said and cleared her throat. "We are honored here at West Austin to have four wonderful sponsors. I would like to introduce them at this time and have their representatives join me here on the mound for recognition. First, Mr. Louis Shanks of the Louis Shanks Furniture stores."

A rotund man of sixty years came out of one of the dugouts, raised his hand to the fans, and walked over to Tildy, who gave him a hug.

"Next, representing City National Bank, is the Administrative Vice President, Bob Kinnan. Mr. Kinnan." A bespectacled, gaunt gentleman ducked as he came out of the dugout and joined the others.

"Next, we have Mrs. Gerald Rylander, wife of the founder of Rylanders. Ethel would you join us please. I understand Gerald is hunting and fishing in Alaska. I suppose he's stocking up your grocery store shelves, huh Ethel?"

The crowd laughed and Mrs. Rylander smiled gratefully at Tildy, and then shook her hand before she stood next to the others.

"And last, but by no means least," Tildy continued, "representing the Seven Up bottling plant, is the son of the late owner Joseph Sawyer, Sr., Joe Sawyer, Jr."

A man of thirty-five, well built and tan, exited the dugout and stood by the others. The applause started to die down until Tildy raised her arms for more, "Please folks, give them their due. In addition to paying for their teams' uniforms, they have each donated two hundred and fifty dollars to our general operating fund. "

Tildy waited for the applause to die down and then continued, "To perform our national anthem on his trumpet is Denny Simpson, who played on last year's All-Star team that came so close to winning the city title. Denny."

A redheaded, freckled scrawny thirteen-year-old teenager walked to the microphone carrying his instrument. He licked his lips and all of the people around the park rose to their feet and placed their caps over their hearts. Denny brought the trumpet to his lips and began. He did a pretty admirable job of it, and was better than most expected. As he finished, Tildy congratulated him and turned to the microphone and screamed, "Ladies and Gents, let's play ball!"

CHAPTER TEN

On a similar spring afternoon, fifteen years before our opening day at Bishop Field, the course of human events for all Americans took a dramatic turn. For the first time since the 1880's, a black baseball player broke through the unwritten color barrier that the white Major League baseball owners had supported and sustained. On April 15, 1947, twenty-eight year old rookie for the Brooklyn Dodgers, Jackie Robinson, strode to the plate to face Johnny Sain of the Boston Braves. Sain was one of the two excellent starters on the Braves during the late forties -- Warren Spahn being the other. They had become famous with the popular jingle, "Spahn and Sain, pray for rain". Sain won the battle on that April afternoon by getting Jackie to ground out three straight times and keeping the fleet-footed runner off of the bases. But Jackie Robinson won the greater battle that historic day having succeeded in beating Jim Crow himself by demolishing the color line. Normally a second baseman, Jackie debuted at first base and showed off his fielding prowess without an error. He would further prove Brooklyn's General Manager, Branch Rickey, to be a man of great foresight; as Jackie would handle with silent class, the pressure, ridicule, racial slurs, and cruel invectives hurled his way during a season in which he would win the Rookie of the Year award, now named in his honor.

At 1:30 in the afternoon on the first Saturday in May 1962, at Bishop Field, I was finishing my warm-ups on the mound preparing for the start of the inaugural game of the West Austin Little League. The lead-off hitter I was about to face was, ironically enough, Willie Veils. In my mind, Willie looked a little out of place in his new blue and gold uniform with the City National patch on the left breast. I guess it was because I had never seen a black face sporting the insignia before. I had finished throwing my warm-ups to Don, our wonderful new catcher who replaced our previous version of "Dizzy" Dean behind the plate. After yelling "coming down," Don threw to second base and my Rylanders infield teammates finished throwing the new Rawlings baseball around the horn. Willie strode toward the plate at Bishop Field just like Jackie Robinson had done fifteen years before in Brooklyn. I reached for the resin bag and tossed it in the air a couple of times before wiping the excess dust off on my uniform.

Tildy announced from her perch above the concession stand, "Ladies and Gentlemen, batting for City National, number 24, Willie Veils." There was light applause as Willie stepped into the box and took a couple of practice swings with his thirty ounce Louisville Slugger. He took a deep breath, as if he was breathing in the historic moment.

I didn't think about making history at the time, though maybe some fans in the grandstands were considering the thought. They may have seen Elston Howard, the first Yankee of color, playing alongside Mickey Mantle on a weekend game or a previous World Series. They probably saw Willie Mays or Henry Aaron on the tube one weekend or another. Maybe they witnessed Jim Brown on the football field on a Sunday in the fall. But these were images on television and not an issue that would affect their community of Tarrytown. However, now was the true test, for in the dark-skinned flesh, the first Negro player stood right in front of them, readying himself for the first pitch. He wore a confident determined grin on his face.

Before the game, Don and I had discussed how I wanted to pitch the hitters we'd see, so we'd be on the same page. I had told him about my only experience with Willie during the try-outs, and after he heard it, Don said, "Maybe we should walk him." No way, I thought, my pride was involved, so our strategy relied on off speed pitches in the dirt or low outside fastballs if I got behind in the count. That discussion still resonated as I toed the pitching rubber and looked in for my signal. Don put down two fingers calling for the curve ball and I nodded affirmatively. I went into the wind up I had practiced in The Clearing all those many winter days, and released the first pitch of the 1962 Little League season.

Perfection is an interesting goal to have. It is by its definition almost beyond achievement. We strive for it, we practice to get it, we hope to be it, yet always, we know we've never quite experienced it. But all along our journey, we are sure of its presence. In the beauty of a rainbow, the cast of the moon's shadow, the scent of a rose, the golden hues of another gorgeous sunset, or even in the implications of truth, we find the existence of perfection. It is fleeting, maybe, but it is most assuredly something truly beautiful.

The almost perfect curve ball starts over the plate and then drops off the planet out of the strike zone as the batter whiffs at it weakly and totally off balance. As a pitcher, I had experienced this infrequently, but on opening day 1962 my first pitch to Willie was as close to a perfect curve ball as I had ever thrown. The ball broke off the center of the plate just catching the outside corner of the strike zone and nestled in Don's mitt about an inch off of the ground. "Strike One" called out Dale Bakers, our aforementioned brisket-making umpire. Don returned the ball to me and I was feeling pretty good. I had a strike on Willie, so now I could play with his head a little bit. The next pitch Don called for was another curve ball, but I shook him off. I wanted to throw a little chin music, high and tight, to back Willie off the plate a little bit. I wanted to come back with another curve on the outside corner later. It's called setting up the batter, practiced by the best of pitchers in the Big's, like Drysdale or Gibson.

But, I guess Willie had heard of it too, because when my fastball aimed at his shoulder ended up just off the inside corner of the plate, he swung and slammed a line drive down the third base line. The ball rolled into the corner of the field and Willie ended up on second with a double. As the ball returned to me after the play, I looked at Willie who tipped his hat to me and I had to smile. Then he took off for third base. I was flabbergasted, caught unaware as he flew down the base path. Our third baseman, Bob, was not paying attention and obviously not prepared. He never moved toward the base and Willie slid in safely. Nobody had ever stolen a base like that on me. Willie just took it upon himself to run to the next base and dared me to throw him out. It was a new experience, and one I was afraid I might see a lot more of during the coming year.

I managed to strike out the number two hitter while keeping my eye on the fleet-footed jet on third. Willie would not steal home on me -- I was going to make sure of that. In Little League, a runner could only leave the base after the pitch had crossed the plate. There was no conventional lead like in the majors, so a runner had to be a jet, or maybe a burner, to consistently steal bases throughout the season.

After I struck out the second batter on three pitches, Tildy announced Danny as their third hitter. He made contact with my first pitch, lifting the ball high to center, just in front of the fence, allowing Willie to score on the deep sacrifice fly. Danny crossed over the pitcher's mound area after his run batted in, pinched his thumb and forefinger together, and said, "I missed it by *that* much."

"Better luck next time," I said, as I picked up the resin bag and glanced at the scoreboard. Ed Knebel's handicapped nephew, Ricky, placed the number 1 in the top spot of inning number one -- across from the placard for City National Bank. Ed Knebel watched proudly as the youngster suffering from muscular dystrophy managed the scoreboard numbers and his crutches at the same time. Ricky had been working with his uncle for three years, and had really mastered the job. Tildy added over the P.A.

"Yes, ladies and gentlemen, it is our pleasure this year to have the scoreboard talents of little Ricky Knebel. Let's give him a hand."

Instead of tipping his hat, he raised his crutches in the Victory signal and the crowd hooted. Back to the game, I thought, reprimanding myself for being distracted. Focus. I turned to face the batter, Jeff Snowden, their left-handed hitting first baseman. Even though he was big and slow, Jeff had hit a homer off of me the year before. I was crafty this time around, and after four pitches, I had my second strike out and it was our turn to do some hitting.

Stepping to the mound for his warm-ups was the pitcher for City National Bank, a solid lefty named Greg Roberts. He was their best pitcher with the possible exception of Willie, who I had yet to see throw. Roberts had won four of the five victories for City National during their miserable year before.

It seemed he had put on a few pounds during the previous twelve months, but he was throwing really hard stuff as he finished his warm-ups. I glanced around the diamond to see Danny in left field tossing a ball back and forth with Willie in center.

"Coming down," yelled out Jeff Snowden. Roberts' catcher threw down to second and their infield began to throw the ball around the horn.

From my perch on the top dugout steps, I yelled, "All right, Marky, start us off!"

Our second baseman, Marky Anders, stood about four feet and four inches, but despite his diminutive status, he was solidly built. He was our fastest runner and therefore, our lead-off hitter. He strode to the plate and glanced back toward the dugout for his signals. In Little League, baseball rules prohibited managers from occupying coach's boxes during the game. Therefore, Travis gave signals to his batters and runners from the corner of the sunken dugouts.

All managers had different ways of giving their signals. However, without exception, Mac, the manager for Louis Shanks, was the least subtle -- using one finger for take, two for bunt and three for hit and run. Everyone else in the league knew this, but Mac was sort of set in his ways and not about to change. He was an institution, not only to the league which he had served as a coach since its inception, but also to the city of Austin. MAC'S was a great downtown cheeseburger joint that he had opened during the great depression. Everyone in the city had been there at least once. No one really knew how old Mac was, but we suspected he was closing in on eighty.

Travis was more conventional with his signage than Mac but, for that matter, so was everyone else. At some point in his gyrations, Travis touched his hat with his right hand as key indicator meaning the next signal would be the one; then either the chest for bunt, the face for squeeze, the thigh for steal, or the belt for take. I glanced over at Travis as he touched his thigh, his belt, his hat, and then his chest. Marky touched his helmet recognizing he received the sign and then he got into the batter's box to face Roberts.

On the first pitch, Marky laid down a perfect drag bunt along the first base line and passed the ball on his way to the base. One on and nobody down. Next up was Fish. Travis flashed the sign and Fish touched his helmet, Marky did the same over at first. Fish took the first pitch low in the dirt for ball one, and Marky faked a steal and drew a throw behind him by the catcher. Marky slid back into first base headfirst and was safe by a whisker. On the next pitch, Fish sacrificed Marky to second with a nice bunt to the charging third baseman. Man on second, one out. Our burly left fielder, Ras, was next to the plate. Travis wouldn't be bunting anymore. After a couple of pitches in the dirt, Ras tagged a fastball into left field for a clean single. Marky didn't challenge Danny's arm though, and stopped at third. Runners on first and third, one out. Our clean-up hitter, Don, strode to the plate. He turned to look at Travis for a signal and our manager simply pointed toward the outfield. Don touched his helmet and stepped into the box. Roberts tried a big slow curve ball that lingered a little too long in the strike zone. Don connected and Danny and Willie just turned to watch the ball land high up in an oak tree beyond the fence. Don trotted around the bases and the entire team met him at home plate. Our fans went wild as little Ricky Knebel placed a three in the bottom of the first slot on the scoreboard. Three to one, one out. Bob and I batted fifth and sixth. Unfortunately, we both flied out to end the inning. But we had the lead, thanks to our new star catcher.

I managed to keep the lead for the next four innings. Going into the sixth and final inning, I had only given up a single to Danny and Willie had beaten out a bunt for his second hit of the game, but City National hadn't scored again. Roberts seemed to find his groove as well, and held us hitless during that same stretch. I walked to the mound to start the last inning knowing full well the first batter was now my new arch nemesis -- Willie Veils.

As Tildy announced Willie's name, we heard scattered, light applause. One by one, a few other parents and friends joined them. Then to my surprise, I saw my mother stand up and clap vigorously, aiming all of her attention and support toward Willie. Others around the park immediately noticed and one by one, followed her lead, applauding more heartily. After a few seconds of this growing support, a number of the people in the stands were standing and clapping. It was an amazing moment of growing acceptance, and I was very proud of my mother for what she had started. I was proud of my friend, too. He deserved this show of support.

Willie backed out of the batter's box and sheepishly looked around at the crowd and acknowledged their ovation. He tipped his hat toward the throng of spectators and then he looked at me, winked, and exhibited his pearly whites in a bigger smile than I'd ever seen on his face. As the fans started to settle and sit down, Willie stepped back into the batter's box, and I toed the rubber.

I was determined to get him out this time. My first pitch was low and just off the plate for a ball. Then I broke a curve ball off of Willie's waist and he chased it in the dirt. I hung a curve a little bit too much on my third pitch and Willie pulled it over the fence. Luckily, it was foul by about three feet. Now, I was ahead of him in the pitch count. It's my turn, I thought. Don called for an outside curve ball. I nodded and threw an almost perfect curve ball once again. Only this time, Willie lunged for it at the last second, hit it on the end of his bat, and sent a spinning top of a ball down the first base line. Dean closed on it from first base, but the slow roller found its way through his legs and into short right field. Willie never thought of stopping at first and by the time our second baseman had retrieved the ball, Willie was sliding into third. A swinging bunt triple. Hadn't seen that one before either. Tildy scored it as an error, so at least Willie wasn't hitting a thousand off of me anymore.

Forget about it, I thought to myself. His run doesn't matter. We still have a three to one lead. Let's focus on the batter. I turned to see Don approaching the mound. He told me the same thing I had just told myself.

"Forget about the runner," he chided. "The play is the batter. And remember, he can't hit the curve." With that he returned to his spot behind the plate and signaled for three straight curve balls. There was one out and Danny, the tying run, was coming to the plate. This is what we play for, I thought -- to get out their best at the most crucial time; to survive the pressure of the moment and succeed with what I had practiced all those days in The Clearing. I looked up to see Travis call a time out and approach the mound. I took off my glove and rubbed the ball. Our shortstop, third baseman, and catcher joined Travis as he stepped onto the mound. He looked me in the eye and said, "Mickey, let's be careful here. Too good a pitch to Dan and we're all tied up. Stay low and away. If we lose him to a walk, we'll turn two."

"Yes sir," we all said. Travis returned to the dugout and the players trotted to their positions. I looked in for the signal -- Don put down one finger and touched his right inside thigh. I reared back and threw as hard as I could. To my amazement, the ball went straight down the middle of the plate, but Danny was a bit surprised by the location and was late on the swing. "Strike one!" yelled Dale Baker. The next pitch was so far outside, Don had to lunge sideways to catch it. Danny didn't swing of course. I shook off the fastball and decided to throw an outside curve ball on the next offering. Danny went for it and looked kind of silly missing it by a foot. Don asked for an outside fastball and I responded by overthrowing once again. The ball flew over Don and Dale Baker's heads and hit the screen behind them. Willie scored before I could get to home plate to cover it. Three to two, one out, sixth inning, tying run still at the plate.

My next curve hung a little on the outside of the plate and Danny got just enough of it to stay alive. Then a fast ball off the outside corner -- Danny contacted it weakly and sent a fly ball to short right field, which Marky shagged easily. I breathed a heavy sigh of relief. We were one out away from starting the season with a victory. Jeff Snowden sort of limped to the plate. He had turned his ankle covering first base in the previous inning and I could see he was hurting. Since it was his right leg bothering him and he was a left-handed hitter, I figured he wouldn't be able to step into the ball, so again I decided to keep it low and away. It worked. After four pitches, I recorded my seventh strike out and Rylanders put its first game in the win column.

The teams formed two lines and passed one another shaking hands, saying, "nice game" or something in the way of congratulations. As I passed Willie, I reached out my hand to shake his, but he just slapped at mine, then turned his hand up toward me for a return slap. I did it without thinking, but only later realized it was the first time I had ever given anyone "five" in my life. In fact, I had never seen the gesture before and I first thought maybe it was a slap in the face, before I heard Willie say with the motion, "Great game, way to go, bro!"

"Good game," I said lamely in response.

Danny was next in line, saying, "I missed it by *that* much."

The teams gathered by the dugouts and listened to a final speech by their respective managers. Travis looked at us and said, "Well boys, we can't win them all if we don't win the first one. So, we're on our way. Good game. Game ball goes to our new catcher, Don, the Waco Kid. Great game Don. You too, Mickey. Great pitching, Mr. Charles. But, we all learned something today. That Veils kid is one hell of a ballplayer, isn't he?"

No one answered out loud, but we nodded our heads in agreement. We didn't know how to say it, but we certainly felt that we were witnessing something special. It must have been like the time when most of our nation came to admire and love Jackie Robinson fifteen years before. Even if it was begrudgingly in some cases. It had been horribly difficult for him to break into the Major Leagues, but he did it with class and more dignity than anyone could've asked of him. As with Jackie, Willie's amazing abilities and qualities born of a loving family, finally started to extinguish the worst of the fires of prejudice and racism in our little part of the planet. Yeah, Willie was good. So good, in fact, his accomplishments and his style led to a color-blindness that eclipsed the narrow-mindedness of bigots, and created an image on the field of a young man who was absolutely gifted at what he was doing. What the Jackie Robinsons and the Willie Veils did for Americans and the West Austin citizens, was nothing short of miraculous, and they certainly earned much greater historical importance than any single game of baseball. Sometimes, it seemed, a boy only started out to play a little ball, but ended up changing the world.

CHAPTER ELEVEN

There are moments in all of our lives that are watershed events -- birth, death, marriage, graduation, or that first real job. These happenings have a major if not absolute effect on the paths our individual lives etch upon the world. They can mark the beginning of a new journey on the road of life, which is pursued to the fullest until that next watershed moment redefines the direction of our path. I was beginning to feel this was the case on my last day of school at Casis Elementary. Somehow, at the end of the day, I knew my life would never be the same again.

Once that final bell rings on our elementary school days, we could no longer live at the top of the food chain like we had as sixth graders. Rather, we would be demoted, taking a back seat to our elders once again, at O.Henry Junior High. However, I was going to fight the onslaught of adolescence as long as I could. It appeared I had a lot of company -- my friends all wore cut-off jeans to the last day of classes at Casis. It was a tradition started a few years before when my oldest brother's class had left their mark on the school by starting the fashion trend. Ms. Vance was far from happy when I entered her classroom with my cut-offs, which were slit up the sides of my legs to reveal the bottom of my jockeys.

"Mr. Charles! You have a mind. I know you do. But going through life ragged, unkempt, and sloppy is not the way to get ahead of the game," she said after she stopped me at the entrance.

"Ms. Vance -- we're celebrating -- loosen up," I said indignantly.

"Young man, I'm still your teacher. And, last day or not, I won't take that attitude from anyone, at any time. March yourself down to the principal's office and let him decide whether to send you home or not. Do not return without a note and proper respect for this institution." Ms. Vance pointed down the hallway.

Luckily for me, Mr. Robbins was in a much better mood than Ms. Vance. He was about to spend his summer as a camp counselor near one of the best fly-fishing streams in the whole state. When I entered his office, Mr. Robbins was tying his flies, copying a master's example in a fishing magazine lying open on his desk. He glanced up at me and spotted my torn cut-offs. He chuckled under his breath and said, "Like your brothers, huh, Mick? Got to swim against the current every once in awhile, just so others will know you can."

"Mr. Robbins, it wasn't my fault. Ms. Vance is a b-- well, she's just mean. All I said to her was this is the last day of school, so can't you loosen up a little bit."

Mr. Robbins leaned back in his chair and reached for the unlit cigar in the ashtray. He placed it in his mouth and chewed on it for a moment or two, looking at me like he was thinking of whether or not to share some information. After a bit, he said, "Mickey, you are not aware of this, but our Ms. Vance has been a trooper this year. It is amazing she has been able to keep her focus at all, considering what has been going on in her personal life. You see, her husband is dying."

I dropped my jaw, and whispered, "Ms. Vance is married?"

"Last week, she celebrated her twenty-fifth anniversary with her husband in Breckenridge Hospital after his second surgery in two months. It was unsuccessful and I'm afraid he only has a few weeks to live -- if that long." Mr. Robbins replaced his cigar and picked up the dry fly again. I stood there stunned by these revelations. I immediately felt a twinge of guilt for the times I caused problems for Ms. Vance during the past nine months.

"Mr. Robbins, I didn't know. I wouldn't have been such a heel."

"Mickey, teachers are under-appreciated and underpaid for the services they provide our community. They earn their dignity, and should be respected by all, but especially by the students for whom they are striving to make better, smarter, and more rounded individuals. Your teacher deserves more. Don't you think?"

"Mr. Robbins, sir, may I have your permission to go home and change into something more proper for the rest of the day?"

"Mr. Charles, you certainly may. And make it snappy. There's still some time to learn something before the day comes to an end," Mr. Robbins replied.

I stood up and mumbled "Yes, sir," and started to leave the office. Mr. Robbins cleared his throat behind me and I turned back around as he stood up and approached. He stuck out his hand toward me and we shook. He said, "Mickey, it's been a pleasure having you at Casis. I especially enjoyed our times together with Jill. You two make a great couple," he said as he winked at me. I didn't know what to say because I didn't know what he really meant; I just stood there with mouth agape. Then he added, "Yes sir, probably the most efficient pair of fire officers in my memory. Congratulations on a great job. Good luck at O. Henry."

I let go a heavy sigh, before mumbling, "Thank you, Mr. Robbins."

On the way to my house I walked through the woods and thought about what my principal had told me. Suddenly, I felt a tear release and run down my cheek. I wiped at my face. Now, where did that come from, I wondered. I guessed it was a reaction to my total misread of Ms. Vance. The guilt must have compressed my emotional base enough to overflow my dikes.

I thought out loud, "I better think about something else." That brought me back to baseball. As I completed my loop from school to home and back to school -- sporting proper jeans -- I reflected on the three weeks since we started the baseball season with a victory over Willie, Danny, and their City National teammates. As the first half of our regular season was nearing completion, Rylanders had only lost one game after sweeping our first three from City National and Louis Shanks. We had split two games with Seven Up, but they had two losses because Willie beat them with a one-hitter in one of his rare pitching appearances. So we were one game ahead of Seven Up with the only one left that afternoon. If we could win, we'd guarantee ourselves a spot in the championship game at the end of the season against the second-half winners. That is, unless we sweep both halves making us consensus champions. But if we lost today, we would have to play a first half championship game tomorrow.

It's funny how things work out. Here it was the last day of school and the last day of the first half of the Little League season. Despite what the calendar said, all the kids considered this the beginning of summer. Every year, that last week in May, as soon as that final bell was heard, screams of delight filled the halls and everyone seemed to gain a step on the game. The time of leisure was about to be upon us twelve-year-olds with three whole months of freedom at hand. Time to weave the fabric of our adolescent coming out. Leaving childhood behind for good. But, first I had to deal with getting through the rest of the day. I approached Ms. Vance's room, gathered my composure, and opened the door to enter.

The room was in chaos. I walked in and quickly shut the door, trying to close off the extreme amount of noise generating from my classroom so other teachers down the hall wouldn't hear the clamor. Ms. Vance was absent and it seemed the students had turned the classroom into an asylum. Paper airplanes floated in the air, spitballs shot out of straws and stuck to blackboards or walls, chalk erasers were being sent screaming through the air by rubber band catapults. Noah Parkes was conducting arm wrestling contests on one side of the room, while girls were exchanging gifts on the other. While I stood in the doorway, I noticed Kitty trying to get my attention through the mayhem. I dodged several erasers on my way to meet her by the door that opened to the playground. She motioned for me to follow and we stepped outside; she closed the door behind her.

"Wow," I said, "what is going on?"

Kitty ignored my question with one of her own, "Where have you been?"

"I mouthed-off to Ms. Vance and she sent me to Robbins, who suggested I go change out of my cut-offs. You'll never guess what is happening to Ms. Vance," I declared.

"Her husband is dying," she offered matter-of-factly.

"How did *you* know that?"

"Mr. Robbins called her out of class for an emergency and he stayed for a few minutes and told us all about it."

"Damn," I said quietly.

"There was nothing you could have done," Kitty said sympathetically.

"It's not that," I said, "it's just that I wish I had a chance to say something to her after Mr. Robbins told me what she had been going through. I felt so bad, you know."

"Me, too," Kitty added, "but we didn't know what was happening, so we can't feel guilty. It's like my mother always says, 'guilt is nothing more than a useless emotion'."

It was just like Kitty to be logical at a time like this. I reached over and took her hand in mine and looked deep into her eyes. We smiled at each other in a moment that crystallized in my mind so much so, that many years later it could resurface from the memory caves and shine brightly in my soul again. Kitty leaned forward and kissed me gently on the lips. As we broke the embrace we heard jeers and applause from inside the classroom. We turned to see most of the class standing in the windows watching us. To hide our embarrassment, I bowed and Kitty curtsied to our amused audience.

"Who's taking Ms. Vance's place?" I asked while shielding my red face.

"Mr. Robbins left me in charge until he could figure something out. That was ten minutes ago," Kitty said with a laugh. "I lost control nine minutes ago."

I looked at my watch. It was half past ten and by my estimation the classroom might make it another half-hour before it exploded from the force of disorder. Either that, or someone might bore of spitballs and try to figure out how to blow up the building or something worse. I definitely wouldn't put it past the devious mind of Noah Parkes to organize some additional chaos.

I bit at my lower lip while trying to think straight. Then it hit me. I knew what I had to do. I turned to Kitty and said, "I've got an idea." With that I sprinted down the sidewalk and ran around the building to a hallway entrance at the end of the wing. I entered there and ran down the hallway until I reached the first fire bell, which I rang six quick times to alert the school of a fire drill. I figured this would get them out of the room and buy us some time. We needed a plan to restore enough order to enjoy the rest of our last day without destroying the school in the process.

Students all over the school heaved a collective moan. I heard it reverberate through the empty halls after the vibrations from the bell faded away. The classes were especially slow to exit their rooms, as most teachers and students didn't believe the drill was for real. I rang the bell again six quick times and yelled "Fire". Finally, all of the students began to filter out into the playgrounds.

"Good thinking," Kitty said as I turned to see her walking down the hallway toward me. "Now what?" she asked.

"We'll leave that to Mr. Robbins. That is, if we can find him. He'll probably think this is a real fire," I declared a little sardonically.

As we entered his office, Mr. Robbins had just hung up the telephone. "Fire engines are on the way. Where's the fire?" he said as he leapt to his feet.

"There's no fire, sir." I said a little sheepishly.

"No fire?" Robbins responded.

Kitty decided to share the heat as she stepped forward and offered, "Mr. Robbins, after you left our class, I kind of lost control, and since no substitute showed up, we figured a fire drill might be the only answer."

"I see -- well, Jill, I guess that's my fault then. I forgot to send a replacement. I'll take care of it immediately. Let's bring everyone back in and I'll send a counselor down to sit with the class until the substitute arrives." Our principal was already going through his Rolodex as we left to ring the students back into the building. In the distance, I heard the sirens of fire trucks speeding closer and closer to our school. As I rang the fire bell, I marveled at the mystery of my last day at Casis. It proved to be more than a watershed moment, it had turned into to an enigma all its own.

That last day at school was interesting, even entertaining, but the afternoon would be the topper. Bob pitched a sensational game against the league's best-hitting ball club. Seven Up had a devastating middle to their line-up with Dave Looney, Jack, and Stan batting in the three, four, and five positions. Dave's .525 was second to Willie's .595 in the batting statistics for the first half. While Jack and Stan each had six home runs, they were also hitting over .400. But on that day, Bob had his stuff working. He had developed one hell of a curve ball over the past year, to go with his screwball and fastball that were as good as any in the league. Nevertheless, Jack managed to hit an early inning homer off of Bob. But our catcher, Don, matched Jack the next inning with a long distance blast of his own. In the fifth inning, Don hit his second home run of the day to give Rylanders a 2-1 lead over our nemesis. Bob shut down Seven Up in the last inning for the victory. We had won the first-half championship of the 1962 West Austin Little League. What a way to start the summer!

After the game, our teams lined up and passed each other exchanging 'high fives' like Willie had taught me after the first game. The act had caught on and now the whole league was using the congratulatory greeting, both after good plays and at the end of the games. Willie, who had been watching from the third base line, jumped over the fence and came up to me.

"Brother, you da' champs," Willie said. "Give me five to stay alive." He held up his hand for mine to slap, which I did. And then, I held mine up, and he slapped it back and said, "But we'll give you a run for the money in the second half."

"We'll be here," I said smiling. "By the way, To Kill a Mockingbird tomorrow, right?"

"I'll meet you in front of the Paramount, five minutes before two," Willie said as he waved, ran down the sideline, hurdled the fence, and disappeared into the woods beyond left field on his way back to Clarksville. I turned and joined my teammates in the celebration feast of cherry-flavored snow cones and chocolate Nutty Buddies that accompanied each win -- compliments of Tildy.

When Willie and I walked out of the Paramount Theater the next day, we realized, we were taken on a very serious ride that would prove to be more important than we could have known. In the lobby, after purchasing a large box of popcorn and sodas for each of us, I started for the door to the center aisle, where I always entered. Willie stopped me and pointed at a sign above the stairs leading to a distant balcony. It said, '*Negroes*, **UPSTAIRS ONLY**'. I was shocked. Not only by the sign's degrading intent, but also because I had been coming to the movies for five years, and never noticed it before.

"That's not right," I said.

"Let it be," Willie said softly. "It's what it is."

"Doesn't make it right, does it?"

"Ain't that the truth," he replied, and started for the stairs. I looked up at the sign again, then around the lobby.

"Hey, Willie," I whispered. "It'll be okay, come on." And with that I waved him to follow me down the center aisle. We opened the door and entered the darkened theater just as the curtain was parting. The cartoon started as we walked down the aisle and settled into seats about half-past center. I didn't notice anyone paying any particular attention to Willie at all. After the cartoon ended, a preview for Lawrence of Arabia followed. As it was winding down, Willie leaned over and said, "We've got to take that one in."

"For sure," I responded.

Suddenly, a figure appeared above and behind us. It was a man who seemed huge, but I wasn't sure if the shadowy theater was tricking my eyes, or if adults always seemed big to twelve-year-olds. The large man reached down, grabbed the two of us by the necks of our T-shirts, and lifted us out of our seats. We started to protest, but he kicked us both in the butt and said, "Get in the balcony. No Coloreds down here and you know it." Out of fear, we both ran up the aisle, took a left, and ran up the stairs, never looking back at the Goliath who had badgered us. We stopped after the third turn in the stairway to catch our breath.

Willie looked at me, "You happy now."

"It still ain't right."

"Come on," he said, "see if the movie looks any different up here."

We entered a part of the theater that was foreign to me. It was an upper balcony, which in all of my years of movie-going, I never remembered seeing. I once sat in the spacious second floor balcony with my grandparents to see the re-release of Gone With the Wind. Looking down on the sold-out theater, I remember wondering what would happen if I spilled my Dr Pepper on all those folks below. But Willie's race was delegated to a separate balcony above and though there were only five Negro patrons, it seemed kind of jammed. I will say it proved to be apropos when about halfway into the movie, the screen depicted Scout and her brother, Jem, as they settled into their nests at the feet of the black citizens of their small southern town.

In the movie, they sit in the 'Black Only' balcony to watch the closing argument by their father, Atticus Finch, in the trial of a Negro man wrongly accused of raping a white woman. Atticus (Gregory Peck) proved that only a left-handed person could have perpetrated the abuse, and the black defendant, portrayed by Brock Peters, had lost the use of his left arm in a cotton gin accident when he was twelve years old. Actually, Peters' character, Tom Robinson, was charged with kissing the girl, an offense considered equal to rape in author Harper Lee's 1930's southern Jim Crow world. It was an extremely poignant moment when Atticus wound up his closing argument to the jury. I'll never forget what he said -- part of it went like this:

> *"...The witnesses for the State with the exception of the Sheriff of Macom County have presented themselves to you Gentlemen, and to this Court...in the cynical confidence that their testimony would not be doubted. Confident that you Gentlemen would go along with them on the assumption...the evil assumption – that all Negroes lie. All Negroes are basically immoral beings. All Negro men are not to be trusted around our women. An assumption that one associates with minds of their caliber. And which in itself Gentlemen, is a lie...which I do not need to point out to you. And so, a quiet, humble, respectable Negro has had the unmitigated temerity to feel sorry for a white woman. Has had to put his word against two white people. The defendant is not guilty! But somebody in this courtroom is. Now Gentleman, in this country our Courts are*

*the great levelers. In our courts all men are
created equal. I'm no idealist to believe firmly
in the integrity of our courts and our jury
system. That's no ideal to me...that is a living,
working reality! And I am confident that
you Gentlemen will review without passion
the evidence that you have heard. Come to a
decision and restore this man to his family. In
the name of God...do your duty. In the name
of God, believe Tom Robinson."*

I looked from my buddy down on my fellow white folks sitting below. No one was coughing or moving. You could've heard a pin drop. Willie and I waited with those in the movie for the verdict to come in. Finally, the Foreman for the jury announced, "We find the defendant guilty as charged."

"What!" I yelled out, not realizing I was breaking the silence of the entire theater. Everyone below and in our section turned to look at me. I shrugged, "That ain't right." The black folks applauded me in our balcony. But in the distance, from way down below came a loud declaration, "Shut up you crazy nigger!"

I sat back in my seat stunned by the vicious slur directed at me. It slammed me like someone had just kicked me in the stomach. What a horrible way to go through life, I thought. These honest, caring black people sitting in the balcony with me surely had to deal with this on a day-to-day basis, had to deal with the many ignorant imbeciles they come across in their everyday life. What character it must take to endure the abuse. To turn the other cheek so to speak, like it said to do in the Bible. My interpretation of history had told me the Negroes had been turning that cheek for more than a century, and that was way too long.

I sat silently and watched the rest of the movie. Then Willie and I walked out into the sunlight on Congress Avenue totally speechless for the first time in our collective lives. We stood below the marquee in silence for the longest time. Finally, I managed, "You want to go to MAC'S and get a bacon cheeseburger?"

"Right on," Willie said. We started walking down the street toward the Capitol building. After a block, I broke the silence.

"Atticus Finch is one hell of a guy, ain't he?"

"Everyone should have a daddy like that," Willie said as he took a toothpick out of his pocket and stuck it in his mouth. "Only in the movies, I guess."

"Did that make you mad? You know, the way the jury dumped on Tom Robinson?"

"Mick -- it kind of made me feel like -- even though it was awful, it was true. I sort of understand this whole thing a little better. It showed me there are a lot of honest, good, white people out there who care about our situation and do their part to make it better for us. That's good, I think, so I really liked the movie. I want to see it again."

"That's neat. I want to see it again, too," I said. After that we walked down the street in silence.

A few minutes later we were devouring our bacon cheeseburgers at MAC'S, continuing our exploration into issues related to the movie, to race, and to life in general. I was getting excited about topics I never considered before I met Willie. It was one of my most important watershed moments, and one I still treasure to this day.

CHAPTER TWELVE

For as long as I remember, from the time I originally arrived in Austin at the age of four, until I moved out of the house as a freshman at the University, Daisy Belle Alexander was our maid. She belonged in the state of Texas, that's for sure, because everything about Daisy was big. She weighed about three hundred pounds, stood close to 5'11" in her stocking feet, and was the color of dark chocolate. Her son, who was 6'10" and practically weighed more than scales could calculate, had played football against my oldest brother in high school the previous year and had made his mama proud by sacking David five times during their game. That gave her bragging rights with my mom for a couple of years. Daisy loved to talk about her son because he was the first in her five-generation Austin family not only to get into a college with a football scholarship, but the first ever to graduate from high school. Daisy was a single mother with one large child. They lived in East Austin and my mother bought her a slightly used car every three years so she could commute to Tarrytown to help with the household cooking, cleaning, and transportation needs.

Daisy was amazing. The first five years in Austin, before my mother remarried, Daisy alternated with my mom as my escort. I would normally see my mother at breakfast, which she would cook -- all the while letting go some expletives that would still be deleted on the radio or T.V. today. She would never admit it, but I learned more bad words from my mom cooking breakfast than I did from my peers or brothers. Daisy would usually show up after my mother's daily morning verbal assault on the kitchen utensils, while we were eating breakfast. Our maid would immediately clean the pots and pans, silently pick up any broken dishes, and then feed Napoleon his breakfast. When I was attending kindergarten at Good Shepherd, Daisy would walk me to the church if my mom couldn't take me in route to one of her many volunteer jobs.

Almost every day at 1:30 when we were let out, Daisy would be waiting to walk me the five blocks back home. When we arrived, she would make me a plate of fried chicken, potatoes, vegetables or cole slaw, with homemade biscuits and gravy. Sometimes she would build me a creative sandwich with all kinds of ingredients. I always yearned for lunch. While I ate whatever she prepared, Daisy quizzed me about my day. In a way, it was a rehearsal for when my mom would return from the hospital or cancer center after another day of volunteerism. I always felt those talks helped me develop into a better communicator in my later childhood and adolescent life. Daisy would remain a friend and confidant throughout my formative years.

On the morning of July 10th before leaving for the Cancer Headquarters, my mother notified Daisy that I would be having a few friends over for lunch and play. She asked our maid to prepare a large amount of fried chicken and cole slaw. It was a special day for us because the annual game when the All Stars of the American League, led by Mickey Mantle, played those from the Willie Mays led National League squad. The game would be televised in black and white for the seventh season in a row, and Willie and I had been anticipating it for several weeks, since they had announced the players.

On the morning of the 10th, as previously arranged, I rode my bike up to the pink house on the hill where Willie's mama worked as a domestic. I knocked on the back door expecting Teresa or her son to answer, but in their place stood a man with a flamboyant scarf around his neck. It flowed down his body hiding vital areas and I suddenly realized it was the only stitch of clothing he had on. The strange sight in front of me said, "Oh my -- what have we got here? Tasty."

From behind the mostly naked man I heard another male voice, "Fletcher behave. Go to your room and dress for crying out loud. We're already late for our showing."

The man in the scarf smiled at me and whispered, "Bruce is so officious."

"Uh huh," I mumbled.

"Fletcher!! I'm serious," the unseen man screamed.

"Okay, don't get your knickers in a twit. See what this cute little boy wants -- would you? I'll be ready in five," he said as he turned dramatically and marched away.

After a moment the other man appeared wearing a white suit with a pink tie, a pink handkerchief jutting out of his breast pocket, and was pinning a pink carnation to his lapel. I figured it had to be his favorite color.

"Yes, young man, and how, pray tell, may I assist you?" he asked.

"Well," I started slowly, "I was picking up my buddy, Willie. I thought he was here with his momma, Teresa."

"Are you Mickey?" he asked.

"Yes, I am."

"I heard you were coming. I know your mother," he said as he finished pinning on the carnation. He glanced in a mirror on the wall and adjusted his tie slightly, then gave his attention back to me. "Yes, Gracie and I go way back."

"I didn't know."

"Well, how could you darlin'? I doubt she would want to bring me up around you or your brothers," Bruce said this matter-of-factly.

"Uh -- is Willie here?" I asked, becoming a little creeped out by his manner.

"He's with his mother in the back yard helping us through our latest domestic catastrophe. Come on in, walk through the kitchen and you'll find them," he said. I entered and started down the hall mumbling a thank you under my breath. He called after me, "And, oh, Mickey -- tell your mother that Bruce says hello from 'the girls'."

"Okay." I said, kind of wondering where the girls were as I walked through the kitchen and out the rear door.

In the back yard of the brilliantly landscaped house I found Willie helping his mama polish a ton of brass vases. Apparently, Willie was not enjoying the work or was really glad to see me, because he jumped up and rushed over, saying, "Mickey, give me five." We exchanged slaps and I turned my attention to his mother who was picking up the polishing rags Willie had discarded.

"Good morning, Teresa," I said politely.

"Mickey, it sure is good to see you," she replied. "How have you been?"

"Just fine. I met the people you work for. They seem kind of -- different," I stated cautiously.

Teresa let go a belly laugh and motioned toward the house. "That, they are for sure, Mickey. That, they are for sure. But I love working for them. Now you boys go do what you do. I have to get on with the polishing."

Willie and I left the back yard, walked through the kitchen and out the garage door entrance without seeing either of Teresa's employers, whom I assumed shared the house. In my youthful naiveté I had no idea what was going on, but I was intrigued. I started to ask Willie about it, but he spoke first, "Boy howdy, I'm glad you got here when you did," he said as he started to mount my handlebars. "I was afraid I was going to polish all that brass forever. I hate woman's work."

"Well, you're out of there now, so forget about it, Kemo Sabe," I said. "Hold on tight, here we go."

And we were off. I pedaled around the corner, up one hill and down another, and then turned onto my street. At the third driveway on the right, I turned and pedaled to the carport of my house. As soon as we dismounted and Napoleon had gotten acquainted with Willie for the first time, Danny arrived on his brand-new, fancy five-speed Schwinn. We all exchanged 'high fives' and then I ran inside for a football to throw around in the yard. As I entered the kitchen, Daisy was sitting at the counter reading the sports page. She looked up and said, "I thought you had some friends coming over for the All Star Game?"

As I grabbed a football out of the utility closet, I answered, "They're out front. The game doesn't start for another half-hour. So we're going to throw the football in the front yard."

"Alrighty then, have fun," Daisy said. "When do you want to have lunch, Mick?"

"Probably around the third inning, if that's okay?"

"Oh, fine darling. I just wanted a ball park time so I could have everything ready."

"Okay, Daisy," I said as I left the house to rejoin my friends. "Thanks."

For the next half hour, we took turns guarding one another, while the odd man played the quarterback. We ran down-and-outs, and caught passes just inside the street curb, and dragged our feet as we left the yard for the pavement, mimicking what we'd seen Raymond Berry do for the Colts on Sunday afternoons. We also ran crossing patterns, post patterns, flag routes, corner routes, buttonhooks, and the occasional out and up. Of course, the hardest for me was playing defense when Willie was receiving because of his unusual jets and Danny's perfectly directed passes. I enjoyed throwing the football, but knew my arm was better suited for baseball and besides, at my slight weight, I knew I wouldn't be playing a contact sport like football -- unless it was of the touch or flag varieties.

We were having a lot of fun as kids emulating our adult heroes. It was a hot, humid July day, but to us, that didn't matter. It's hard to believe, but we didn't even perspire all that much. To our adolescent minds, sweat was for older people or fat kids. Every once and awhile we had to interrupt our games to yell at a driver of the car that Napoleon had stopped in the middle of our street. I would scream to the driver, "Floor it, you'll never hit the dog." Sometimes I would offer money if they could. Invariably, Napoleon would intimidate the driver into freezing in fear they were going to hit him. In these cases, we would have to grab the boxer, who was attacking the bumper, and allow them to move on down the road. I always wondered why people who experienced this situation every time they drove through my neighborhood, ever bothered to come down our street at all.

That beautiful summer morning of our idyllic young lives everything came to an arresting stop for the stupidest of reasons. Danny threw a touchdown corner route to Willie just out of my reach. After congratulating Willie, I turned and raced Danny to the hose by our front door to get a drink of water. Willie wandered out into the street after catching the TD pass, and was tossing the ball into the air in celebration just as a car traveling at a great rate of speed grabbed Napoleon's attention. Our boxer charged into the street like always, and the cherry red Plymouth Belvedere predictably slowed to a stop for the brave, but somewhat stubborn dog.

"Napoleon," Willie yelled, "come on buddy, get out of the way. You're gonna get killed."

Danny and I looked up from our drinking to see my dog, about one hundred and fifty feet away, as he stopped the vehicle.

"Uh oh," Danny said, with some trepidation.

"What's wrong?" I asked.

"I think that's Noah Parkes's new car."

"How could Noah be driving?" I asked. "It took him three tries to pass the sixth grade."

Danny jerked his head at me and said with enthusiasm, "Well, test or no test, he's old enough to drive and there he is. His stupid drunk mother bought him a car so she doesn't have to drive the jerk around. I'm pretty sure that's the car."

"Damn, we may have a big problem. Come on." Danny followed me toward the street where Napoleon had stopped the car and Willie was still yelling.

The window of the car rolled down to reveal the demon himself, Noah Parkes, in the driver's seat. He looked at Willie, and then at the dog attacking his bumper, and then back at Willie. He started to get out of the car as Danny and I approached.

"Noah," I yelled, "get out of here or I'll have Napoleon attack you and not your damn car."

Noah stopped short of getting out of the car because, as stupid as he obviously was, even he knew he couldn't take on my snarling boxer and *three* of us. But he did yell out toward me, "You got it comin' to ya', ya' damn nigger lover! You'd better watch more than just ya' back from now on." And with that he peeled out, barely missing Willie and my dog. Napoleon lunged out of the way at the last moment and then chased the red Plymouth down the street until it was out of sight.

"That boy is plumb crazy," Willie said. "We got to stay away from his racist cracker ass."

"You got that right, blood brother," I said.

"Noah Parkes is what happens when animals mate. He's stupid, but I think he's harmless. Let's go inside, the game's about to start."

Willie looked back at our dog laying in wait for his next vehicular victim and said, "Should we bring Napoleon with us, Mick?"

As we headed for the garage door to the kitchen, I started to yell for my dog but another car got his attention and he was off to do his chase detail. Danny entered the house first and said hello to Daisy. Then I entered with Willie.

"Daisy, this is my friend Willie Veils. His momma is a maid like you, around the corner and up the hill a ways. Willie, this is Daisy."

"Hello Daisy, it's nice to meet you," Willie spurted out.

"Oh sweet Lord, what have we got here? In all my days I never -- Well, what do you know. Oh, I'm sorry, where have my manners gone. Welcome, Willie. Y'all go make yourselves comfortable in the den. The game's about to start."

There was a small television on in the background behind Daisy, but the sound was turned down. On the silent screen I could see Dizzy Dean and Pee Wee Reese announcing the starting line-ups as the players appeared from the dugouts and joined their teammates along the base paths.

Danny yelled, "I get the General's chair."

He ran out of the kitchen and down a hall toward the den. When Willie and I started to follow, Daisy cleared her throat. I looked back at her and she held up her hand, saying, "Mick, could I see you for a moment before you get involved in your game."

"Sure. Willie you go ahead and join Danny. It's down the hall to the left, and I'll be right with y'all," I said, pointing the way for my buddy. He left the kitchen and Daisy immediately questioned me.

"Does your momma know what's going on here?"

"What's going on, Daisy?" I asked, bewildered.

"You know, bringing a Colored boy into the house," she said.

"Oh, Willie, sure -- she didn't tell you? His family had me over for ribs one day last month, and now I'm paying him back."

"Did your momma say where you should have lunch?" Daisy asked in a very concerned voice. "Did she say it was all right to feed a Colored boy in your den?"

"No. She didn't mention anything special."

"You are sure she knows Willie is here?" she asked.

"Of course."

"Well, then I'm going to give her a call and see what I should do with this situation. You know I dearly love working here, Mickey, and I wouldn't want to endanger my position," she said as she reached for the phone hanging on the wall by the refrigerator. She glanced at the number written on a piece of paper on the counter and slowly dialed the number for the Austin Chapter of the American Cancer Society. Ever since my father died of stomach cancer, my mom volunteered for the local organization and served as its treasurer for several years.

"Hello," our maid said into the phone. "Could I please speak to Mrs. Gracie Lilly? Yes ma'am, thank you."

"Daisy, I would have thought you would have no problem with this," I said while she was holding for my mom to come to the phone. "Willie is your kind of peoples."

"Your kind of *people*," she corrected. "Speak properly, Mick. Don't you start turning *Colored* on me. It's not that I have a prob -- Oh, hello Ms. Gracie, it's Daisy -- No everyone is just fine. But I had a question concerning the little Colored boy Mick brought over today -- Oh yes he is very nice -- Well, I was wondering where should I feed the boys lunch -- in the kitchen or sunroom?"

"No," I blurted out, "we want to eat off the TV tables while we watch the game in the den."

Daisy held up her hand to silence me as she listened to my mother on the other end of the phone. "Yes ma'am, I was just checking. Didn't want to upset the apple cart. Okay, I'll see you then, Ms. Gracie. Sorry to disturb you. Bye-bye."

"Well?" I asked.

"She said it would be all right to feed you boys in the den," Daisy said with a chuckle. "In all my days I never. Oh Lordy. Mick, go join your friends and I'll bring in some snacks after the National Anthem."

"Thanks Daisy. I still don't see what the big fuss was all about, but you're okay now, right?"

"I'm just fine, Mick. You are still only a child with no big worries of your own yet. When you're a little older and look back on this, I think you might understand my situation. But, for now, you go enjoy the game with your young friends."

I left the kitchen and walked to the den. Danny was sitting in my mom's chair, which was off-limits if she was home, especially when the Cowboys were playing on Sundays. Willie was sitting Indian-style on the floor about five feet in front of the tube. I plopped down on the couch, choosing not to bring up the topic of my kitchen conversation. On our 20-inch black-and-white Magnavox television, the great blues diva, Ella Fitzgerald, was performing the National Anthem at home plate while the players and coaches of the two teams stood in lines that stretched along the base paths.

After it was over, Willie whistled and smiled. "That lady has got some voice!"

"All right, let's go American's!" I shouted out.

"Come on National's!" screamed Willie.

Danny asked, "Either of you know when the first All Star game was played?"

"Before I was born," answered Willie.

"It was 1933," Danny said, showing off his extensive knowledge of baseball trivia. "Okay, who hit the first home run in an All Star game?"

"I'll guess. Let's see, 1933 -- it must be Lou Gehrig," I said.

"Close. It was The Babe, in the third inning off of Wild Bill Hallahan," Danny said with authority.

"Okay, what did Carl Hubbell do in the 1934 All Star game that was unbelievable?" Danny asked.

"I know that," I said sitting up in my position on the couch. "He struck out The Babe, Lou Gerhig, Jimmy Foxx, and a couple of other Hall of Famers, in a row."

"Who were the other two?" Danny wanted to stump me again.

"I don't remember. Who?"

"Al Simmons and Joe Cronin." Danny smiled.

"You white boys amaze me," Willie barked. "You must spend all of your time memorizing stuff? I remember next to nothin' I read."

We returned our attention to the T.V. as Pee Wee Reese interviewed the recently-retired, nineteen-time All Star, Ted Williams, in the booth before the game. Williams told Reese, "They invented the All Star Game for Willie Mays."

With the three of us watching intently, Don Drysdale and Jim Bunning, two of the premiere pitchers of their respective leagues, started the game and each gave up only one hit during their three inning stretch -- the two pitchers left the game with the score tied 0-0.

As the fourth inning ended, we were finishing off our second helpings of Daisy's glorious fried chicken, potato salad, baked beans, and homemade biscuits with gravy. Willie spoke through a full mouthful, "Jesus, this is great fried chicken. I wish my mother could make it like this. Delicious."

"Mention it to Daisy," I said. "She loves compliments."

Willie stood up and grabbed my empty plate to help clean up, then started to take Danny's before he said, "Keep away, Kemo Sabe. I'm having thirds."

"Say what!" Willie exclaimed. "How you two stay so skinny with all the food you stuff down yo'selves? If I ate like this all the time I would be as big as that new Goodtime blimp flying over the field."

"That's Good-Year," I said, "like the tire, dummy."

"I knew that," Willie said, and walked out of the room.

"The Mick must still be hurting," Danny observed, "if they're gonna run Colavito for him."

"Probably hasn't recovered from the hamstring pull. He needs the four days off to recover so he'll be ready for the rest of the season."

Willie returned and plopped down in his spot on the floor. He said to me over his shoulder, "Daisy doesn't like me, but I won't hold it against her 'cause she makes some awful good finger-lickin' chicken."

The game continued and was highlighted by Willie Mays saving the victory for the National's with a home run-robbing catch of a Roger Maris' blast to right center in the eighth inning.

A few minutes after the end of the All Star game, Danny and I were engaged in a wicked Gnip-Gnop game in the upstairs playroom. Willie was standing by the window looking beyond the roof to the street in front of our house. Suddenly, he stiffened and yelled, "That Cracker's back!"

Danny had just slammed one off our soundproofed ceiling, right wall, and into play on my side of the table for a winner. I started for the window to see what Willie was screaming about. Suddenly, he said, "Oh, no!" and turned, sprinting between us down the stairs. Danny and I looked at each other, and then quickly out the window. We saw Noah Parkes's car, but Napoleon wasn't biting at the bumper as per usual but was positioned a few feet away from the car on the driver's side. The dog seemed to be chewing on something. Willie entered our view and sprinted toward the street. Noah Parkes must have seen him coming because he suddenly floored his Plymouth and Napoleon gave chase with whatever he had been gnawing at still sticking out of his mouth. Willie chased after the car and dog but slowed down a little before my boxer gave up the chase. Willie walked over to the boxer and yanked away whatever was in his mouth and threw it down the gutter.

"Let's go," I said. We ran down the stairs and out the kitchen door. As we approached the street, we saw Willie struggling toward us carrying my dog in his arms. When they reached us, I noticed Napoleon was frothing at the mouth, with an ominous white soapy substance running out.

"That Cracker tried to kill Napoleon," Willie snarled. "He fed him some bad meat and we gots to get him to the vet."

I looked from Willie to my dog to Danny. I guess I was in shock because I couldn't think or move. Danny took charge like the QB he was to become, and directed the offense with calm and courage. He instructed Willie and me to take Napoleon to Daisy's car in front of my house. He said he would get her and meet us there. We obeyed and a few long moments later Daisy followed Danny up our driveway to her car. As she got in, she was huffing and puffing and praying. "Oh, Lord," she said as she looked at the sickly boxer. "Look what they done to our dog. Where do I take him, Mick?" I couldn't answer. I was shaking so badly, afraid that I was losing my friend.

Danny elbowed me in the ribs. "Tell Daisy where to take Napy, now! The vet can still save him."

"Uh -- it's near Two Jays Hamburgers. About a block the other side -- it's called West Austin Animal Clinic or something like --" I was lost and rambling.

"It's on Lamar north of 38th Street," Danny added, "about five or six blocks."

As she turned onto Exposition Boulevard, Daisy screamed out, "Okay little darlins', hold on! We're not stopping for nothing." Daisy put the pedal to the floor, accelerating past fifty miles per hour, probably for the first time in her life.

As we tore down the pavement, I looked over at my faithful friend who seemed to be slipping away. His breathing had sped up and the foam coming from his mouth was flowing like a great gusher. Willie sensed my uneasiness and placed his arm around my shoulder.

"Napoleon's too tough to let a little bad meat take him out," Willie reassured. "I think I got to him before he ate too much."

I finally realized what Willie had done. If he hadn't seen the encounter with Noah Parkes and grabbed the tainted steak as quick as he did, Napoleon would be as much a part of history as his human namesake. "Thanks," was all I could muster.

"Don't mention it."

Suddenly, we were pulling into a familiar parking in front of McCloud's Animal Clinic. "This is it!" I shouted.

The next thing I knew, Willie had the dog out of the car and was racing toward the door which Danny held open. Daisy and I followed. At the front desk, Daisy rapidly explained what had happened and the veterinary assistant immediately sprung into action. She directed Willie to place the dog on a lab table in the back room and notified the vet, Dr. McCloud, of the situation. Then she showed us all out to the waiting room and told us to be patient, trying to reassure us that everything was going to be okay. My last sight of Napoleon was of him lying on his side, breathing erratically, and his mind too scrambled to notice I was leaving, or hear me say I loved him.

The time spent sitting in the waiting room seemed interminable. The four of us sat there silently for several minutes, but it was like an eternity to me. We could hear Dr. McCloud and the assistant talking mutedly through the paper-thin walls of the clinic. After awhile, I thought I heard Napoleon barfing. Not knowing what the sound meant, I thought it was my dog's last gasp at life and tears sprung into my eyes. Daisy saw this and put her arm around me, saying, "That's a good sign, Mickey. The poison is coming out. They is pumping his stomach, you see, dear."

"You mean he's going to live?" I asked, wiping at the tears.

"He just might. Put your faith in the Lord, Mick, and everything will work out just fine." Daisy seemed to speak from experience.

After a couple of minutes, Dr. McCloud showed up in the doorway and the four of us all stood up. He approached us, smiling and said, "We have to thank God for Napoleon's really strong stomach. He's going to be okay. Rest assured of that. We've given him a sedative and an antibiotic to fight any infection that might accompany the substance he ingested. I suggest you leave him here overnight for us to monitor. You can give us a call in the morning and probably come pick him up then."

Daisy shook his hand and said, "Thank you, Jesus."

"Can I see Napoleon?" I asked.

"Sure, Mickey, but you understand, he's sleeping," Dr. McCloud reiterated.

"I just want to tell him I'm sorry I gave up on him. I should have known better." I was sobbing, still suffering shock from the whole event.

Dr. McCloud escorted me into the lab where the assistant was securing my dog in his kennel. As I looked down at Napoleon, I was so glad to know he was alive. He looked peaceful in a way. His breathing was so slow from the sedative that at first glance, he didn't appear to be breathing at all. I reached out and patted him gently on his shoulder. He didn't move or respond -- he was out for sure. I hoped he could still feel my love.

Daisy was in the doorway behind me. She whispered, "Let him heal up, Mick. We need to get back home, son."

I took one last long look at my dog lying so still before me and sighed. We left and drove home in a silent vehicle. As she parked in front of our house in her favorite spot under the shade of an oak tree, Daisy finally said, "God Bless that po' boy who done this. He's gonna have nothing but trouble his whole life, I'm afraid. We'll tell your mama, Mickey, and she'll decide if she wants to call in the police, okay?"

"Sure, Daisy, whatever you say," I stated somberly. We all got out of the car and watched as my maid waddled her large frame down the driveway and through the carport entrance to the house.

"Is this going to be Tom Robinson all over again?" Willie asked.

Danny looked at Willie like he was Greek, blurting out, "What are you talking about?"

"From To Kill A Mockingbird. Keep up with the program, dummy," I said sarcastically. Good, I thought, my sense of humor had returned. I guess I was coming back from the shock. I continued, "No Willie. Noah's going to get what's coming to him."

"He sure is 'cause we're going to give it to him," Willie said with a mischievous smile on his face. "How many ping pong balls you got?"

"Say what?" I asked, confused by the question.

"Give me three ping pong balls," Willie continued, "and we'll give Mr. Parkes something to think about."

"What are you going to do with three ping pong balls?" Danny asked, suddenly interested.

"Something my older brother showed me once. Trust me. We'll get the best of Mr. Cracker," Willie said. "Now where does that po' white trash park his car at night?"

"I know how to find out," Danny said. "I'll be back in a bit." And with that he left us in a hurry, running across the street.

Willie and I decided to wait for Danny in our playroom. While we were listening to Sam Cooke on the hi-fi, and deriding the Cracker, Daisy interrupted us, yelling from below that my mother wanted to see me. As I started down the stairs, I met Danny coming the other way. As we passed, he said, "I got it."

"Great. I'm going to ask my mom if you two can stay over," I said. "Keep Willie company until I get back."

I found my mother sitting at her desk in the bedroom. Plopping down on the bed, I sighed and said, "Can you believe what that jerk did to Napy?"

"It's too horrible to accept," she stated simply.

"We can pick him up in the morning?" I asked. "He looked really bad there for awhile."

"That Noah Parkes is a no good, ignorant, boy, who is going nowhere in his life."

"Are you going to call the cops, Mom?"

"If we file a complaint with the police, then a whole bunch of issues come into play that I am not prepared, at this time in my life, to drag in front of the public. Besides, Mickey, you and I both know Noah Parkes will get his justice from God, which will be much more powerful than any Travis County Courts could ever bring to bear."

"I guess -- is it all right if Willie and Danny stay over tonight?" I pleaded. "They said it was okay with their folks."

"I don't know honey. Steve and I are going to a party tonight and --"

"Please!!!" I begged. "You can get Nanny to come over, can't you?"

"I suppose," she said sternly. "But, you three have to promise to not give your grandmother any trouble. Deal?"

"No problem. We'll stay upstairs all night."

"When Daisy first told me about this mess, I was going to ground you," my mother said, startling me.

"Ground me?"

"I'm thinking you were the cause of this uproar by bringing Willie into the neighborhood. I realize you two are becoming good friends, and I see nothing wrong with it. However, there are some people around here --" she trailed off, lowering her head and shaking it.

I walked over and placed my hand on her shoulder. "It's all right, Mom," I said reassuringly. "We can take care of ourselves."

She put her arm around me like any good mother would. "Oh, Mickey. I'm sure you can. Go tell Danny and Willie I want to hear from both of their mother's that it's okay to stay over."

"They haven't really talked to them, yet. But, I'm sure it will be okay. I'll tell them to call right now." I leapt from the room before she could accuse me of manipulation and mendacity.

So, here we were in the playroom as the evening set in with Willie telling Danny and I about the great ping-pong ball illusion. His late brother, the one run over by the train when he was eighteen, had gotten especially mad at a rival for his girlfriend. He decided to fix the challenger who drove a fancy car, which sadly outclassed Willie's brother, who only had a beat up single-speed bike built from scratch with spare parts from the junk yards of South Austin.

Willie's brother took three ping-pong balls and inserted them into the gas tank of this fellow's fancy car. The guy started his car the next morning, just like always. The car ran fine at first, but before long the soft plastic balls got sucked into the internal ports for the fuel, stopped the flow, and stalled the car. When the engine died, the suction force holding the ping-pong balls in place released them to float harmlessly in the tank again, awaiting the guy's next attempt to start the car. When Willie's brother had done this, the fellow ended up trashing his car because he never figured out what the problem was, in spite of the fact that he made his living as an auto mechanic. Danny and I agreed immediately that the ping-pong ball prank would be perfect revenge.

My mom arranged for my grandmother, whom I called Nanny, to stay with us while they were at an anniversary party at the country club. I called her Nanny because my oldest cousin couldn't pronounce 'Granny' when she first spoke as a two-year-old, and all the grandchildren adopted the moniker. She was in her eighties and very sweet, but extremely hard of hearing. In fact, when she was sitting in front of the television with its single speaker blaring out the Huntley-Brinkley report, I could stand behind her yelling as loud as I wanted and she never heard a thing. So, needless to say, Danny, Willie, and I were excited by the prospect of sneaking out of the house unseen and unheard, and having a couple of uninterrupted hours to seek our revenge on the brutish, dog-poisoning, "Cracker" Parkes.

However, his whereabouts between 8 and 10 p.m. was key to the success of our prank. We knew he lived near O. Henry Junior High, but couldn't be sure he'd be home. If he wasn't, it would only leave us about an hour and a half to find him and even if we did, it wouldn't mean we could find the opportunity to tamper with the tank unnoticed.

Danny, who previously retrieved Noah's address, was also smart enough to get the bigot's phone number as well.

"You know," Danny said, "we should call him and say he's won something and if he's by the phone at 9 p.m. this evening for the live radio call, Wolfman Jack will announce his prize."

"Neat plan" I said. "Who makes the call?"

Danny thought for a moment, then said, "What about your brother, David? He might like the idea of getting even -- don't you think?"

"Yeah, maybe. I'll go ask him," I said.

I walked down the stairs and through the sunroom into the den where my grandmother sat watching her nightly news. I yelled out a "Howdy!" from directly behind her and she never moved. As I came into her peripheral vision she looked up and I waved. She blew me a kiss. I turned down the hallway and found my oldest brother in the bedroom he shared with Larry. He was finishing dressing for a date, but after explaining the situation to him, he immediately followed me past Nanny and joined us in the playroom. He was never one to waste time. When there was a task to do, you didn't think about doing it or wait to do it later, you simply took the time to do it right then.

My brother made the call, Noah Parkes answered, and David led him to believe he was the luckiest guy on the face of the earth, having his phone number picked at random for a chance to win a prize. He was told that he would receive a telephone call at 9 p.m. from none other than the Wolfman, himself. The famous DJ would ask him a question on Chubby Checker, and if he answered it correctly, he would receive $1,000. We were on the floor in laughter after my brother ended the call with his best Jackie Gleason sign off.

"Well, thank you, Mr. Parkes, now you wait for the Wolfman's call -- and a—waaaaaaaayyyyyyy we go."

It worked. At 8:45 when we arrived at his apartment building behind O. Henry Junior High, we saw the red Belvedere parked exactly where Jack had told Danny it would be. Willie stealthily approached the car, opened the lid to the gas tank, and dropped the three ping-pong balls into the opening. Then we ran to our bikes hidden behind a neighbor's hedges and pedaled away. We didn't know if it was going to work, but we had pulled off the most difficult part, and the sense of the accomplishment and rush of adrenaline invigorated us. Around the first corner, the three of us pulled our bikes to the side of the road and exchanged high fives before continuing on toward my home.

We arrived home a short time later and found Nanny sitting in the same position as always, watching the television. She never looked up as Danny and Willie walked behind her and up the stairs. I walked in to say "goodnight" and as I walked up beside her, she surprised me by spurting out, "How was your little bicycle excursion, Mickey?"

"What," I said in a stunned mumble, "uh, I di...di..didn't -- think you --"

"You didn't think I heard you yelling behind my back all those times, either. What do you think I have," she asked, "one directional hearing? Might as well tell me where you've been, so I can decide what I'm going to do about it?"

"Please Nanny, don't say anything. We had to go out. We had something really important to do. I'll come rake your leaves for nothing."

"You should have asked permission. Did you ever think of that?" she asked.

"Not really."

"Well, next time you better. You hear me," she said sternly.

"Yes, ma'am."

"Okay, this one time, I won't say anything. But, if I catch you sneaking around again, I will not go easy. I have a responsibility to your momma, you know," she said, and I nodded. "And, Mickey, stop yelling at me. I hear just fine. It's called selective hearing and older people have the privilege to practice it. Now, come here and give your old grandmother a kiss."

I leaned down and kissed her gently on the side of her cheek and she gave me a big hug. Then she said, "Go play with your friends and stay out of trouble."

"Yes ma'am, Nanny. And thanks for letting me off the hook," I said as she let go.

I returned to my friends, and on the way I remember thinking how lucky I was to have family and friends that looked out for me. The contrast between what my grandmother had done, and what I'd seen the two fathers do at the Little League park. I was truly a lucky kid.

CHAPTER THIRTEEN

Glory day moments -- we hope to achieve them, and if we do, they never leave our minds for long. Anything brilliant, noble, and beyond the reach of normal achievements in the world of sports for most participants constitutes a glory day moment. As a young athlete, one strives for: an elusive championship, an undefeated season, a batting or scoring title, a no hitter or a perfect game, a hole in one, bowling a three hundred game, scoring the winning touchdown, reeling in a trophy fish, breaking a record in the pool, or winning at a state meet on the track. This separates the average to above average from the master or the professional, for the latter is exceptional at a particular sport and they may realize many a glory day moment. But, when one of the average players experiences one or two such moments, in the teen or pre-teen years, that athlete is not likely to remember anything except the minutiae of the entire event.

On the second to last day of the 1962 Little League season, Rylanders was playing Willie, Danny, and their City National team. If we won the game we could sew up the second-half championship, and since we had won the first half, we would be the first undisputed champions of our league in five years. If we lost, Seven Up could end up tying us and we would have to play a one game playoff for the second half. If we lost that game, we would have to play a final championship game. In other words, this was shaping up to be an important day. I was scheduled to pitch and I woke up in the morning feeling like I was going to throw an exceptionally good game. All day the feeling kept up -- at lunch I had a premonition that I was going to make the headlines the next day.

By the time I got to Bishop Field for warm-ups, I had gone over the batting order in my head and figured out how I was going to pitch to each of their players. They only had three All-Star caliber players, unlike the six or seven on our squad. Of course there was Willie, the leadoff hitter, who was still topping the league in batting average, stolen bases, runs scored, and doubles. In fact, because of his jets, he was the *only* player with a triple! Batting second was a weak-hitting second baseman, Freddy, who tried to bunt Willie to the next base as a sacrifice. Danny batted third behind Freddy and was fourth in the league in homers and in the top five in most of the other categories of hitting statistics. Behind him in the clean-up position was City National's other All-Star, the left fielder, Billy, who was a gifted hitter, made contact all the time, and never struck out. He didn't have the power of the normal clean-up hitter, but Mr. Paul, the manager of City National gambled that he was their best contact hitter and would knock in the most runs. It appeared he was right, for Billy was second to Jack in RBI's for the season and had the third best batting average in the league. Due to injuries and a general lack of experience, the remainder of the team was as weak a line-up as I had faced all year.

The first three innings were cake. I had my curve ball breaking both sideways and down and it was unhittable. I also had better control of my fastball than I'd had all year, hitting the corners keeping the ball away from Willie, Danny, and Billy. Accordingly, I took a no-hitter into the fourth inning. I lost the chance for a perfect game, as Willie led off the bottom of the fourth, walked after fouling off five pitches to stay alive at the plate. With Willie at first base, of course, I knew Freddy would try to bunt him to second. So with my first pitch, I threw a sinking curve ball that bounced in the dirt. As Freddy lunged for it and missed, the ball ended up in Don's mitt. However, Willie was off as soon as the ball crossed the plate and slid into second just ahead of Don's off-balance attempt to nail him. My next offering was a carbon copy of the first one and Willie once again decided to run on the pitch in an attempt to steal third. This time Don almost got the jet, but Bob whiffed with his swipe at the tag out. I struck out Freddy on the next pitch, but with Willie at third and only the one out, I would have to throw really well to keep either Danny or Billy from knocking him in with a hit, a fielder's choice, or sacrifice fly. I got ahead of Danny in the count with two quick strikes. On the third pitch, I decided to waste one outside to see if he would chase it, but he didn't. After the pitch, Don stood up and took a few steps toward me, shouting some encouraging words before he gently tossed the ball to me on a floating arch. While it was in the air, out of the corner of my eye, I saw a flash going down the base path toward home. It was Willie attempting to copy one of his idols, Jackie Robinson, who loved to steal home. As I caught the ball, I had a little trouble getting it out of my glove before firing it back to Don who was still standing a little bit in front of the plate. Don caught the ball and swiped at Willie, but it was too late. Willie Veils executed a perfect hook slide across the very back edge of home plate to score the first run of the game.

I was fuming. I couldn't believe I had a no hitter going and we were suddenly behind one to nothing. Out of my instant rage I was able to recover enough to strike out Danny on a wicked curve and get Billy to hit a line drive directly to Bob at third, who barely had time to raise his glove before the ball miraculously found its webbing. Then in the top of the fifth, Don made up for his earlier mental error with Willie, by homering to deep left field and tying the game. In the bottom of the inning, I struck out the side keeping the no hitter in tact. We couldn't even get a base runner in the top of the sixth, so I had to make sure City National scored no runs in the bottom of the frame to ensure extra innings and a chance to preserve a victory.

The first two batters were the eighth and ninth spots in their line-up. I struck them out on seven pitches, and with two away, you know who was coming to bat. Willie strolled to the plate to face me for the third time in the game. In Little League, a pitcher could only pitch six innings every week, so if I kept the game under control and City National scored no more runs, then I had to leave the mound and hope our next pitcher could hold onto the momentum I had generated. The Lord and some luck were on my side this time. I struck Willie out for the first time this season on an excellent mix of curves, fastballs on the outside corner, and a final drop that made him look a little silly.

The inning was over and I had my first no-hitter, however, since the score was tied it seemed to go unnoticed by my teammates. There was no rush to the mound by the catcher, like Yogi Berra in the 1956 World Series. My other friends on the squad knew we were still in a dogfight and most of them immediately ran for the dugout. Only Bob, my fellow pitcher, seemed to comprehend the magnitude of my achievement as he met me at the third base line and patted me on the shoulder, more like a condolence than a congratulations. If it hadn't been for Willie and his jets, I would have won the game – and been carried to the dugout on the shoulders of my teammates. Someone I had convinced to play in our league ruined my dream game, and I failed to find the justice in that.

For the extra innings Travis chose Dean to relieve me and I moved to first base in his place, since Bob was over at third. Dean was a mediocre pitcher. He threw left-handed and had a big slow fastball and an even slower curve that sometimes baffled hitters. He did all right for a while, though he gave up successive hits to Danny and Billy to lead off the seventh. After that, the bad luck of City National allowed them to reach the bases but held them scoreless. The score was still tied, when Willie came to bat an inning later. He crushed a double to right field and stretched it to a triple after the only throwing error of the season by Fish. Travis called time out and walked toward the mound. He motioned for Don and Bob to join him for a conference. I decided to listen in and approached the group.

Travis said with extra care, "Now, Dean, there's two outs, so Freddy will not be bunting. But, there is no doubt that Willie will attempt to steal home on you. When Don throws you the ball, which he will fire back while guarding the plate, you need to turn toward third and keep an eye on Willie and your hand on the ball because he may dash for home at any time. Do you understand?"

"K...k...k..Keep an eye on Willie. I...uh, I...uh, g...g...get it," Dean stammered in slow motion.

"There you go." Travis slapped him on the butt and headed for the dugout.

"Come on," I said with encouragement. "You can do it, Dean. Throw strikes, Freddy can't hit. Just keep an eye on Willie."

"Ok…k…kay Mickey, I'll throw strikes," Dean said as slow as usual but with a strange sense of confidence.

On the first pitch to Freddy, Dean threw a fastball that the kid missed by two feet. Don fired the ball back at Dean, who caught it almost nonchalantly and turned his back to Willie, slowly starting back toward the rubber. All the time he was walking eleven voices in unison were yelling, "He's running!" But, this seemed to confuse Dean as he looked at first base where I was yelling the loudest and pointing at home plate urging him to throw the ball to Don. Dean caught on but it was way too late for us to have a chance for a play at the plate. Willie scored the winning run without sliding. After a second, I walked over to Dean who had his head down and seemed on the verge of tears. I put my arm around his slumping shoulders, and said, "We'll get him next time. It's not your fault. Forget about it."

By the way, I made the headlines like I projected I would. On the first page of the Austin American-Statesman, near the bottom, was a one-inch declaration:

CHARLES LOSES NO HITTER!!

Not "Willie Veils Steals Home to Win Game," but "Charles Loses No Hitter!" I was a loser and a winner at the same time, but I was not a happy camper. And though it was a marginal glory day moment, one I've never forgotten, it would take a few more games before my major glory moment would arrive.

As things turned out after that fateful day when I lost the no hitter, Seven Up was able to tie us for the second half with a last inning victory on Jack's home run in the final game of the regular season. So we would have to play them for second half championship in a single game. It would be my turn in the rotation, as Bob had followed my no hitter with a splendid pitching performance of his own against Louis Shanks, winning our final game.

Unfortunately, I didn't wake up in as good of a mood as I had the week before. It only got worse during the day. Leading up to the late afternoon debacle ahead, I made the immense error of attending a picnic with some friends at the remote location of Spicewood Springs, where Danny's parents had some property where we could play in the rushing low-water stream.

After swimming for hours in the hot sun, I scarfed down about eight hotdogs and swigged down three or four Dr Peppers.

When I arrived at Bishop Field that afternoon I was feeling a bit queasy. The sun had baked the contents of my stomach into a soufflé of growing proportions, and it was sending butterflies to replace my nerve as I approached the mound to start the most important game of my life. Toeing the rubber, I couldn't focus, my stomach was grumbling, muscles were in light spasm, and I was having trouble sighting the catcher's mitt through the waves of nausea and pain. I walked the first three batters and then Jack connected on a towering home run to center field, probably the longest ball I had ever seen leave the park. All of a sudden, the score was four to nothing and before I realized what was happening, I lost my lunch on the side of the mound. Coach T came running out to me and placed his arm round my shoulders, trying to ease the pain as the hotdogs were reversing their trip through my esophagus. I was embarrassed because my family and friends were all watching my demise. I noticed Kitty out of the corner of my eye, and all she could do was stare at the ground.

"Here, Mickey, get down," urged Coach T, "put your head lower and relax -- breathe, you'll be all right, the worst is over -- there you go, just breathe."

I was trying, trust me I was trying, because I knew I had to calm down. But every time I tried to take in a deep breath -- out came more hotdogs. And those types of exhales can really hurt. Our esophagus has thousands of tiny cilia, which like to run in one direction, and can cause major pain when forced to reverse field. A series of dry heaves followed, before I finally had control over my digestive tract again. I glanced up at Coach T through watering eyes, and muttered through my discomfort, "Too many hotdogs."

"That's all right, Mick, you're going to feel a lot better now," Coach T said. "You want to come out of the game?"

The game, oh yeah, the gawd dang game. My mind raced at mach speed with bizarre thoughts. In the name of Dale Evans and Roy Rogers, why did I eat all those hotdogs on the day of a championship game? I wonder what my mother was thinking? Why won't Kitty look this way? Jesus, my stomach hurts. Why is everybody staring at me? I looked around but everything was a blur -- I almost fainted for a moment before I rescued whatever courage remained in my aching body.

"No, Coach," I said. "I'm okay. I want to stay in."

I would come to regret those words of illogical bravado -- for the rest of the game was nothing less than a complete massacre. Custer suddenly had company as I led my guys into a slaughter of legendary proportions. When the dust settled, Seven Up had crossed the plate fourteen times while we only scored three runs. I gave up three home runs to Jack, two to Dave Looney, and two to Stan. To my credit, however, I stayed in for the whole debacle, and survived to live another day, unlike Custer.

We had won the first half, so we were relieved to know we would play again and I could have a chance to redeem myself in the championship game. The next day, we played Seven Up, again. This time Bob was on the mound and I was at third base. Jack was pitching for Seven Up. He threw really hard, in fact, as hard as any Coach in the league. However, Jack was not as much a great pitcher as he was a natural athlete, so he had no earthly idea where the ball was going. To say Jack was wild would be an understatement. Jack's pitches behaved like the funnel of a tornado, because nobody knew what direction it was going, but it was destined to arrive there as fast as it could.

Surprisingly, Jack and Bob were both on their games, and it was a pitching duel par excellence. The score was tied 0-0 going into the fifth inning when some of Jack's legendary wildness returned. After getting two quick outs, he walked our next three batters, which loaded the bases, and I was coming up to bat. Here was my chance to make up for the previous day's stupidity. But I had never hit Jack very well. In fact, I had looked horrible while striking out during an earlier inning. Knowing he had no control seemed to unnerve me, as I was usually "stepping in the bucket," bailing out toward left field, before he released the pitch. Today though, the baseball gods were shining their light on me as Judge Looney, the manager of Seven Up, stepped out of the dugout to replace Jack with their steady left-hander, Rupert Andrews. I loved hitting against Rupert because he had such good control. While Rupert started to toss his warm ups, Jack walked dejectedly to his new position at first base, and Travis approached me in the on-deck circle.

"Mick, I want you wait for the pitch in your zone. You know, a little inside and just above your waist. Just wait for that pitch. Keep focused on that spot -- and when you see it, go for it. This is your time to shine." He patted me on the butt and added, "Have fun."

Travis always knew what to say, and how -- that's probably the most important thing an adult can know about communicating with kids. He knew he didn't need to talk down to his players. This was the key. When he spoke, you got it because he treated you like an equal. We were all ballplayers with a shared experience and balance of knowledge, and we knew Travis had more than all of us, so we all knew to listen. That day, I not only listened – I actually heard.

Up to that time in my baseball life, I had concentrated all of my attention on becoming the best pitcher I could be, and practically ignored the art of hitting. So, I can honestly tell you, I never knew I had a zone. When Travis described it, I suddenly felt a sense of rightness, like I should have known this all along.

The first pitch was a little inside and above the waist, just as I had pictured it before stepping into the batter's box -- and right in my zone. I watched until the ball seemed as big as a watermelon, then I swung with a gut-ripping uppercut and blasted the ball. It was a feeling unlike anything I had ever experienced as a batsman. The ball struck the wood with a great crack and exploded off the bat. I was stunned a little and didn't mean to show up the pitcher by standing and watching, but I couldn't move. My eyes followed the ball up as it rose toward the billowing clouds and over the heads of all the fielders, who were all apparently as shocked as I was with the blast. When it started arching down, I heard Travis yelling at me to run, so I started down the base path. About three-quarters of the way down the first base path, the ball cleared the left centerfield fence by about two feet and my body left the planet. When I returned, only because of the force of gravity, I landed near first base right in front of Jack, who gave me five and said, "Touch 'em all, Mick. Nice hit."

I touched first and that was the last clear thought I had for the next two or three minutes. The grand slam was the only home run I had ever hit in my life, in a game or in a practice. It was so unexpected that I went into a stunned state of blissfulness. After making the circuit, I arrived at home plate to meet up with all my teammates who lifted me on their shoulders and carried me to the dugout. I caught sight of Kitty who was applauding with a huge smile across her face. I pointed at her and then at the fence, and could only laugh at the absurdity of what had just happened. I noticed my mother's proud smile as she stood with the others in the grandstands, giving me an ovation the likes of which I would never hear again. Bob finished off the shut out and we won the game 4 to 0. Rylanders was the 1962 West Austin Little League Champions. The next day's American Statesman described it best in its blurb report of the big game:

Mickey Charles has a Glory Day Moment

CHAPTER FOURTEEN

The regular season was over, but for some of us, there would be plenty more baseball. Immediately after Rylanders had won the championship game, the four managers and their coaches selected the best players to represent our league on an All Star team to compete in the state championship tournament. Travis and Coach T would serve as manager and coach, as a reward for Rylanders' first place finish.

Across from the River City's world-renowned jewel of waterworks, the Barton Springs Pool in Zilker Park, is the home of the South Austin Little League. Wright Field is situated just off of Robert E. Lee Road and the ballpark's left field fence is almost spitting distance to the clear, cool waters of the fourth largest spring in the state, separated only by a beautiful grove of elegant, aged pecan trees. Those pecan trees received the ball from my friend Jack's home run swing in the All-Stars' championship. With the walk-off blast, our West Austin All-Stars won the South regional title and our next destination would be Houston where we'd play for the state championship.

Our All-Star team was made up of all of the quality ballplayers from the league. Willie was our lead-off man, of course, followed by Billy, Danny, Jack, Don, Ras, or sometimes, Stan, Dave Looney, David McKendrick (the only player selected from Louis Shanks), and either Bob, Fish, or me, depending who was scheduled to pitch that particular game. We had a good, balanced ball club and we sailed through the city league playoffs with two shutouts and a blow out. Then we traveled to San Antonio to the district playoffs where we squeaked by a very good San Antonio club and then beat the defending state champs from Seguin. From there we returned to our roots and played a great team from Corpus Christi, which stretched us to the max -- into extra innings -- until Jack's thunderous blast into the pecan trees won the game.

We were set to play the Northern regional winner in Houston the following weekend for the state championship, but first we were to attend a celebratory picnic courtesy of our sponsors and Dale Baker's BBQ at Zilker Park. Before eating, we planned to swim at Barton Springs with friends and family, and on that particularly hot, humid July afternoon -- still buzzing from our successes -- leaping into the sixty-eight degree spring waters of Barton's would be a refreshing rush and richly deserved.

Arriving at the Barton Springs Pool parking lot in my mother's station wagon, Kitty and I raced to the bathhouses where we could shower and change into our trendy swimming suits. Then Kitty and I met at the box office where we paid our twenty cents to enter the historic pool. We walked through the old original stone and metal turnstile that every swimmer had passed through since the City commissioned the park in the 1920's, rushed down the side of the green-grass hill through the hundred-year-old pecans, and jumped down the three-foot retaining wall to the concrete deck below. Paying no attention to the hundreds of patrons in the pool, we dove with total abandon into the cold water. I felt instantly energized. Every time I swam at Barton's I seemed to feel better afterwards. Maybe it was no coincidence that the Indians living nearby in the 1800's thought these springs were a source of healing.

Kitty and I swam over to Philosopher's Rock, a limestone outcropping where two Texas legends, noted author J. Frank Dobie and historian Walter Prescott Webb, both in their seventies, sat discussing some major topic with what appeared to be depth and feeling. They were two of the most influential, important chroniclers of Texas history, culture, and folklore.

Kitty's father, as I mentioned before, was a famous local artist and called these men friends. He introduced his daughter to them several years before on an outing at the Springs. Kitty, in turn, had introduced me to these great gentlemen of Texas letters and I was immediately taken into their confidences on their weekly debates on Philosopher's Rock. Today as we swam up to the writer and the historian, they both gave us their biggest grins and a hearty wave of welcome.

"Hello, Mr. Dobie, Mr. Webb, what's the topic today?" I asked as I pulled myself onto the rock outcropping and helped Kitty out of the water.

Walter Prescott Webb spoke up first, "Well, Mickey, Jill, it just so happens we are discussing my favorite topic in the world."

"What's that happen to be, Mr. Webb?" Kitty asked seriously.

"Honey, don't you know?" he said softly, without intimidation.

"The pioneers of the west, maybe?"

"That's right, Jill," J. Frank Dobie said. "We were discussing the first major historical concept that W.P. here brought to the consciousness of the masses. It was called the Great Plains thesis."

"Wasn't that about the Great Plains stopping the pioneers, or something like that?" Kitty asked Mr. Webb.

"That's part of it, honey – I see you've been paying attention to our past discussions," Webb said. "Progress across the West stalled at the ninety-eighth meridian until they developed technological advancements like the six shooter, barbed wire, and the windmill. These innovations and others were needed before the westward trek of the brave pioneers could continue -- allowing them to leave the woods and rivers of the eastern United States and face all of the situations associated with an arid desert environment in the west."

"Wow," I said. "That's interesting."

"It's damn brilliant is what it is -- excuse my French," Dobie said with a grin and a chuckle. Kitty and I shared some nervous laughter at the sound of the familiar invective. We loved these old men. They were wise, humorous, and kind and what could be better than that.

"On more important matters, Mick," Webb said, shifting the topic, "who won the game?"

"We're packing our bags for Houston!" I exclaimed with so much pride I almost burst.

They both declared simultaneously, "Congratulations!"

I replied, "Thank you. It feels pretty damn great."

All four of us laughed. Across the pool, I spotted Willie sitting on the rock retaining wall that held back the beautiful grassy hills above Barton Springs. He was sitting with a white girl, about our own age, who I had never seen before. Kitty and I exchanged goodbyes with the old wise men and dove into the water, racing to the other side of the thousand-foot long pool. We jumped onto the deck and joined Willie and the mystery girl sitting on the wall.

"Mickey, Jill," Willie said happily, "I want ya'll to meet Mary. We went to Mathews Elementary together."

I hope all of you will be lucky enough to experience the unexpected, irrational, colossal, incredible power of a force beyond anyone's control, known as love. In my case, it was love at first sight -- for the moment, I looked into the deep brown eyes of Willie's friend, Mary, beside the Springs of Barton Creek that late afternoon, worlds collided, universes exploded, and lightening struck our souls simultaneously. A most dramatic moment happened in the lives of two young people, and because of it, we would never ever be the same again.

A twelve-year-old is never completely equipped to deal with such a force, for it is beyond definition, understanding, or comprehension for the pre-teen mind and, for that matter, most adults. It is more than a feeling. It's a combination of energies, where the depths of two souls are connected through our constant compassionate conduit with God.

In this connection, the strengths of our natures are realized, the bond of humanity is consummated, and the hope of perfection is born. In a perfect world, one might see beyond that powerful initial surge, to glimpse the increasingly irrational view of life that love and madness can harness. However, when the intellect loses the driver's seat to the near-sightedness of love, one has to watch out for the road ahead. But, how could I as a twelve-year-old child, ever know the full ramifications of this powerful emotion -- I couldn't even drive yet.

"It's really nice to meet you," I said to Mary as I shook her hand, even though I wasn't aware that the words were coming out of my mouth.

Kitty also greeted Mary, but I wasn't paying attention. My mind was consumed with the beautiful image of the brown-haired girl in front of me. Our eyes connected for only a second or two, before I was oblivious of anything, and everything, around me. There were no people, no beautiful pecan trees, no lifeguards, no philosophers on their rock, no friends, no baseball. In my world, in that moment, there was only this stunning brown-eyed angel.

Mary's smile pierced my heart as she said, "Willie's told me all about you."

"I hope," I said in a haze of immediate infatuation, "he only told you the good parts."

However, even after that promising start, an awkward moment of silence surfaced. I tried to avoid dominating the conversation with wit or some intelligent yarn -- for I was content gazing into the eyes of this newly discovered beauty.

In a delayed shift in my awareness, I suddenly realized Kitty was watching me. She sent daggers flying at my head. For the first time in my life I felt the pangs of internal conflicts of infidelity, at a time when I barely understood the word. At this age of course, it had a bit of a separate meaning than it would evolve into when I became an adult, however, when the heart is involved it's the same old story.

Kitty had that most incredible attribute of the female population -- a woman's intuition. I felt she was reading my mind. I nodded nervously and made small talk to cover my shame. "Hum, Kitty do you think we should go to the picnic? We don't want to miss out on the ribs. Let's all get moving."

Kitty cocked her head a little to the side like she often did when she was really concentrating on something important. Finally she said, "If you think that's best."

The four of us started down the walkway beside the beautiful pool. Willie and Mary trailed behind us as we walked over the bridge that spanned the waterfall, which cascaded from Barton Springs into the Colorado River below. We walked up the thirty stone steps, crossed the parking lot, and entered a grove of live oak trees with a stone walkway cut through the limestone outcroppings rising through the foliage. We arrived at the Rock Garden, a section of Zilker Park that was covered by a canopy of shade from the lacey and live oaks encircling a picnic area. Dale Baker and his employees were catering the event and they had organized an assembly line of delights. We slid right into the end of the line as the last person was being served by the huge jolly genius of barbecuing.

Kitty leaned over to me and whispered, "I saw that."

"What?" I asked, trying to sound ingenuous.

"You like that girl," Kitty said with authority. "Maybe more than me."

"What?"

"You can't even talk, Mickey! My sister was right. You can't trust boys," Kitty whispered in my ear so no others would hear. "They're all creeps."

"Wha…Do we have to -- talk about this now?" I asked.

"Answer one question," she said. "Do you like that girl more than me?"

"No way," I barked incredulously as I lied to protect her feelings. I was a heel. I felt it, but an irresistible force had taken over my thought processes. Kitty gave me that look of disbelief. I shrugged my shoulders, "What?"

"Oh just forget it. You're impossible," she said and walked away from me. I watched her for a moment, then shrugged my shoulders and turned my attention back to Willie and Mary.

Willie knew what was going on. He smiled at me and said, "Isn't Mary the prettiest girl in Austin?"

I looked her up and down as she twisted for me like a model posing on the platforms of Paris. Then she giggled like the little girl she was, and I melted into mush. "She just might be," I said.

Mary blushed and smiled, "You're so kind, really."

It had officially started. I didn't know where it was going, and I wasn't focused on my girlfriend's feelings, but I was determined to take the ride. I hoped against hope she wouldn't get hurt any further, but I knew full well that Jill wasn't going to be a happy kitt.y

CHAPTER FIFTEEN

Other cities in Texas definitely do not have the hipness, beauty, and soul that Austin exhibits -- in fact, most are downright depressing. For example, there is the hot, humid, mass of turmoil and angst of the largest city in Texas, Houston. Some people who lived there, survived, and relocated, refer to it as Abuseton. I spent a lot of time in the Bayou City during my youth, especially before my mother remarried, because my grandparents lived there. My father, who died of stomach cancer at the age of twenty-eight, was their only child. So, I spent a lot of time with them until my grandfather's unfortunate cosmic accident. He was killed by lightening while fishing on the intercoastal canal. Before that particular meteorological event changed the spiritual path of my youth, I spent a couple of weeks every summer in the big H.

My grandfather worked for Humble Oil for forty-four years. His mother, who was a Cherokee living on a reservation in the desolate plains of Oklahoma, died during his childbirth. His father left to become a hobo and a tramp when my granddad was in the third grade. We never found out how he survived his youth, but he did. Somehow, he applied for a job as a toolie at the Humble Camp near Burkburnett in East Texas, in the early twenties. Because of his amazing communication skills and leadership qualities, my grandfather rose up at an amazing speed through the company ranks. After a mere nine months he was promoted to field foreman. Two years later he was the superintendent of all of the operations in the Burkburnett area, and performed those duties until the field dried up.

However, Mr. Shiltess, the Chairman of the Board of the company that was the oil-producing wing of Standard Oil of New Jersey, had special plans for my grandfather. The moment the two were introduced, the CEO knew he had met a man who was an honest, hardworking gentleman. He told me this in person on one of my vacations with my grandparents a few years before. We spent three glorious days fishing beside the Shiltess's cabin on a beautiful mountain lake high in the Rockies. On the CEO's insistence, Humble brought my grandfather to Houston for a position at the corporate headquarters. He was put in charge of production for all the West Texas fields that were producing about one third of all of the oil the huge company was collecting in America.

By the time World War II came around, he rose to Vice President in charge of all production for the company, overseeing the recovery of about one quarter of the oil drilled by the West for a war-crazed nation and its allies. He stayed in this position until his retirement, at which time the company presented him with a book about his life, which I still treasure today. It's called <u>Pumper's Progress</u> and there is a testimonial at the beginning that helps to explain this great man and all he meant to the people of a company and the friends and family he lived his life to serve. It read:

Presented

To

Russell C. Charles
Who for over 42 years gave the best of himself to
Humble and its people and in so doing set new
horizons of integrity, courage, and kindliness in
industrial statesmanship.

Champion of the right, he bore his part
In unyielding fealty to his trust;
But humor keened his swiftest dart
And kindness tempered every thrust.

My grandfather taught me how to fish, hunt, bowl, and golf, but more importantly, how to learn from my mistakes. He drilled me on proper posture, a firm handshake, looking people in the eyes, keeping a cheerful, positive disposition, enjoying life but remaining firm to your convictions, and the importance of having faith in God. I really loved him for all he did for me in place of my missing father.

He was on my mind as I traveled to the biggest baseball game of an incredible season. "It's going to be a thrill to pitch in front of my grandfather for the first time in my life," I thought to myself as our team pulled out of Columbus, Texas, halfway on our trek to the state finals.

Willie sat beside me in the last row of the bus as the mid-summer worn Texas countryside passed by the window. We were playing Twenty Questions using only famous baseball players, when we noticed Travis approaching down the aisle.

"Well, boys, tomorrow you find out if you're men," he said to no one in particular. Then he leaned over to Jack, who was sitting across from us and asked, "Jack, do you mind if we trade seats for a little while, I need to discuss some things with Willie and Mickey."

"Sure thing, Coach," Jack said as he jumped up and lumbered to another seat. Travis sat down and turned to face us.

"Willie, Mickey, we need to talk about a decision we made. The area of Houston where we're going to be playing the next couple of days is restricted. Do you know what that means?"

I didn't, but I looked over at Willie who had a pained expression on his face as he grimaced and said, "No Coloreds allowed."

"That's right. We know it's not right," Travis said. "It's downright backwards, but it is a fact. One we have to deal with and then move on. Hopefully, Willie, your play and attitude may wake up a few of the folks in the stands tomorrow, but it's not going to help us get you into the motel where we are staying. Even though it won't make you feel any better, I want you to know that all the great Negro ballplayers had to suffer this indignation. Willie Mays, Hank Aaron, Frank Robinson and Jackie Robinson have all told horror stories of traveling and playing in the South."

I interrupted him, asking, "You mean Willie can't stay with the team?"

"Unfortunately, yes. But, we have a solution that will work out and allow us to concentrate on the ball game tomorrow. I spoke with your mother during the lunch break in Columbus, Mickey. Your grandparents have agreed to put you boys up with them for the next couple of days to avoid trouble. So, we're going to drop you fellas off first so you can get situated and your grandfather is going to bring you to the practice later this afternoon."

"Practice?" I spurted out.

"Light hitting. No hard throwing. No running. We need to get the jitters out of the way," Travis said sternly. "So, yes, Mickey, we are going to practice."

"I'm sorry Travis. I love to practice. I just thought since we had a big game and all," I said apologetically.

"You leave the thinking to the coaches for now, Mickey. You concentrate on what is important -- staying relaxed and taking care of your arm. I think we're going to ride it to victory fellas. I've got a good feeling." Travis stood up to start for the front of the bus. He paused, turned back to us and said, "Willie, you know, if there was anything I could do to alter this mess, I would."

"I know Coach," Willie said. "It's not your fault. My pop says prejudice is like a disease. We have to stand up to it, and be patient."

"Your father is right, and he's obviously a good role model for you, son. You should be proud of your papa. It's too bad he hasn't got to see you play, but I've had detailed conversations with him on the church telephone about your abilities and performances, which have rivaled any of the great kids that ever played in our league."

"Thanks, Coach," Willie said simply. And with that Travis moved back up the aisle.

A little later, as we were nearing the outskirts of Houston, the comfort level of everyone on our bus was beginning to ebb. We passed through the pinewood veil of East Texas and entered the famous dome of humidity known as Harris County. We immediately felt the impact of the climate, as the bus filled with a mist of steaminess, which seemed like you could cut it with a knife. As we passed my boyhood home near Katy, where my father worked at a Humble Camp as an engineer, I pointed out the special place to Willie, who had sunk into a sullen mood for the first time since I met him.

"That's where I was born, Willie," I said, trying to get his mind off his latest funk.

"Oh," he said without any emotion.

Suddenly I had an idea. "Why don't we have the whole team stay with my grandparents, so everybody can be together?"

Willie's disposition rose like the Old Faithful geyser at Yellowstone. He looked at me and asked, "Do they have enough room for all of us?"

"Of course, they have four empty bedrooms and a servants quarters. The house is so big we can even have the coaches stay there, too." I said, exaggerating a little -- a Texas custom.

"Why don't we ask the Coach?" Willie asked.

"I'll go ask him right now," I said and jumped up, sprinted down the aisle, and approached Travis at the front of the bus.

"Travis," I said. "I was thinking Willie and I shouldn't be separated from the team, so what if everybody stays at my grandparents' house. They have plenty of room."

Travis looked me up and down and then smiled, "Capital idea, Mickey. But, I'll have to talk to your grandparents first when we get to the house."

"They'll do anything for me. And I want the team to stay together. It's important, don't you think? You're always saying the sum of the parts is more than the whole," I said profoundly.

"If it's all right with your grandparents, then it's all right with me," Travis replied.

Twenty minutes later we exited the highway and entered the edge of River Oaks. This part of Houston is exceptional in its beauty from expansive landscaping including huge pines, elms, pecans, and maple trees. Though, due to the abundance of moisture in the air, on the ground, and running through Buffalo Bayou, the mosquito is ever present and that is part of the annoyance that is Houston. Pulling up to the front of my grandparents' sprawling, red brick house underneath their enormous pine and oak trees, I spotted my grandmother and grandfather standing in the driveway, apparently waiting to meet us. I jumped out first and gave my grandmother a hug and kiss on her cheek, then turned and gave my grandfather a firm handshake.

"I am so glad you two are finally going to see us play. We're really good," I said to brag a little.

"Mickey," my grandfather said, "it's good to see you. And we're proud to have you and your Negro friend stay here with us."

"Grandbaba, Grandmama, I was wondering if the whole team could sleep here. We don't want to split up the team. This restricted business is for the birds," I pleaded. "It'd really mean a lot to us."

"We have enough room, sweetie," my grandmother said with a smile. "Why not!"

"Why not indeed," said my grandfather. "The team should not have to separate the night before its biggest game." He noticed Travis step down off the bus and my grandfather stuck out his hand for the famous firm handshake of his and said, "Russell Charles, this is my wife, Mattie. You must be Travis."

"Yes sir, Travis Bowie, sir, and it's a real pleasure meeting you two," our coach said with simple dignity.

"Well Travis," my grandfather replied, "Mickey's request for the team to stay here is an excellent idea."

"We have plenty of room," my grandmother confirmed. "We can put the team up in the four spare bedrooms and we can put you coaches over the garage in the old servants quarters. We only use it for storage now anyway."

"That's right kind of you, Mrs. Charles. Mickey suggested you would be open to taking in the whole team, but I don't want to impose. I think it's best if the other coach and I stay at the motel."

"I won't hear of that," said my grandmother. "You are part of the team as well, so you both stay here. It's not an imposition at all, seriously. We insist."

With that it was a done deal. The team unloaded, picked up their suitcases, and followed as my grandmother assigned them to the various bedrooms in the massive house. Willie, Danny, Ras and I shared one of the bedrooms, which had two large double beds. After the team got situated, we all hopped on the bus for the late afternoon practice. And Travis was right. It was a good idea to practice, because the sun was situated in a totally different spot than the other parks we'd seen. At Hobby Field, off Westheimer Road, the sun was in the batter's eyes making it extremely difficult to pick up the ball as it came off the pitcher's arm. Travis brought out some pitch black, which we applied underneath our eyes to cut the glare of the bright Houston sunshine. It seemed to work as during batting practice that afternoon, Jack, Don, and Danny all crushed one ball after another over the fences, two hundred feet away. Well, I thought, so much for light hitting.

After practice my grandfather took everyone to play miniature golf and eat hamburgers near Memorial Park. When we returned to the house on Overbrook Lane, we were supposed to go straight to bed, yet some of us were too amped up to go to sleep immediately. In our room, to my surprise, Willie and Danny were sleeping like babies. They could sleep anywhere, it seemed, and had absolutely no problem relaxing in the luxury of my grandparents' comfortable house. Ras and I, however, could not sleep -- the game was on our minds, so we snuck out of the bedroom and slipped out the front door. We headed down the street to a nearby park and sat on a bench under a pine tree canopy.

Ras lived in the same neighborhood as Jack, Bob, Stan, Dave Looney, and me. In fact, the six of us were within one city block of one another growing up. Ras was a boy of insatiable appetites, with a quest for adventure. He had inherited these traits from his three hundred pound wonder of a father, who happened to be the last of the father figures in my life. Ras' grandparents also lived in Houston near Rice University, in another wealthy enclave of the humid city. After we settled into our positions on the park bench, Ras turned to me and said, "My grandparents would never allow a Colored to stay at their house. My grandmother doesn't even let the Negro milkman walk up to the house. He has to leave their stuff at the gated entrance with the security guard and she picks it up every morning on her walk."

"Why do you think some people don't get it?" I asked.

"I don't know. My dad says we are growing up in a changing time, that things won't stay the same."

"I hope so," I concluded. "Willie is just like us. The only difference is the color of his skin."

"My dad says people don't change when it comes to race, religion or politics," Ras said, "and you shouldn't waste your time talking about it."

"I guess so. That's what my mom's been telling me ever since I met Willie. One good thing is nothing can keep him off the field tomorrow."

"We have to win," Ras said, obviously giving into the pressures surrounding the game.

"We will," I said with authority.

After thirty minutes in the park, Ras and I returned to my grandparent's house and retired for the night. That doesn't mean we went to sleep, at least I didn't, because massive ugly butterflies were swimming in my stomach. Anything resembling rest was out of the question. I tossed and turned during the night, thinking about my expectations of the next day's game. I probably fell asleep around three or four o'clock in the morning. When my grandfather came into the room the next morning at nine a.m. to wake up the four of us for an early lunch before the afternoon game, I was sleeping like a log. I guess once I fell asleep it was a deep sleep, because I don't remember experiencing any dreams or nightmares, and it took my grandfather and all three of my roomies to get me moving that morning. When I finally opened my eyes, the first image I saw was my grandfather, who had a very stern look on his face. First, he addressed the others in the room.

"Boys, there are choices of bacon and eggs, or cheeseburgers and fries, with all the milk you can drink in the kitchen," he said. "Mickey and I are going to have a little chat. So go ahead and enjoy the meal fellas. You want to be strong for the game. Mickey and I will be along in a few minutes."

Danny and Ras said, "Thank you, Mr. Charles."

Willie looked at my grandfather and said, "Mr. Charles, I wish I had met you a long time ago."

"Thanks, young man, I enjoyed our talk last night about the deficiencies on our Colt-45 team. You have a great baseball mind for such a youngster," my grandfather said, as he looked Willie in the eye. "I have a feeling you'll go places, Willie, if you stay out of trouble. I look forward to watching you play today. Enjoy your breakfast and have a good game, son."

After my roomies left the large bedroom, my grandfather closed the door and surprised me with a broad smile.

"Mickey, your father would be so proud of you for all you have accomplished as a ballplayer and a young man, but especially because of your friendship with a boy like Willie. I want you to know we will be proud of you this afternoon. Your father will be watching from Heaven and your grandmother and I will be in the stands applauding you, no matter what happens. But, I want you to concentrate on each pitch you make and each pitch you try to hit. Keep your head in the ballgame, focus on the task at hand, and give it the best you can."

"Yes sir, Grandbaba. Don't worry about me. I'm going to pitch the best game of my life. Travis told me he had a good feeling," I mumbled, as I sat up in the bed.

"All right, son. I love you because you're a young man of responsibility and principles. Now, come get something to eat and good luck with the game today."

"Thank you, Grandbaba," I said sleepily just before he closed the door on his way out. I sat up in bed and rubbed my eyes. I smelled bacon and it suddenly made me very hungry. I leapt from the bed, threw on my clothes, and rushed off to join my teammates for the pre-game feeding.

After breakfast, Willie and I walked out the front door to check the weather. I asked him if he wanted to walk around the block. There were some interesting houses to check out. He thought he needed to walk off the eggs, bacon, and cheeseburger he scarfed down. We started down a sidewalk in front of the houses. Hearing a strange noise behind us, we turned to see a large truck coming slowly down the street. At the back of the truck, huge sprayers were distributing an insecticide mist into the air covering the yards in search of the pesky mosquito. We immediately changed our minds about the neighborhood tour and dashed back to my grandparents' house, so we wouldn't inhale the poison. We just managed to close the front door behind us as the truck passed by with its billowing cloud of mist dissipated over my grandparents' yard.

Willie looked out the window as the truck passed, and said, "Man, that's gotta be bad for you."

Jack appeared dressed in his uniform, with a bat slung over his shoulder. He said, "Hey y'all, we're leaving in ten minutes. Don't you think you ought to go get ready?"

I looked at the grandfather clock in the corner of the living room to see it was 12:05. I looked back at Jack, and stated, "Travis said 1:15. We have an hour and ten minutes."

Jack looked at his watch, the clock, and then, at his uniform. He smiled and said, "Oh – guess I'm a little anxious. Well, I might as well get another cheeseburger."

He walked through the living room and into the dining room toward the kitchen. Willie and I looked at each other and laughed. I think everybody was ready for, not to mention nervous about, the state championship.

At game time that afternoon as the depressingly humid summer in Houston reached its most horrid peak, I strolled up to the mound at Hobby Field. It couldn't have been any more uncomfortable at this ballpark with its flat, windless, treeless background. The sweat ran down my back, face, and off of my fingers. As I reached down and picked up the resin bag in my hand, I worried that the dry powder would turn to Mississippi mud. I tossed it in the air a couple of times and the resin dust mixed with the moisture to provide a reasonably good grip on the ball.

I looked in at Don squatting behind home plate and everything was blurred as the perspiration ran down from my cap and into my eyes, stinging them. I turned from my catcher and tried to wipe my face and eyes, finally managing to squint directly into the late afternoon sun. I was encouraged, because it was the same glare that the batters would be facing the first four innings, and it was fierce. I closed my eyes and concentrated for a moment before realizing the obvious. Since the batters wouldn't be able to see my pitches very well until later in the game, I thought it would be a huge mistake to walk anyone. With the sun's help, I had to make sure they earned every base.

After nine warm up pitches, the umpire said something to Don, who in turn yelled "Coming down." I threw one more pitch -- a deliberate three-quarter fastball so the three batters in the warm up circle couldn't time my real fastball. Then I would bring on the curve and the drop after the sun was no longer to my advantage and hope their late inning timing couldn't recover.

An hour and fifteen minutes later, I strolled to the mound in the top of the sixth inning with a 3-0 lead, due to Billy's base-emptying double in the fourth inning, just after the sun got below the horizon and our hitters were finally able to focus on the ball. Following the strategy I developed after my epiphany with the sun, I had held our opponents, a team from Dallas Trinity Little League, to one hit through my first five innings. Now I only had to set down their second, third, and fourth hitters and we would be off to the desolate Texas Panhandle for the regional playoffs to see who would represent the West United States in the annual Little League World Series.

Dallas Trinity's first batter that last inning, was a left-hander who had gotten the only hit for their team in the fourth inning when I hung the first curve I threw in the whole game. He stepped into the batter's box and I looked at Don for the sign. Fastball, outside, and I nodded. I went into my wind up and threw strike one, hitting the low outside corner. Next signal from Don was the same and the pitch was a little off the plate for a ball. The third pitch was too much of the same thing, as the lefty strode into the outside low pitch and pushed it into left field for a clean single.

After that, the big lug of a first baseman on Trinity stepped to the plate. I thought he was salivating like a wild dog. He stepped into the batter's box without even looking at the coach for a signal. Well, that made sense, since he was never going to bunt anyway, especially with the score at three to nothing. I knew I couldn't hang a curve to the big palooka, for fear the ball would transform into a rocket and leave the park. The first pitch was the best curve ball I had thrown that afternoon. However, the second pitch was a little bit too inside and a little bit too high and he pounded it down the third base line to the fence, sending the base runner to third and leaving the sluggish big lug standing on first.

The next batter was their clean-up hitter and the best all around player we had faced during the state playoffs. He was a lean muscular fellow named Waldo, of all things. He almost took my head off in the second inning when he sent a hard line drive through the middle. Somehow my reactions kept up with it, incidentally sending my glove in front of the path of the ball for an out, but driven by the intention of avoiding a decapitation. Representing the tying run in the sixth, Waldo strode to the plate.

The evening shadows were creeping into the infield as the sun's rays hid behind the right field scoreboard. Travis called time-out and motioned for Don to join us at the pitcher's mound for a conference. Travis gave me a serious look, then looked at my teammates around the field. "Mickey, I was thinking we should walk Waldo."

"You want to put the tying run on base?" I asked incredulously. "Isn't that breaking a cardinal rule of baseball?"

"Son, sometimes the situation warrants it. If this were Willie Mays, they would walk him because one swing could tie the game. If we put Waldo on and load the bases, we have a force out at home and a possible double play."

"Whatever you think, you're the coach," I said.

"We have a three run lead, Mickey, let's walk him. I believe you can set down the next three," Travis said and turned to my catcher, "Four balls - way outside, Don." Then, he turned back to me and stated, "Mickey, I got no one warming up. We're going with the horse that got us here, and you've got some talented teammates that will be backing you up."

Travis patted my rear end and returned to the dugout. When Don was back behind the plate, he held his arm out like a hitchhiker, calling for me to throw the intentional pass. Waldo gave me the dirtiest look I've ever seen from the mound. After four high and outside, the bases were loaded. There were no outs and number twelve, their shortstop, was strolling to the plate. Don came out to the mound for a quick conference, saying, "Let's come right at him. Mick, everybody's behind you -- so you go with your best stuff, we get three outs, and then we all go for pizza and Dr Peppers at Westies."

I laughed. Don's little diversion had worked. With one comment my catcher had immediately put me at ease with the situation ahead of me. As he returned to his catcher's position I glanced around the field, starting with Willie standing in center, and then Danny in left, McKendrick at shortstop, and Ras scratching the dirt with his shoe at third. The next thing I saw was Travis standing on the dugout steps smiling at me, giving the "Hook 'em Horns" sign, which meant I should go right after him with the fastball.

My attention turned to the stands and I spotted my grandfather and grandmother sitting next to my mother and older brothers, all with grimaces that indicated they were suffering more agony than I was at the time. It's kind of funny how parents are sweating out the moments on the field more than the kids that are actually playing. Suddenly, I heard Don yelling at me to concentrate and get my head in the ballgame.

"Focus on the target," I mumbled to myself, "just like in The Clearing."

I went into my wind up and released the ball. It was right down the middle of the plate and surprised the hitter, who took the perfect pitch. Strike one. The next pitch was a fastball on the inside corner of the plate, which he bent to avoid and took for strike two. My last pitch to this particular batter was one of those semi-perfect curve balls that completely fooled him and made him look like a circus clown falling off a wagon. "One out!" yelled Don as he threw the ball back to me with vigor. "Now, that's pitching, Mickey. There you go, Mickey. Come on everybody, let's turn two and get this thing over with -- right now. Turn two, everybody, force at all bases."

The second batter walked toward the plate with a menacing look in his eye. Three more pitches, three more strikes, and the menacing look of the tiger had been reduced to the confusion of a frightened lamb. The kid slinked back to his dugout.

One more out and we would be the Texas State Little League champions, instantly qualifying as the latest West Austin heroes. I told myself to breathe and everything else would work out fine. I had my teammates behind me -- that was all I needed -- well that and oxygen, maybe.

I looked to Don for a signal and he gave me a fastball on the inside corner. I took my wind up and released the ball -- it followed like on a string directly toward the target for a perfect strike one. The second pitch was a curve that dropped off the face of the earth, which the batter fanned for a quick strike two. I turned and took a deep breath and looked at all my teammates again -- the thought of a state championship trophy, and all of the fame that would come with it, was dangling right in front of us.

I looked in for the signal, and Don wanted the curve ball. One would think I'd remember that exact moment with crystal clarity. But I went into my wind up and the next thing I knew my teammates were lifting me up on their shoulders. Don, Jack, and Ras were holding me in the air while Danny, Willie, and Billy arrived from the outfield full-sprint and joined us, creating a wriggling, jumping pyramid of joy that tumbled over spilling everybody into a pile in the center of the field. Smothered at the bottom, I managed to get my head free in time to see my grandfather standing proudly, clapping hard along with my grandmother, mother, stepfather, and brothers in the stands. I got immediate goose bumps from the flash sighting, like being surrounded by thousands of tiny unseen spirits that were blessing me with the electrifying touch of God. I was so proud of myself and so happy for my teammates.

The next day, our bus passed out of the humid veil of East Texas and headed for the land of the Palo Duro sun. After an eight-hour bus ride, we rolled into the antithesis of Houston. The Western Regional of the National Little League World Series was to be played about fifty miles west of Lubbock, just this side of New Mexico, in the windy desert town of Levelland. Along the highway, we learned we would stay with all of the other teams competing for the championship and the resulting trip to Williamsport, Pennsylvania, for the Little League World Series. The magnitude of the situation started to sink into our travel-weary group as we pulled up to Levelland Christian Seminary on East Cactus Drive where we would spend the next three nights.

The first day in the arid town of 13,000 people was spent meeting the players from the other Little League All-Star squads. The California team was from Stockton in the North Central agricultural area of that state. It was the only team, other than ours, with kids of color. A team represented Nevada from Henderson; a town we learned was the gateway to Lake Mead and Las Vegas. Arizona's team was from Scottsdale and New Mexico sent a team from Truth or Consequences, which was a strange tag for a town and seemed even more bizarre when we learned it was named after a game show. Utah's team was the strangest, though. Their players were standoffish, stuck-up, and a little hard to deal with. The teams that were easiest to communicate with hailed from Oklahoma and Colorado. The Colorado Springs' team had a couple of guys on their team with whom I corresponded for years afterward. The last team, one from Commerce, Mickey Mantle's hometown, was the cream of the crop. According to Travis, the scouting report on these Okies was downright scary. Every kid in their line-up could hit with power and run like burners, with some even rumored to have jets like Willie's.

Since it was a single elimination tournament, our goal was not to lose. We would have to win three games in a row to advance to the Little League World Series in Williamsport starting the following 17th of August. The thought of spending August in Pennsylvania – where we would escape the brutal heat and humidity of my hometown's hottest month and get to play the game of baseball in the cradle of the Little League organization – was foremost on our minds.

The first day in Levelland, after we got situated in our rooms, was spent swimming in the pool at a nearby city park and meeting the ballplayers from the other teams. It was my first experience talking at length with someone other than a Texan, and that was a little hard to get used to. You see, Texans by birthright are not really able to adjust to folks who don't get Texas. For Texans, Texas is a state of mind, a reality to some, a nightmare to others, but always and constantly an independent, relentless, restless, radiant state of being. To a non-Texan this can appear to be arrogant, abusive, illusive, and just plain downright out-of-this-worldly. But Texans, given the chance, will only grow on you like the meadows that feed the cattle, that in turn, fill the trucks and trains that roll to feed a hungry nation.

Trying to explain this to the players from California, Colorado, and the other states would be like trying to decipher Pythagoras's Theorem. However, Willie, Jack, Ras, and all of us tried to do that very thing during the late afternoon swim and get-together. I don't know if we succeeded, but we at least tried. Some of us thought we should have been practicing, like we had before the Houston game, but Travis thought it best after the long bus ride that we take some time off and relax.

The next day was the opening games for all of the teams on two adjoining fields. We were to play the team from Ogden, Utah, and California would play Arizona following us on the north field. Nevada was scheduled to face Oklahoma and Colorado would play New Mexico on the south field. Fish pitched a really good all-around game against the Mormons and we survived a late inning rally to win the game 5 to 4. Don, Danny, and Jack led the way with two hits each and we had sent the Ogdenonians packing. In the late game at our park, the lads from California dispatched the team from Scottsdale, so we would play the kids from the Golden State the next day.

Travis took Bob and I aside, telling us he was changing the rotation this time around. Bob would start if we made it to the championship game and I would pitch against Stockton in the semi-finals the next day. At first, Bob was disappointed he wouldn't get to pitch in his regular spot in the rotation, but Travis helped him realize that he would be getting the chance to pitch us into the Little League World Series, if indeed, I could help us get a victory in the game against California. The strategy worked for the team as I pitched another pretty good ballgame against the Stockton outfit and Jack provided a key RBI, knocking in Willie who had doubled to start off the sixth inning. We squeaked out a 3-2 victory. The next day we would play the boys from Commerce, Oklahoma, for the opportunity to advance to the ultimate dream and challenge of every Little Leaguer -- a chance to play in Williamsport.

None of our team got a lot of sleep that third night in Levelland, especially Bob. But he was up to the task, and proved Travis to be a prophet, by pitching the game of his young life against the monsters from north of the Red River. Bob had his curve working and master control of his fastball. He didn't walk a single batter during the game. The only rally the Okies managed to come up with was in the fourth inning and that was snuffed by a home run-robbing catch by Willie in left centerfield. Billy, Dave Looney, and Danny led the way, hitting safely their first two times at the plate.

We took a three to one lead into the sixth and final inning. Bob had to face their number two, three, and four hitters and he didn't falter. He struck out two of the three and coerced the last hitter to ground out to Jack at first, which launched our delirious celebration. Williamsport, here we come!

CHAPTER SIXTEEN

I felt like I was waking from one super incredible dream as I opened my eyes to find out, in fact, what I thought was my sleep time vision turned out to be my true reality. I looked out the window of the bus as we passed a sign saying: Durant, the Magnolia Capital of Oklahoma. I pinched myself. Yes, I was awake. Our team was on its way to Northern Pennsylvania to participate in the 16th annual Little League World Series in Williamsport. We left the arid Texas panhandle late, the evening before. Collectively exhausted from the ordeal and celebration, the entire team had fallen asleep immediately after selecting our seats. I glanced around at all of my sleeping teammates, then looked out on the countryside of Oklahoma as we were entering the Choctaw Indian Reservation. The densely forested topography strangely resembled Central Texas, which was quite a surprise to me -- I had always thought of Oklahoma as dust bowl country. I stood up, stretched, looked out the back window and was surprised by the sight of twenty cars following our chartered school bus in the dawning morning. I later learned that Tildy had led a caravan of Austinites up to Dallas to meet our team and the dedicated parents who had followed the bus from Levelland.

I moaned as I stretched, which had the unfortunate effect of stirring up a few of my teammates. Jack, Willie, and Ras all opened their eyes, as did Danny, who grunted and threw his pillow at me.

"What did I do?" I asked rhetorically.

"Oh shut up!" he said, turning back over to face Billy, who was still sleeping soundly beside him.

Jack told me he had experienced an uncomfortable, sleepless night and had gotten off the bus to see his parents and brother who had followed Tildy to Dallas. His parents had been unable to make the trip to Levelland, but no one, other than Willie's parents, of course, would be missing the trip to Williamsport. This was going to be historic and all close relatives wanted to witness such grand heroics. Jack suddenly rose up in his seat and got all excited, getting our attention.

"Hey, Willie, Mickey," Jack whispered loudly. "Listen to this." Willie and I leaned toward him, as he continued, "You won't believe what my brother, Bill, told me happened to Noah Parkes."

"What happened to that jerk?" I asked.

"Bill said he heard Noah tore his car apart twice, and still couldn't find out why it kept stalling. He figured the guy he's been cutting cedar for sold him a lemon on purpose. So, you know what Noah did? He went to the man's offices in Westlake Hills, punched him a couple of times, and broke his nose. The man's considering pressing charges. Willie, I never thought your little trick would actually work, but boy howdy -- it did!"

Jack held up his hand, Willie slapped it and smiled, saying, "That Cracker had it coming for trying to kill Napoleon."

"And, Mickey," Jack continued, "you know who the man was -- the one that got his nose broke?"

"Who?" I asked.

"Trudy Prentice's father." Jack smiled.

I thought about the irony for a moment and said, "Perfect. That jerk deserved it for starting all that fuss about Willie."

"Say what?" Willie looked at me confused.

"Never mind. That was a long time ago," I said, trying to play it down a little bit, not wanting to rehash old history, especially now that such a wonderful new chapter had been written.

"What did I do?" Willie asked a little concerned.

"Nothing, really. But, remember the day you played touch football with us at Westenfield?" Willie nodded and I delicately continued, "Well, Trudy Prentice's father heard about it and raised pure hell. Racist stuff you know.

He caused a lot of problems in the neighborhood by sticking his big nose in the middle of something that had nothing to do with him."

"Oh, I didn't know," Willie said smiling. "Guess we got a twofer."

Willie and I exchanged high fives.

After crossing the Arkansas River, the landscape of Oklahoma began to resemble what I had pictured in my mind. The green cliffs and hills of the Southeast transformed into the flat, parched farmlands of the Northeast. We soon stopped for lunch at a truck stop along Highway 69 for chicken fried steaks, mashed potatoes, and salad, a meal known far and wide as the traditional dinner of a traveling Texas sports team.

Four hours later, we pulled up to the Louisville Slugger Factory in that famous Kentucky city along the banks of the Ohio River. We got a tour of its patented flame-tempered manufacturing process as we followed the progress of the personalized bats the factory produced for all of the players on our team, compliments of Tildy's bankroll. We learned that all of the raw wood needed to process the bats comes from both Pennsylvania's and New York's unique forests of white ash. Each tree provides enough lumber for about sixty Major League bats. After a tree has been milled down to what the company calls billets (sixty inch long four by fours), they are then individually hand turned into a bat in about twenty minutes, by one of the employees working a factory lathe.

Before the tour started, they took our signatures and, by the time we had watched a billet hand-turned into a bat, a metal stamp was made from our signatures. A technician placed the metal stamp with our signature with the logo for the Louisville Slugger Company, and the two were burned into the new bat. The bats were sanded, flame-tempered, dipped in bonding fluid, and set to dry as they rolled over a bed of heat. The end chucks were cut off, sanded smooth, and *voila!* We each had a personalized bat made to our specifications, to use at the Little League World Series. We all thought maybe this would provide the edge we needed to win the championship. As we were returning to the bus, several teammates expressed little prayers that they wouldn't break the treasured keepsakes.

After the factory tour, Tildy took the team to a local cafeteria in downtown Louisville where we were allowed to choose our own meal. Almost the entire team chose chicken fried steaks, mashed potatoes, and salads and, this time, each added Jell-O and a huge dessert. We were fully satiated as we boarded the bus for a second night of travel. Tildy hired a second driver so we wouldn't have to stop along the way. After several games of cards, chess, or Twenty Questions, we all fell asleep despite the growing anticipation.

I woke to the sight of the early morning sun shimmering off of the Susquehanna River and spotted a sign designating the city limits of Williamsport. I yelled for everyone to wake up -- I felt like they would want to see the field as we came upon it for the first time. Everyone enthusiastically got up to take in the sights, except for Danny who again moaned and turned over, trying to return to his private slumber land. This time pillows pelted him for his laissez-faire attitude and he was forced to join the rest of the team as we witnessed the beautiful Susquehanna River Valley pass into view.

The north-central Pennsylvania countryside was spectacular with huge tree-laden hills rising from the low gradient body of water that flowed along the highway. We exited off Highway 322 and took State Road 15, crossing the wide, shallow Susquehanna River, and approached the Little League complex in South Williamsport. Our anticipation was border-line crazed, almost off the scale, as we turned into the team dormitory area known as the "Grove." The first thing we all saw as we entered the driveway to the Grove was a quote by the highly-revered journalist, Grantland Rice, one of the most famous sportswriters ever, who coined many classic phrases while covering decades of our national pastime's Golden Era. Blocked letters on a stone marker near the entrance said:

> *When the one Great Scorer comes to write your name – He marks – not that you won or lost – but how you played the game.*
> *Grantland Rice*

On the other side of the driveway, again etched in stone, was the motto of Little League Baseball:

Character   Courage   Loyalty

"Character, courage, loyalty --" we all screamed out in unison as we drove down the driveway to the Grove, our home for the upcoming week of competition.

Up until 1958, the previous twelve World Series had been played at the original Little League field in West Williamsport, where Carl Stotz had first created the game for the local boys of his neighborhood. However, at the end of 1958, the Organization had evolved into a worldwide concern. If the township of Williamsport wished to keep the international championship, it would have to expand its facilities. Along came Howard J. Lamade, a very successful local merchant and farmer, who donated fifty acres of land in South Williamsport, below the tree-covered ridges rising from the valley, to be utilized by the Little League Organization. The new space would provide ample room for dormitories, practice fields, and the new 6,000 seat state-of-the-art stadium. To show their gratitude, the Organization included Mr. Lamade on the Founder's committee, and agreed to name the ballpark in his honor.

Our first glimpse of the Howard J. Lamade World Series Field was distant, through the trees around the Grove's parking lot as our bus pulled to a stop in front of a wooden barn-looking building, which had a sign posted in front that simply said "WEST". One by one, we marched off the bus, squinted through the foliage at our future ballpark, grabbed our suitcases, and raced for the building to pick out the most suitable bunks for the week ahead. Travis came into the room as we were debating who was to sleep where for the week. He said, "Boys, I have a couple of announcements. I'd like you to acquaint yourself with the Grove and all it has to offer for the next hour. There's a game room with ping-pong, pool, chess, and cards, which is next to the mess hall where all the teams eat their meals. You may want to take your pins with you to trade with your counterparts on the other teams from this country and around the world. This is a special time for all of you. A week that will forever give you the most cherished of memories, no matter what happens on the playing field. So, please, enjoy it, soak it up, make friends, and then, when it's time to practice or play the game, leave the memories for later and concentrate on the task at hand. One of the best things you do, as good as any bunch I've ever been associated with, is play quality, fundamental team baseball. Let's try and keep it up for three more games, what do y'all say?"

Everyone yelled, "Three to go -- three to go -- three to go --"

Travis held up his hand to silence us.

"First things first," he said, "our game with France is on Wednesday afternoon. We've been on a bus for practically 48 hours and we need to get some serious work in to be prepared for the game. In a couple of hours from now, at 11 a.m., we are scheduled for our first practice. It will be held at field number six at the far bottom end of the complex. Anyone who is late will have to give me ten. If there was ever a time to take everything seriously about the game, this is that time, boys. I'm proud of all you have accomplished up to now and even if we don't go any further, we could still call this season nothing but a success. However, that's not our goal, is it?"

Everyone yelled, "No!"

"Good! That's what I want to hear. Now, enjoy yourselves exploring the complex and I'll see you at practice on field six at eleven o'clock." Travis gave a thumbs up and left the barracks.

Willie, Danny, and I walked over to play a little ping-pong, hoping against hope it would be a closed-in room so that we could teach the world the game of Gnip-Gnop. We were lucky. When we got to the game room, we found the ping-pong table was enclosed in a square glass room with a ceiling of eight feet, perfect for the game my brother and I invented in our playroom in Austin. Danny and Willie played game number one as I stood outside the glass partition and watched. Pretty soon a young guy about my age sheepishly approached the window and watched with fascination. After watching a very competitive rally, the kid exclaimed, "Magnifique!"

I turned to him as he watched in awe, a game I figured he didn't understand. Sticking out my hand, I said, "Howdy, I'm Mickey," as I pointed at me, so if he didn't speak the language maybe he would still know what I was saying.

The French boy shook my hand and said in very broken English, "Hullo, Mickeee, my nam iss Francois."

"Nice to meet you, Francois. Would you like to learn this game?" I said, more with hand motions than with our native tongue.

"Oui, oui," he nodded.

I knocked on the window and waved at Danny and Willie to stop. They did reluctantly. We entered the square glass room and I introduced Francois to the two, asking them if I could use the room to teach him the game. Danny and Willie relented, reluctantly handing us the paddles on their way out. I explained to Francois in broken English and sign language the rules of Gnip-Gnop. I figured he understood because Francois nodded and said "Oui, oui." After a few practices, we started the game. I decided to take it easy on him at first, thinking the game would be completely foreign to him. That was a mistake. He schooled me in the fine art of the overhand slam on several occasions in a row. I had to struggle to stay even with the French kid and I was trying to save face in front of my buddies on the other side of the glass. Pretty soon we had other interested parties as more and more kids stopped at the window to observe this fascinating new game. Now, I had been playing Gnip-Gnop for about four years, since Larry and I invented it. I was very good at it and hardly ever lost, however, this day I met my match. With the score tied 19 to 19 and Francois serving, I thought I saw an opening, but it was closed with two topspin aces that left me bewildered. Danny and Willie razzed me long and hard about the defeat, but I took it in stride. I congratulated Francois, who said it had really been fun. He then informed us he was the junior ping-pong champion of his little town in France. I had played a ringer.

A half-hour later, our entire team was tossing the ball back and forth at five minutes to eleven on field 6. No one would dare be late for this practice. During the two-hour workout, Bob, Willie, Fish, and I ran wind sprints at three-quarter speed in the outfield while the other players had some batting practice. Everyone was concentrating seriously, and though there were some laughs, they were born of a release of tension rather than any comedic intent. Though Willie had only pitched a total of three innings during our All-Star streak, Travis was leaning toward pitching him against Poitiers Post, France, the team on which Francois played. He wanted to save Fish, Bob and I for the final two games. As it turned out, Francois was one of only two French boys on the team. The rest of their squad was made up of American service men's boys who had only played together as a team for this one year. They were good enough to sweep through the European championships, but in 1962 there were about as many Little Leagues in the entirety of France as were found in the city of Austin. In the post-practice speech, Travis said, "Boys, we can't take any team lightly that makes it to this level. I know some of you have heard that this French team is inexperienced. Don't be fooled -- this Poitiers All-Star team is as American as apple pie with a little French custard on the side. Air Force kids have got it pretty rough, because their fathers get reassigned to a new base every other year. That's the only reason they haven't played together as a team as much as you guys. However, they all have individual experiences in Little League, just like you. They play on the same field, with the same ball, and the same wooden bats. And just because they play in Europe, their bases are still sixty feet apart and the pitcher's mound is 46 feet from the plate. So, what I'm saying, boys, is Poitiers plays the game of baseball just like you. And we all know the winner is not necessarily the one that looks the best on paper, or we'd never have to play the games."

He looked up and noticed another team, one from Ontario, Canada, approaching the practice field. He quickly concluded, "Here comes another squad, so everyone help the coach bag the equipment and then you can have the rest of the day to horse around. Just don't be stupid and get hurt. An injury at this time is not what we need. We eat at six in the mess and, again, don't be late. Practice tomorrow at the same time and our game is five o'clock Wednesday afternoon."

We spent the afternoon swimming in a public pool located about three blocks from the Grove. A couple of years after we made the trip to Williamsport, the Organization added a beautiful pool in the Grove so players would never have to leave the complex. However, with plenty of adult supervision, we frolicked in the public pool alongside the residents of South Williamsport. Playing pool games like Splash and Marco Polo, we whiled away the hours of the afternoon under the hot August sun.

By six we had returned, showered, and joined all of the teams in the mess hall for our dinner. The President of the Little League Organization welcomed us. Then he said he had a little surprise for everyone -- while eating we were to see a famous baseball routine from the comedy team of

Bud Abbott and Lou Costello. Costello plays his typical character, the idiot, but this time as a new peanut vendor at a baseball stadium managed by Abbott. He wants to familiarize himself with the names of the players:

Costello:	*Now look, I gotta know all of the baseball players' names. Do you know the guys' names?*
Abbott:	*Oh sure.*
Costello:	*So you go ahead and tell me some of their names.*
Abbott:	*We have Who's on first, What's on second, I Don't Know's on third.*
Costello:	*That's what I wanna find out.*
Abbott:	*I say Who's on first, What's on second, I Don't Know's on third.*
Costello:	*You know the fellows' names?*
Abbott:	*Certainly!*
Costello:	*Well, then who's on first?*
Abbott:	*Yes.*
Costello:	*I mean the fellow's name.*
Abbott:	*Who!*
Costello:	*The guy on first!*
Abbott:	*Who!*
Costello:	*The first baseman!*
Abbott:	*Who.*
Costello:	*The guy playing first!*
Abbott:	*Who is on first.*
Costello:	*Now whaddya askin' me for?*
Abbott:	*I'm telling you Who is on first.*
Costello:	*Well, I'm asking YOU who's on first.*
Abbott:	*That's the man's name.*
Costello:	*That's who's name?*
Abbott:	*Yes.*
Costello:	*Well, go ahead and tell me.*
Abbott:	*Who!*
Costello:	*The first baseman.*
Abbott:	*Who is on first.*
Costello:	*Have you got a contract with the first baseman?*
Abbott:	*Absolutely.*

Costello:	When you pay of the first baseman every month, who gets the money.
Abbott:	Every dollar. Why not? The man's entitled to it.
Costello:	Who is?
Abbott:	Yes. Sometimes his wife comes down and collects it.
Costello:	Who's wife?
Abbott:	Yes.
Costello:	All I'm tryin' to find out is what's the guy's name on first base.
Abbott:	Oh, no – wait a minute, don't switch 'em around. What is on second.
Costello:	I'm not asking you who's on second.
Abbott:	Who is on first.

Willie and I were constantly laughing out loud throughout the routine. I had heard of "Who's on First", but had never actually seen it. And, by the reaction from all of the kids in attendance in the mess hall, they hadn't either and were breaking up as much as us at the true genius of the comedians. I really loved the finish:

Costello:	Look, you got a pitcher on this team?
Abbott:	Tomorrow.
Costello:	You don't wanna tell me today?
Abbott:	I'm telling you now.
Costello:	Then go ahead.
Abbott:	Tomorrow.
Costello:	What time?
Abbott:	What time what?
Costello:	What time tomorrow are you going to tell me who's pitching?:
Abbott:	Now listen, Who is not pitching. Who is on fir...
Costello:	I'll break your arm if you say Who's on first. I wanna know what' the pitcher's name.
Abbott:	What's on second.
Costello:	Whaaaaa! You got a catcher?
Abbott:	Oh, absolutely.
Costello:	The catcher's name?
Abbott:	Today.

Costello:	Today. And Tomorrow's pitching.
Abbott:	Now, you've got it.
Costello:	All we've got is a couple of days on the team.
Abbott:	Well, I can't help that.
Costello:	Well, I'm a catcher too.
Abbott:	I know that.
Costello:	Now suppose that I'm catching. Tomorrow's pitching on my team and their heavy hitter gets up.
Abbott:	Yes.
Costello:	Tomorrow throws the ball. The batter bunts the ball. When he bunts the ball, me being a good catcher, I wanna throw the guy out at first base. So I pick up the ball and throw it to who?
Abbott:	Now that's the first thing you've said right.
Costello:	I don't even know what I'm talkin' about!
Abbott:	Well, that's all you have to do.

Needless to say, we were in hysterics the rest of the evening, performing the routine with each other in our dormitory right up to the moment we fell asleep with smiles on our faces.

The next morning we continued to relive "Who's on First" during breakfast at the Grove. We spent a couple of hours playing games with various members of the other teams. I got my revenge against Francois, beating him in another competitive game of Gnip-Gnop, 24-22. I was looking forward to the rubber match later in the week.

At eleven o'clock we reported for practice. We learned Willie would be pitching the opener against the transplanted Americans and French from Poitiers in the opening game of the 1962 Little League World Series. We had a relatively light session with no running, since Travis said that if we weren't in shape by now, we never would be. Everybody looked at Don who shrugged his shoulders and said, "I'm going to really miss the laps." We all laughed.

After practice, we boarded our bus and headed for the original Little League field across the river in West Williamsport. There was a game in progress between the local area Little League All-Stars and a team from San

Jose, California. In a five-year-old tradition, the San Jose team had accepted an invitation to come play a three game series with the home team, in what was termed the Carl Stotz Memorial series.

Carl Stotz had built the field on West Fourth Street for that first season of Little League in 1939, less than a mile from his house where the inspiration for the game had dawned on him the autumn before. Behind home plate was the press box and behind the press box was a small museum dedicated to the inception of the game, which housed paraphernalia from those original days of the organization. We met Al "Sonny" Yearick and Bill Bair, two of the Lycoming Dairy players that played on the league champion that first year, twenty-three years before when Carl Stotz' managed. Willie and I really hit it off with Sonny and he spent about a half hour with us, going over all the mementos from those first years when he played for the first three "national champions." Even though all of the teams in the country were actually located inside the state of Pennsylvania, it was still an incredible accomplishment in my young eyes. Willie and I got a big kick out of seeing the original lilac stump that Carl Stotz had kicked, leading to the inspirational moment of creation on the back stoop of his home while watching his nephews play catch. Also on exhibit were the original uniforms, bats, balls, and statistics from those early years in the development of the organization.

"Sir," Willie asked Sonny, "how did y'all do it -- that first year, you know?"

"Well, Willie, I'll tell you. Carl Stotz had a vision and he figured to follow through on it. He came to the church that Bill and I went to, about four blocks east of here. He asked to see all of the boys between ages nine and twelve after Sunday School for a few minutes. When we all gathered, he asked how many would like to play baseball in uniforms with umpires on a field more our size. I think only one boy didn't raise his hand. Carl had us come out to this spot, where this park is now, and he timed us from stake to stake until he figured out the best distance for the base paths. Then, he pitched to us one after another, to see how far we hit the ball, which helped him set the distance for the fences. And, after more experimenting with pitching, he decided on forty feet from the pitcher's mound to home plate."

"But, it's 46 feet," I said with cautious authority.

"Oh, he moved it back to the distance it is today after the first two seasons."

"So," Willie asked, "why isn't the field that the World Series is played on named for Mr. Stotz?"

"Carl believed the game should stay pure," Sonny explained. "He didn't want his ballplayers, who were only kids, to be exploited by the Organization. He believed the corporations of America should support a game that was creating the future leaders, for its industry, teaching them all of the principles important to become good, productive citizens in our society. The Little League board of directors, in the Fifties, was being led astray by greed, and forced the kids in each league to raise money door to door to support the Organization. So Carl hired an attorney and sued Little League to take back the control he had granted the board. He lost, and they kicked him out of the Organization he created. So, after a year or two, we originals got together and decided to honor Carl with this series and small museum. Someday, the world will know the truth about this great man again, and understand what he did for the youth of America."

At the end of the Memorial game, a San Jose player slammed a three-run game-winning homer. Al turned and wished us all the best of luck in our upcoming series. Willie and I shook his hand and thanked him for the wealth of information. In the back of our minds, we were hoping a little bit of his success would rub off on us. One thing was for certain -- we would find out the next day.

CHAPTER SEVENTEEN

"Babe Ruth," Jack said with authority. He was answering a question Billy had posed to our group about who was the greatest Major League ballplayer of all time. We were at breakfast the day of our first game in the Little League World Series, and I was sitting with Jack, Willie, Danny, Billy, Stan, and Dave Looney. Jack had gone first and, in my opinion, picked the obvious.

"There's no question about it, y'all," Jack continued. "He was the most dominant player of all time. Two times in his career he hit more home runs than all the players on the other teams in the American League. He also hit for a high career average and I know we're not supposed to include pitchers, but come on -- what other great hitter was one of the best pitchers before they switched him to the outfield. He still holds some World Series pitching records. It's definitely Babe Ruth."

Danny looked at all of us and said, "All I have to say is – fifty-six. No one will ever break that record. Joltin' Joe DiMaggio. He made it look so easy. He led the Yankees to five straight World Series titles and nine by the time he quit. He was smooth and a great athlete, not a big out-of-shape slob like the Babe." We all laughed.

"If we're talking numbers," said Billy, "then what about .401 to knock your socks off. The best pure hitter in baseball -- ever -- was Ted Williams. We've all read his book. He was smart about the game and then he got real good at it. If he hadn't been in the Air Force during World War II and

Korea, no telling how many records he would have shattered. Missed four seasons. Can you imagine?"

"You guys are way off," Dave interrupted. "What about Ty Cobb? He led the League in hitting, twelve times. His career average is twenty points higher than the losers you guys named. And even though Maury Wills may break his stolen base record this year, Cobb was still the greatest base runner ever. He was also a pretty good coach. I don't think those other guys did that. I say it's 'The Georgia Peach'."

We all looked at Stan, but he only shrugged his shoulders.

"Well, this is hard," Stan calculated. "They're all great players. But, I'm thinkin' Lou Gehrig. Played 2,130 straight games -- 'The Iron Horse' of baseball. He hit behind Ruth or he might have hit sixty homers in a season. You know, like last year, if Mantle hadn't been switched part way into the season to bat behind Maris. Even batting behind The Babe, Gehrig hit for a higher average. He never missed a game until he got Lou Gehrig's disease."

We all analyzed that last statement. We'd seen the old film clips of his speech. We didn't understand much about Lou Gehrig's Disease, except that he died from it -- and his last public statement confused us: 'I am the luckiest man on the face of the earth.' I could still hear those words echo across Yankee Stadium in that film clip. Baseball was lucky to have him.

After a pause, Stan faced me and asked, "What about you, Mickey, who's the greatest ever, as if we all didn't know who you're going to pick?"

Before I could speak everyone at the table joined Stan in saying simultaneously, "Mickey Mantle!"

After a second, to let them have their moment, I said emphatically, "Without a doubt, he's the greatest switch-hitter of all time, and maybe the most courageous. If he hadn't been injured so much, he would definitely have to be considered the best all around player. A healthy Mantle would have hit more home runs than Ruth, stole more bases than Cobb, and led the Yankees to more World Series championships than DiMaggio. Still, even playing through his pain, he was the last Major Leaguer to win the Triple Crown, and he's probably going to win his third Most Valuable Player award. I don't think any of your guys did that."

"Well," Jack scoffed, "would'ah, could'ah, should'ah, and considering they didn't have any MVP awards until the 1930's, so it's not fair to throw that in our face. Cobb or Ruth might have won six each."

"Besides Mickey," Danny barked, "my Yankee Clipper, Stan the Man, Yogi, Roy Campanella, and Jimmie Foxx all won the MVP three times each."

"Okay, okay, I forgot," I said with a shrug. "Heck, I'm just trying to make a point. Mick's career was great anyway, and it could've been even better. But you have to give me one thing. No one hit tape measure home runs from both sides of the plate like Mantle. I'm sticking with number seven."

"Well, I have to disagree," said Willie, the last to speak up in the group. He paused for a moment to get everyone's attention. "About that courageous stuff, I'm not so sure. Lot's of players had injuries and played. Besides, he didn't have to go through what Jackie Robinson did when he broke into the league. If I can't include Josh Gibson, who hit more homers than Ruth, or Satchel Paige who, when he finally got to play in the Major Leagues, dominated at the age of forty-eight. If I can't choose them, I'd have to say the greatest ballplayer will prove to be Willie Mays. He can field better than anyone, hits for power, runs like crazy, and he'll break the Babe's records someday. On top of all that, he's the captain of his team even though he's Colored."

Dave Looney scowled, "Figures, you'd pick a nigger."

Everyone froze and looked at Dave incredulously, except for Willie who said, "Why did you have to go and say that?"

"Well, it's true, you're a nigger -- you pick a nigger," Dave said matter-of-factly.

Willie grabbed his glass of orange juice and threw the remaining liquid into Dave's face. Dave instinctively jumped across the table and tried to throttle Willie's neck. Dave knocked him off his bench and landed on top of Willie, who instantly whipped his leg up like lightning and knocked Dave to the floor with a blow to his side. Both jumped up and started to face-off when Jack grabbed Dave and lifted him off his feet, turning him away from the lunging Willie. Danny and Billy grabbed Willie's arms and pulled them back as I jumped into the middle, screaming, "Stop it, y'all!"

Travis showed up out of nowhere.

"What's going on here, fellas?" he asked in a surprisingly calm voice. "Letting off a little steam are we? Now, I don't care who or what started this mess, but real men know when to apologize and move on. You two shake hands and then let it go. We need to support each other as teammates, if not forever, at least for the rest of this week."

Willie and Dave both started to protest but Travis raised his hand to stop the objections. "No arguments on this, y'all! I want you to shake hands, now. Let's go."

Jack, Danny, and Billy let go of their grasp and the two reluctantly held out their hands to each other and shook briefly without making eye contact.

"There you go," Travis concluded. "Now, finish your breakfast and go rest up for the game. Mickey, I would like to talk with you when you've finished with breakfast."

I looked at my empty plate and said, "I'm done, Travis. What do you want?"

"Come walk with me for a few minutes."

As we made our way outside and down the sidewalk toward the stadium, Travis turned to me and said, "What was going on back there?"

"Well, we were discussing the best ballplayers, and when Willie picked Willie Mays, Dave said something like 'it figures a nigger would pick a nigger.' Willie threw his juice in Dave's face and it was on."

Travis stopped me and looked me in the face. He said, "Mickey, you have to make sure they get over it, all right? They'll listen to you. So, when you go back to the dorm, I want you to check things out and get everyone on the same page. I don't care how you do it, but you have to make them see our goal is too important to let it slip away because of differences we may have off the field. I don't fault either player. I'm glad to hear Willie stood up for himself -- it shows he has a lot of fight in him. If he can funnel it the right way, he might have a great series. As for Dave, it's no excuse, but he's going through a tough time with his parents divorce. I'm sure he knows in his heart what he said was wrong, but he may not be able to see it clearly at the moment. The best thing to do for the next few days is to keep the two apart when they aren't in uniform, so we don't have a repeat of today's fiasco. Got it?"

"Yes sir. I'll do what I can do," I said.

"I trust that will be enough, son. You have a certain quality, Mickey. People will follow your lead. I have chosen you for the honor of reading the Little League Pledge before today's game. Do you know it?"

"I think so," I said tentatively.

Travis smiled and handed me a piece of paper, saying, "Here. Work on it."

"Yes sir," I said.

"And, Mickey, if your teammates ask you why we talked, then that's what you tell them. Not the other -- you keep that to yourself and work your magic. Okay?"

"Yes sir, Travis," I said. "And thank you for the honor."

"You deserve it, son. I'm counting on you, Mickey. Keep everyone's eyes on the prize."

"Yes, sir," I said and turned back to join my teammates as they were filing out of the mess and heading for our dormitory.

During the next couple of hours I alternated my time between Willie and Dave, making sure they were over their hostilities and ready to concentrate on the first game. I felt like I had been pretty successful when Willie told me he had already forgotten about it. Dave told me he knew he said something stupid and didn't know where it came from because he truly liked Willie. I suggested to Dave that the way we were taught to refer to other races needed to evolve with the changing times. I pointed out to Dave, in a very delicate manner, Willie was a person just like us. What we thought maybe as just slang, to him was a vicious slur, and an attack on his people. I probably didn't word it that well at the time, but I got the point across.

On my way to batting practice before the game, I came across the large, covered board, which displayed the brackets for the upcoming tournament. I stopped for a moment to study it -- first of all looking for our West name among the eight teams participating. There we were, the second name, the home team of Game One. And our opponent was Europe, Francois' team from Poitiers Post. The other half of our bracket included the East team from Manchester, New Hampshire, who would follow our game, playing under the lights against Central America, with players from Monterrey, Mexico. I glanced over at the other bracket revealing the two games that would be played on Thursday, while we would have a day off. First up the next day would feature Asia, a team from Hilo, Hawaii, that had won an exciting extra-inning game against the defending champion team from Taiwan, to earn their first trip to Williamsport.

It was funny that Hilo was included in the Asia division, even though they were Americans, but it made sense for the Organization to have them participate with teams from Taiwan and Japan, since there were only a few Leagues in both countries -- Little League was just beginning to catch on in the Orient. Asia would play USA's North squad, a group of sluggers from Kankakee, Illinois. We had heard the North team had won all of their games by more than four runs, in their streak to reach Williamsport. The final first-round game would have Canada, represented by a team from Ontario, play an East squad from San Juan, Puerto Rico. Ours was to be a simple single elimination -- you lose, you go home -- you win you advance. Win three in a row and we're the world champions. Just the thought made me tingle.

Willie and I were sitting in the dugout when Jack stepped up to the plate to take his cuts on field number six, by the riverbanks of the Susquehanna. The first four swings produced mammoth "tape measure" home runs. Willie yelled out, "Nice slugging, Moose, but save a few for the game."

"Buck," Jack said as he glanced to the dugout, "I got plenty more where those came from."

The big guy then hit two over the center field fence. He looked ready. Jack and Willie had grown to respect each other from their play on the field during the season; they had their own private nicknames for each other that only they would use. I couldn't really think of anyone ever getting away with calling Jack by the name of Moose, except someone who had earned the right. Jack's name for Willie was Buck because he knew that was what Willie Mays' teammates called their captain.

"Way to go Jackie boy, good hitting buddy," I yelled out from the dugout in support.

When Jack finished and jogged down to first after half-heartedly laying down a bunt, Dave Looney stepped up to take his cuts.

I turned to Willie and asked, "Are you and Looney going to be all right?"

"Sure, Mick. I won't start anything, and I don't think he will either. But, deep down, that boy is a cracker and he's heading for sad days and bad times."

Willie turned out to be prophetic with that statement. Ten years later, Dave Looney would join an underground movement in the U.S. and take part in bombing a post office in San Francisco to protest the Viet Nam war. The incident would accidentally kill a night janitor, and Dave would find himself evading the authorities ever after. But for the time being, he was a kid playing baseball in Williamsport.

At 4:50 that afternoon, dressed in our new West All-Star uniforms, after having taken batting practice on a field adjacent to Howard J. Lamade stadium, we arrived at the third base dugout and got our first look at what a huge crowd of 8,000 looked like. As they saw us emerge from the shadows under the stadium, the attendees applauded our entrance. Goose bumps started at the base of my neck and ran down my entire body, so much so, I even felt them in my toes. The bleachers lining both foul lines were filling up with parents, other teams, and fans, and the hill beyond the fences was packed with people. Behind these masses was a second, even larger hill, where young kids, using sections of cardboard boxes, rode toboggan-like down the ruts on the hillside far above the stadium.

Willie was warming up along the third base line when Travis whistled at him to wrap it up and join the team in the dugout. As he did, we heard the announcer come on and welcome everyone. Then, one by one, he introduced our starting line-up, and then each of the reserves. As they announced my name, I trotted onto the field, gave all my teammates a high five, and took my place along the third base line. After France was announced, we all stood with hats over hearts as the national anthems from both countries reverberated from speakers around the stadium. During the playing of "*The*

175

Star Spangled Banner," with 8,000 plus singing in unison, I had my second goose bump experience of the afternoon.

Everyone left the field returning to their respective dugouts after the anthems, except for Francois and me. We approached a microphone set up behind the pitcher's mound as the PA announced "Ladies and Gentlemen, your attention please. Representing their teams, communities, and countries, Mr. Mickey Charles from Austin, Texas, USA, and Monsieur Francois Pleger, from Poitiers, France, will recite the Little League pledge in English and French. I stepped up to the microphone, cleared my throat and, as I looked out on the masses, I drew a complete blank. I glanced over at Francois who whispered, "I truest in good." I smiled as I relaxed, and my memory returned. Holding my hat over my heart, I recited the pledge written by Peter J. McGovern, the president of the International Little League organization:

I trust in God
I love my country
And will respect its laws
I will play fair
And strive to win
But win or lose
I will always do my best

When I finished, there was a large cheer from the grandstands. I returned my hat to my head, turned and passed by Francois on his way to the microphone. I whispered, "Merci boucoup, for the assist."

"No probleeem, mon ami," he said, stepping up to the microphone. Francois removed his hat and said the pledge in French, and, to my ear, I didn't hear any mistakes. After he finished, the crowd applauded politely. Francois turned to me and we exchanged high fives, which brought a heightened response from the enthralled, anxious throng surrounding the field. As I walked back to my teammates, I passed the Little League mascot, Dugout, a teenager dressed in a uniform that looked like a cross between Yogi Bear and Goofy, who gave me a high five and then sprinted over to Francois and repeated the congratulatory action. Then the PA played Chubby Checker's "The Twist." Dugout pulled the manager of Poitiers out onto the field and twisted with him as the whole crowd howled. Then, Dugout approached our bench and repeated the process with Travis. We all laughed at the sight of our manager twisting to the music.

After a moment of silence, the PA announcer said, "Ladies, Gentlemen, boys and girls, we have a treat for you today. Throwing out the first pitch of the first game of this sixteenth annual Little League World Series is a former Major Leaguer considered by a consensus of sports writers to be the greatest living ballplayer. During a career shortened by his service for our country during World War II, he still managed to win three Most Valuable Player awards in 1939, 1941, and 1947. On June 24, 1936 he hit two home runs in one inning. On August 27, 1938, he hit three triples in one game, which is still a record to this day. Yet, of all of his accomplishments, the one that will live forever may be his unbelievable achievement of hitting safely in fifty-six consecutive games, an accomplishment in 1941 that completely enthralled our country. Ladies and Gentlemen, please join me in welcoming Hall of Fame New York Yankee center fielder, Joe DiMaggio."

As the great Yankee Clipper appeared from under the grandstands, raising his hand over his head to wave at the appreciative response from the fans, goose bumps raced across my skin. Suddenly, Danny elbowed me in the ribs.

"Greatest living ballplayer," he said. "I guess I win."

Jack, hearing this, leaned over me and said, "Living, Danny boy. Remember, he said living."

"Yeah, but he also said greatest," Danny retorted.

Joltin' Joe raised a baseball above his head, then took a slow windup and delivered a perfect strike to Don, who was lucky enough to catch the pitch and return it to the great DiMaggio. Then, they posed for a picture together. Don never looked more content as he beamed at the camera in his catcher's gear, standing next to the Hall of Famer. I was really happy for him. He had moved to a new town and adapted to the surroundings, new friends, a new ballpark, new teammates, a new coach, and all of the running at practice, and had managed to come through with flying colors. I was a better pitcher because he was the best catcher I'd ever had behind the plate.

"Play ball!" screamed the home plate umpire. Our team rushed out to their positions on the field. Willie looked relaxed and comfortable on the mound in the first inning, striking out two, giving up a Texas Leaguer to their best hitter before getting the clean-up hitting first baseman to line out to David McKendricks, who replaced Willie in centerfield while he was pitching.

After Willie struck out the side in the top of the first, he led off the bottom of the inning with a single to left field. Billy laid down a perfect sacrifice bunt that advanced our speedy lead-off hitter to second, who subsequently scored on Danny's double down the left field line. Jack homered to center immediately after, and plated two more runs. Don and Ras followed with homers of their own and the massacre was on. When Willie walked off the mound in the sixth inning, the dust cleared long enough for the scoreboard to reveal: West – 14 Europe – 0. Jack and Don had both hit second home runs, giving the team a total of five; we pounded out sixteen hits and Willie had held the guys from France to four scattered singles. I'm sure we impressed the other teams a little bit with our exceptional power-hitting display. What they couldn't know was that we still had our three "A" pitchers rested and ready to go. Confidence enhances talent and we were exuding it with a capital C.

An hour after the game, I offered Francois a little accidental consolation, when in our rubber match of Gnip-Gnop, he spanked me 21 to 10. But, I found solace in that our West Austin All-Stars were going to get to play another ballgame.

We sat in the left field grandstands that evening to watch the night game between Central America and the East. I watched intently since Travis had informed me that I would be starting our second game against the winner. It was no contest. The team from south of the border had three pitchers combine for a three hitter, pounded out twelve hits, and scored nine runs in the rout against some pretty darn good pitching by the New Englanders.

At noon the next day, we had batting practice on the adjacent practice field three below the stadium. Everybody was loose, but also a little concerned, because we knew we would not be facing patsies in the next game. While our hitters unloaded on the casual pitches from Coach T, Travis went over the order with Don, Fish, Bob, and me in the dugout, giving us his expertise on how to handle their powerful hitters. He had noted that most of their line-up took pitches until they got a strike, except for the three and four hitters, who always swung at first pitch fastballs. He suggested we go right at the line-up with fastballs, other than the three and four batters, until we had two strikes. Then we'd come with the drop, curve, or change-up as the out pitch. With hitters number three and four, he thought we should start off with curves and, when throwing fastballs, make sure they were off the plate, either tight inside or, preferably wasted a little outside, in an attempt to make them hungry for a fastball and lunge for the pitch. Travis reminded me we didn't want give these two players anything good to hit. If runners were on base, he thought that the drop might be the optimal pitch, for these two power-hitters were the slowest runners on the team and we might be able to get a double play on a ground ball.

On the hottest August day in the history of Williamsport, our team sat along the third base line to witness game number three of the first round, between Asia from Hilo, Hawaii, and the top-seeded North squad from Kankakee, Illinois. I was literally wilting in the stands as the temperature hovered around 103 degrees with rising humidity, reportedly being pushed by a Norther blowing in from Canada. I could only think about how glad I was that I didn't have to pitch in this heat as the North squad pounded hit after hit and won a commanding 10 to 4 victory. We all figured that if we could get by Mexico the next day, we would be playing the North team in the finals on Sunday.

That evening we saw the final first-round game between the Caribbean and Canada. Again, it was a wash out as the Caribbean squad cleaned the plate with the team from Canada. We retired to our West dormitory and all I could think about for the rest of the evening was the day that lay ahead, for it would be the most important of my young life.

After a sleepless night and restless early morning, I joined my teammates for breakfast. All of them tried to build up my confidence by uttering those little clichés that have become common in baseball: "Throw strikes, we'll back you up," "They got nothing," "Hold 'em down and we'll win it for you," and "No pressure, Mickey, we're all behind you."

The last statement came from David McKendricks, our shortstop, who had played on the lowly cellar-dwellers, Louis Shanks, and though I knew him as a teammate now, he had never really been a close friend. However, I accepted his high five with the same enthusiasm as my other teammates. And, in a way, I thought David's wholehearted response was a positive sign for what was to come next.

During the previous night while we slept, roaring thunderstorms crossed over the Susquehanna Valley, drenching the grounds and cooling the air. So, as we approached game time, the temperature had dropped twenty degrees from the day before and it was a perfect day to play baseball. At 4:45 that afternoon, under a beautiful, cloudless blue sky, I finished warming-up down the first base line, in front of the massing crowd of 9,000. On Travis's signal, Don and I stopped my pre-game routine and returned to our Visitor's dugout.

We were introduced, and this time I was announced to be batting ninth as the pitcher. The national anthems of the two countries played and the teams retired to their respective dugouts. Willie had the honor of reading the Little League pledge along with the clean-up hitting first baseman from Monterrey. They both did an admirable job; in fact, Willie did much better than me because he never froze. Then, after Dugout had twisted with both managers again, the honorary first pitch was thrown out by Alexander Cartwright IV, the great-grandson of the aforementioned Father of Baseball who had initiated the first ball club with his creation of the New York Knickerbockers back in 1845.

"Play Ball!" yelled the umpire standing at home plate. The team from Monterey sprinted to their positions on the field, began their warm-ups, and the big day was staring us in the face.

I sat down on the end of the bench and tried to fight the nervousness. I grabbed my windbreaker and put it on to keep my arm warm. Willie selected his bat from the box next to me and I said, "Come on Willie, start it off for us. Be the man." Willie smiled and tipped his batting helmet at me. Then, he turned, left our dugout, and approached the plate.

Everyone on our bench was chatting it up, shouting encouragement to Willie.

"Be a hitter, Buck," screamed Jack, "be a hitter."

Willie turned to look for a signal from Travis, who yelled out, "Make it be your pitch, Willie boy."

Willie stepped into the batter's box and settled into his stance, eyeing the pitcher with determination. The tall, lanky right-handed pitcher went into his wind up and let go a fastball that sailed toward the inside corner. Willie stepped toward left center field and produced a beautifully smooth swing that connected with the ball. It soared high into the blue sky and carried over the fence for an opening-pitch home run. Willie circled the bases with a big smile on his face and jumped into the arms of his gyrating, screaming teammates at home plate.

As we returned to the dugout, I patted Willie on the back and said, "You are the man. Way to start us out." The butterflies that had been swimming in my stomach a few moments before had evidently drowned with the immediate lead. The pitcher for Mexico seemed to calm down a little, too, after giving up a single to Billy, he was able to get Ras, Danny, and Jack to pop up lazy flies that ended the top of the first. As I walked out toward the mound, I glanced at the scoreboard. 1 – 0. Okay, Mickey, I thought, you got your lead, now let's hold on to it.

I tossed my nine warm-ups to Don who was firing the ball back with vigor and shouting statements like: "Just like that, Mickey" or "There you go, Mickey." After Don had thrown the ball down to second and it had made its trip around the horn, Ras tossed me the ball from his position at third. I reached down and picked up the resin bag and tossed it the air a couple of times. I licked my fingers and rubbed down the ball a little while I glanced around the stadium. I thought, focus, concentrate, one pitch at a time.

I toed the rubber, and looked in for the sign from Don as Mexico's lead-off hitter stepped in the batter's box. He was a tiny second baseman who I figured would be looking for a walk. My first pitch was a fastball right down the middle of the plate and the little guy took it for the first strike. Then Don signaled for another fastball, but I shook him off. I was ready to see if I had my good breaking ball under game pressure. My second

pitch, a curve, dropped into Don's mitt on the outside corner, and the umpire screamed, "Strike two!" The little guy swung and missed a fastball on the next pitch that I was wasting off the plate. Don threw the ball down to Ras who whipped it around the horn. As I watched the ball make its way to Dave Looney at second, then David McKendricks at short, and finally, to Jack at first, I was thinking, "Keep it up -- trust your stuff."

Their second hitter was a lefty. Don looked over at Travis for a signal and then relayed it to me. Fastball, as planned. I went into my wind up and delivered directly into Don's mitt on the outside corner for strike one. Then I threw a curve that broke into the batter, hand-cuffing him, and he sent a weak grounder toward David at short that Ras cut off coming across the infield from third and rifled to first for out number two. I walked the third batter on four pitches before getting their clean-up hitter to line out to Willie deep in center to end the inning. Fifteen more outs.

The second and third innings were scoreless, but not without incident. In the top of the third with two outs, Willie came to bat again and slashed a ball into the corner down the left field line. As he rounded first base on his way to a sure double, he stepped awkwardly on the side of the base and twisted his ankle, which sent him to the ground in a lot of pain. He managed to get up and limp back to first before calling time out, but then he laid down on the ground in agony. Travis and Coach T rushed out to evaluate the damage to our star player. Willie was on the ground for a couple of minutes as they were moving and probing the ankle to make sure nothing was broken.

Travis got him on his feet to put some weight on it as a test of strength. Willie was still in a lot of pain, but like the trooper he was, he indicated to Travis that he could play on. He limped more than jogged down the first base line to warm up and loosen the tightness in his swollen ankle. Willie told the umpire he was ready when he returned to first, and he took his position on the base. Billy stepped up to the plate and on the first pitch, hit a weak ground ball down the third base line. Willie started to run, but his ankle couldn't take the pressure and their third baseman easily threw him out at second to end the inning.

Between innings, Travis asked the trainer for the Little League World Series to tape up Willie's ankle so he could play the rest of the game. As this was happening, Travis made a decision to switch around our defense so Willie wouldn't have to cover so much territory on a bad ankle. He moved David McKendricks to center, put Ras at short, and told Willie to play third base. He called me over and said, "Mickey, they may try and test Willie's ankle with a bunt or two. I want him to stay deep and you cover bunts down the third base line. Tell Jack to take the first base side and Dave to cover first behind him."

"Yes sir," I responded.

Travis looked at me and asked, "How's the arm?"

"Feels fine. I feel fine," I said.

"Good, stay focused. Throw strikes. Make them hit you," he instructed. "Your teammates will back you up."

"Yes, sir," I said. I called Dave and Jack over, explained the defensive scheme, and went to the mound for my warm-ups.

Willie appeared from the dugout and tried to trot to his new position at third base. He had a little bit of a limp and was in obvious discomfort, but amazingly, as he passed the mound, he tipped his hat to me and said, "Keep it up, Mickey. Be the man."

Travis was right; the first batter I faced laid down a bunt along the third base line. I got a great jump on the ball and cut it off, however, my legs came out from under me and I slipped onto my backside. Somehow, I saw a charging Don out of the corner of my eye and tossed him the ball, and in a flash, he turned and whipped to Dave at first, just beating the runner. As Willie threw me the ball after it had gone around the horn, he said, "Smooth play, bro', there you go." I proceeded to strike out the next two batters to end the third.

In the top of the fourth, Jack got us an insurance run with a hit that is probably still being talked about in the mythology of Williamsport. He caught a low fastball with all of the power he could muster and sent the offering deep over the fence, nearly to the top of the huge hill, some eighty feet behind the 205' sign in dead center field. The tape measure home run brought the biggest cheer of the week from the massive crowd.

Thank God for Jack's homer, because in the bottom of the fourth inning, after having retired ten straight, the clean-up hitter for Mexico belted one of my hanging curves and deposited it half way up the hill behind David McKendricks in center. Don came out to the mound, not so much to console me as force me to think about the moment in front of me.

"Look, Mick, we're still ahead," my catcher said. "Keep throwing strikes. Make them hit you. Stay focused."

"I just left it hanging there for him," I said with disgust.

"Forget about it," he said. "One pitch at a time, okay?"

"You got it, Donny," I replied and reached down for the resin bag to dry off my sweaty palms while my catcher returned to his position. He squatted down and gave me the signal for a fastball on the inside corner. Slowly, I went into my windup and delivered a perfect pitch just inside the strike zone and the batter for Central America whiffed at it. Regaining my confidence, I then proceeded to strike out the Mexican outfielder on two perfect curve balls, ending the inning with my team still leading by one slim run.

The fifth inning was three up and three down for both squads. No harm, no foul. I gave up a couple of singles with two outs in the bottom of the fifth, but struck out a pinch hitter to end the Mexican rally. When I left the mound after my narrow escape, I remember thinking, "Only three more outs."

We came to bat in the top of sixth with a slim one-run lead, three outs away from playing for the world championship. After Danny hit a two out double to the gap in right center, Mexico brought in a relief pitcher. The new thrower, a slender, left-hander, faced Jack and threw a cork ball that our star first baseman connected with on the fists, sending a shot toward the gap in left center. The center fielder made a quick move on the ball, fielded it, and threw to the cut-off man in the infield, who turned and whipped it toward the catcher as Danny barreled down the base path toward home. He and the ball arrived at about the same time, and since the catcher was blocking the plate, instead of sliding, Danny surprised everybody and leapt over the catcher's passing tag and touched the extreme outside of home plate for an insurance run. However, as Danny ran over to our dugout for congratulations, we heard the crowd behind the Mexican dugout screaming out that Danny had missed the plate. We all returned to the dugout when the catcher for Mexico came in and tagged Danny on the shoulder with the ball. The home plate umpire, who had followed the catcher toward the dugout, pointed at Danny, stuck his thumb in the air and yelled, "You're out, number twelve. You missed the plate."

Two or three players had to restrain an irate Danny from running after the ump. In fact, our whole team went ballistic, including Travis, who stormed out of the dugout and confronted the man in blue who made the call. But alas, as blow the winds of destiny, it was not to be -- despite all our pleadings and name-calling, the play stood as ruled. So, instead of a cushion of two, we were back to the one-run lead again.

I walked to the mound in the bottom of the sixth with a ton of confidence after a talk with Travis. He had said, "We're going with what brung us. I'm not going to warm-up Fish or Bob. We'll save them for Sunday, Mick. Go win this game."

The first batter, in the last of the sixth inning, was an outfielder that I struck out on four pitches. As Don threw the ball to Ras for its pass around the horn, he yelled out, "Two more outs, Mickey. Let's get 'em."

The second batter up in the inning was their diminuitive lead-off hitter. After a first strike, the little guy swung wildly at my second pitch and the ball rolled very slowly down the third base line. Since Willie was playing deep due to his sprained ankle, it was my play. I made the decision to let the ball roll, hoping it would ultimately go foul. Unfortunately, the ball came to a stop directly on top of the foul line, which, of course, in baseball should actually be called the fair line. So now, they had a speedy tying run on first base, with only one out.

I picked up the resin bag to dry my hands, then licked my fingers, and toed the rubber. My first pitch to Mexico's next batter, the lefty, was a high inside fastball that he managed to fist weakly over Ras's head at shortstop, for a Texas Leaguer. As the dust settled, they had two runners on base and I was feeling a tightening around my neck. The tying run was on second, the winning run was on first, and there was only one out.

Travis called time out. Don and I joined him at the third base line for a strategy session. He said, "Listen, Mickey, you're pitching really well. They had two lucky breaks. But, you still have your stuff. Believe in it. Don, let's go after them, it's now or never, guys. Now, relax and breathe. Breathe." Then Travis smiled at both of us and added, "Isn't this fun, y'all?"

"I should have fielded that swinging bunt," I said with a frown.

"Mick, you made the right play. No way you could have got him at first anyway. But, forget about it, okay. Throw strikes -- make them work for everything. Stay confident. You're throwing really well."

The home plate umpire walked over and interrupted, "Excuse me, Coach, we still got a game here."

"Sure thing, Blue," Travis said, before facing the infielders and yelling, "You stay alert out there. Turn two."

I returned to the mound, got my signal from Don, and went into my windup. The pitch was inside, just above the knees. The burly right-handed batter took a mighty cut but caught the very top of the ball and sent a chopper bouncing off home plate down to Willie, who had to wait for gravity to bring the ball down before stepping on third for the force out, just beating the slide of the speedy runner from second. Willie checked the runners at first and second before asking for time. He limped over to the mound and handed me the ball.

"One more out, Mickey," he said. "Go after them bro." He patted me on the butt and returned to his position.

As Mexico's clean-up hitter strode to the plate, their manager asked for time and replaced the slow-running player at first with a pinch runner. I glanced at the batter who had hit me hard two times, including a massive homer in the fourth inning. I took a moment behind the mound to gather my composure and give myself a last pep talk, "Focus on the target, concentrate on the pitch." I toed the mound and looked in for the signal from Don. He called for a curve ball. I wound up and let go a good curve that the batter only watched as it dropped out of the strike zone. I overthrew my next fastball and it almost sailed over Don's head. Miraculously, he leapt up and grabbed it out of thin air with his catcher's mitt. Don called time and approached me on the mound, handing me the ball.

"Come on, Mick, throw strikes, let's not lose him, okay."

He returned to his position and signaled for another fastball. As I was finishing my wind up, I slipped off of the pitcher's rubber and the ball came out low, bouncing in the dirt in front of the plate for ball three. Travis yelled from the dugout, "Relax, Mickey, take your time. Hit the mitt."

I nodded toward my coach and then looked to Don for a sign. He put down one finger for the fastball. I wound up and threw a strike down the middle of the plate, and the clean-up hitter for Mexico swung mightily, but missed for strike one. The next pitch was one of the best curve balls I had thrown the whole day. The pitch had the batter bailing out before the ball broke off his shoulder and popped into Don's mitt for strike two.

Two outs, bottom of the last inning with a slim one-run lead, runners on first and second, and I had a three and two count on the best hitter from Mexico. I remember thinking, this was what I lived for -- this moment, where everything was on the line, and all I had to do was deliver one good pitch to win the big game. I took a second, grabbed the resin bag as Willie called out from third, "Come on Mickey, you can do it. One more pitch."

I bore down and, as I went into my wind-up, the only thing I could see was Don's catcher's mitt. I followed through and delivered a fast ball on the inside corner that the batter hit. The ball took off as a soft line drive toward David McKendricks in centerfield. Yes, I thought, it's over. Unfortunately, David, who was playing fairly deep, didn't get a very good jump. He came charging as fast as he could toward the sinking ball, but it landed just inches in front of his extended glove, skipped underneath and past him, and rolled on its way toward the fence.

With two outs, the runners were running on the pitch, and I felt a twinge of defeat as I ran to my back-up position behind the plate. Danny, backing up the play from left field, had to cover a lot of territory to retrieve the ball that eluded David and passed through his legs. By the time Danny had picked it up at the centerfield fence, one run had already crossed the plate and the speedy pinch runner from first was rounding third and heading for home. Willie cut off the ball at the pitcher's mound and wheeled and threw a laser shot to Don covering the plate. The ball and the runner reached home at the same time, but Don's tag was a second too late and their runner scored the winning run. With the suddenness of a lightning strike, it was over -- but it didn't end like it always had in my dreams.

The team from Mexico went delirious with their good fortune. As they ran toward the infield, collapsing in a pile of joy around home plate, I sank to my knees, covered my face with my glove, and was unable to hold back the tears. I looked up after a moment or two to see most of my teammates kneeling, groping to understand the shocking finality of what had just happened. The only player standing and walking toward our dugout on the field was David McKendricks, who seemed to be in a stupor. I stood up from where I had watched the play behind the plate, and walked around the pile of celebrating Central American's and approached McKendricks. He looked at me and shook his head.

"I can't believe it. I let down the whole team."

"David," I said, "it wasn't your fault. We all lost."

"I'm sorry, Mickey," he said, collapsing into my arms in tears. "I blew it for everybody."

"Listen, buddy," I said, sucking up my own courage. "Who would've thought we'd get this far, anyway? Remember what Travis says, 'We win and lose as a team.' You gotta shake it off."

I looked up at the stands and saw my brothers, stepfather, and mother applauding our efforts, despite the loss. Another flood of tears rushed forth. We experienced an uncontrollable agony and sense of grief, as if someone, or something, near and dear had just died. In a way, I guess it had.

After all, we had gotten so close -- so *damn* close.

CHAPTER EIGHTEEN

After our almost unacceptable last out defeat, the next few days in Williamsport reminded me how I felt when my first dog had died. In that instance, the dreadful despair lasted for several weeks. It wasn't until my brother brought home a new dog, a beast I named Napoleon, that my emotional condition recovered and I began to feel normal. Nothing else could compare with the blue feeling I was experiencing as I tossed and turned and tried to get to sleep the night after our dramatic loss at Lamade stadium. I believed we would be playing for the championship instead of watching it from the stands. However, a couple of days after our loss to Mexico, we were only spectators as we witnessed Kankakee, Illinois, win the national title, defeating the representatives from Central America by a score of 6 to 4. My mother had always warned me that "expectations can lead to disappointments." Unfortunately, I finally knew what she had meant.

For me, most of the bus ride home was a long, suffering journey. It had been the total antithesis of the trip north the week before. However, by the time we arrived in Austin, most of us, including me, could laugh at childish things again. It was strange but true. Even though Willie was on crutches, he was rallying the group to look forward to our upcoming football and basketball seasons. He inspired the rest of us with the resiliency of a confident young athlete, as he refused to let the sting of defeat push him down. Ironically, it was Willie on crutches who convinced us there would be plenty of more opportunities to be champions. After his pep talk, I was beginning to feel ready for the next battle.

As a twelve-year-old, I knew that Labor Day marked a rite of passage -- it would designate the end of childhood and the beginning of adolescence. The teenage years were looming. My friends and I were finished with elementary school and facing the uncertainty and mystery of O. Henry Junior High. Before we would attend our first class at our new school, we would celebrate this Labor Day as the end of our most glorious of summers, when life delivered us to the threshold of a wonderful dream, and we were shining All-Stars.

After three weeks of reflection since the disappointment in Williamsport, Pennsylvania, I concluded that we had actually overreached any expectations and what we had accomplished should be recognized and celebrated, not diminished by grieving. After discussing this very point with Danny, he convinced his parents to host a Labor Day picnic for the All-Star team, their parents and guests, at their vacation house perched above the shores of beautiful Lake Travis.

On the way to the party, with my stepfather driving west on Highway 71, my mother was in the passenger seat and I was in the back, observing the awesome Central Texas Hill Country. I was thinking how disappointing it was that Kitty was unable to attend because her family was vacationing in Ruidoso, New Mexico. Kitty's uncle had a horse entered in the All-American Futurity, the richest horse race in the world at the time, and her mother had told her she had to honor the significance of the event with her presence at Ruidoso Downs on Labor Day. I'll never forget her parting words on the telephone the day before, when she had told me to be careful and, laughing through the receiver, I heard her whisper to watch my "wandering eye." Even though she had forgiven me a long time ago for my moment of weakness that July afternoon at Barton Springs, that didn't mean she fully trusted me -- and I thought maybe she had something there.

We pulled up to the side of Danny's parents' A-frame structure, with its huge deck situated between some expansive live oaks overlooking Hudson Bend, and parked beside a slew of cars hidden among the low-lying cedars. I looked down the hill a hundred feet below and spotted most of my friends already swimming in the emerald waters of Lake Travis. As we were retrieving our floats and towels from the trunk of the car, I looked up at the sound of a vehicle backfiring as an old pick-up truck came down the driveway toward us. It stopped among a group of trees and I noticed Walter and Teresa Veils in the cab before spotting Willie and his classmate, Mary, jumping out of the bed of the pickup.

I was glad to see Willie's parents were finally getting the chance to share in the celebration of a team they, unfortunately, never got to witness, for even they didn't have to toil on Labor Day. When I locked eyes with Mary for the first time since I met her a month before, I felt a shiver go through my whole body. A warm sensation surrounded my skin and I had the feeling my face was blushing beet-red. My heart was suddenly pounding and my temperature was certainly on the rise.

Willie took a moment to study the connection between Mary and me, then he turned his attention to my parents, saying, "Mr. and Mrs. Lilly, I would like you to meet my parents, Walter and Teresa Veils."

Steve offered his hand to Walter. "It's a pleasure meeting you," he said as they shook hands. "I understand you didn't get to see your son play ball this summer -- that's a real shame. Willie's a very special player."

"Thank you," said Walter. "Those are mighty kind words, Mr. Lilly."

"Please, call me Steve, and this is my wife, Gracie," he offered.

My mother stepped forward and shook hands with the couple. "I'd like to add," she said, "that I've been watching Little League for the past nine years with my various son's teams -- and your boy, Willie, is the best I've ever seen."

Teresa, sporting a huge grin, replied, "Walter and I have to thank your son, Mickey, for believing that Willie would be accepted to play baseball with the white boys from Tarrytown. Without your son, I'm afraid our boy would still be playing stick ball on the dusty roads of Clarksville, and would have missed seeing those wonderful sights and playing those exciting games. Your son was a blessing."

"Heck, Teresa," I clarified. "Willie was born to play – all I did was get the ball rolling."

Willie chirped in, "Mickey's dad is a baseball coach at the next level for teens age thirteen to fifteen."

Steve smiled and said, "Willie, I hope to see you playing with us in the Austin Lions' Babe Ruth League next spring. It's going to be a pleasure watching you develop. And no matter which team you play for, Willie, I'm sure they'll feel lucky to have you."

I noticed a nervous glance between Teresa and Walter at my stepfather's last remark, but I put it off to the disappointment of not having witnessed their son's unbelievable accomplishments on our field of dreams. Within months that look would crystallize in a moment that would dramatically change the directions of Willie's life, and mine.

"We're all looking forward to baseball, Mr. Lilly. Thanks for the kind words," Willie said simply.

"How's the ankle?" my mother asked.

"Oh, it's fine, just like new. I just wish I'd been smarter when I was roundin' that base. It was dumb," Willie said softly. "We almost had it."

"Don't go blaming yourself, Willie," Steve said abruptly. "It was a freak accident, son. I agree, if it hadn't happened, things would've probably worked out a little better. But hey, as they say in the Big Leagues, that's the breaks. You learn, you grow, you move on. You boys have nothing at all to be ashamed of, and as you get older, you'll treasure what you accomplished as a team this summer."

Mary had walked over near me. I smiled at her. "Hi, Mary," I said after the lump in my throat dissolved.

"Howdy, Mickey, it's nice to see you again," she said. As she stepped out of the shadows and the sun illuminated her beautiful brown flowing hair which, in turn, highlighted her attractive, young face.

The seven of us approached the lake house and met Danny's parents, who tried to make the Veils feel as comfortable as possible. Danny's mother led them to the ultimate-view lounge chairs on the deck while his father treated his guests to cold beers and sausage appetizers fresh off his barbecue. My parents settled in next to Walter and Teresa, and everyone started to make small talk.

Willie, Mary, and I excused ourselves so we could join our friends frolicking in the waters far below. We made our way down along the rock steps that Danny and his brothers buried into the side of the steep hill, creating a walkway leading to their boat dock and floating island. When we reached the flat land leading to the beach, Willie challenged us.

"Race you two to the island," he urged.

We all ran toward the shore and dove into the chilly lake. We dodged teammates and friends and swam toward a floating deck that was tethered to a boulder on the shore by a large cable. Along the way, Mary grabbed my leg and pulled me back in a playful, suggestive attempt to slow my progress. It worked. Willie easily won the race. He was standing on top of the floating deck by the time Mary and I touched the ladder.

"Why did you do that?" I asked Mary as we treaded water next to the island.

"Because I wanted to," she said as she kissed me on the side of the cheek. "Do you have a problem with that?"

"It was a little bit of bad sportsmanship."

"I was talking about the kiss," Mary said with a grin.

"I didn't have a problem with that," I said, treading closer for another kiss. Mary splashed water in my eyes. My boiling blood helped me overcome the sting and I placed both hands on top of her head and pushed her under the surface. As Mary sank, she grabbed my leg and pulled me down after her. Underwater, she planted a kiss square on my lips, which surprised and titillated me so much that I immediately inhaled water and surfaced coughing it up like bad soup. Mary, on the other hand, broke the surface with a gurgling giggle. Suddenly, Willie was looming above us. He wagged his finger like an angry teacher and said, "You two are being naughty."

I didn't say anything as I reached up and grabbed his arm and pulled him into the water. I quickly returned my attention to Mary, who was climbing up the ladder. She was tan and lean and I was captivated by her sparkling aura. Suddenly, Willie pulled me under the water and I swallowed more of the lake. Before our horseplay got out of control, we heard Danny calling us over to the shore for a game of water football. Mary chose to stay and catch some rays on the island, so Willie and I left her and swam over to join the others. I did a backstroke most of the way keeping my eyes on Mary, who in turn, was watching me.

There was a submerged sand bar, only a foot or two deep that ran along the shore by Danny's lake house. It was thirty yards wide and forty yards long, which was absolutely perfect for a game of water football. I had always avoided tackle football and knew, with my gaunt physique, I would probably never attempt the game in which my older brothers shined. But, with the water serving as an equalizer to break your fall, I have to admit that tackle football on the sand bar was a hoot. We chose sides among the boys and girls who wanted to play and usually enjoyed a vigorous game. This day was no exception, and like most, it came down to last minute heroics. On our last attempt to score, Danny hit me on a perfect fly pattern down the shallow side of the field for a game-winning touchdown.

Danny's older brother, Thad, who was four years our senior, had been warming up their twenty-nine-foot-long Glastron motorboat. After the game ended and we were winding down from that madness, Danny asked if anyone wanted to go skiing. Willie, Mary, David McKendricks and his girlfriend, Stephanie, and I were the closest to the boat, and jumped in to join him for an excursion around the beautiful highland lake.

Lake Travis was sixty miles long and in places swelled to three or four miles wide. Most of the time, the lake was very choppy from the large number of watercrafts and the constantly windy conditions. However, Thad took us to the other side to Jogga's Bend, where we entered a huge cove protected from the southeasterly winds by cliffs rising from the shore. The cove was perfect and peaceful and the only movement I could see was a couple of ducks gently paddling across the surface. No other boats were present, and the water was 'smooth as glass' -- perfect for slalom skiing.

Danny threw out a line and turned to our group. "Who wants to go first?" he asked. "Mary?"

"Sure," she said as she jumped up. "Hey, Mickey, do you want to ski together?"

"Okay," I said with a little hesitation. Not having seen Mary ski before, I wasn't quite sure if she would be able to keep up with me. I had been skiing for three years now and was pretty comfortable on the water. "But, are you sure?" I added.

"Come on, I love to go under and over."

"Oh, you do," I said, playing along.

"I do," she said and dove into the water. I threw on a life vest like the one she was sporting and joined her in the water. Danny tossed a ski to each of us and the handles to the ski ropes.

Once we were ready, Mary and I gave the thumbs up. Thad put the boat into gear and we rose up out of the water like leaping dolphins. Mary immediately crossed under my rope and sprayed me in the face. She jumped the wake, flew out to the side of the boat and made a perfect turn. I thought to myself, "She is good." I jumped the other wake and we formed a symmetry of sorts as I was turning off the starboard side while Mary was mirroring me off the port. She gave me the signal to change positions and we turned, racing toward each other. When we were directly behind the boat I lifted my rope high enough to let her slide underneath. Distracted by watching her skiing prowess, I caught an edge as I passed through the boat's wake and took a mighty tumble, ending with a series of summersaults along the water before coming to an abrupt, splashing stop. Thad circled the boat around and brought Mary back to where she released and floated to a halt beside me.

"I wasn't paying attention to where I was going," I said, in a way of apology for my fall.

"Oh, and what were you looking at," she asked playfully.

"I think you know."

"How did it look?" Mary asked.

I chose to ignore the innuendo. "You ski really well. How long ago did you pick it up?"

"My sister, Diana, is a champion junior skier. She taught me a couple of years ago. You knew my sister and your brother, David, have gone out a few times. Right?"

"I didn't know. Is your sister as pretty as you are?"

"Why, thank you. But, no, Diana is truly beautiful."

We spent the next ten minutes skiing back and forth in the cove, before letting the others take their turns. David McKendricks and his girl, Stephanie, skied as a pair like we had. We had been spending a lot of time with David since Williamsport, and we'd largely forgotten the error he made during the crucial play in our elimination from the Little League World Series.

David turned out to be a very funny guy, and Danny, Willie, and I enjoyed his company. After Stephanie and David tired of the fun, they let Danny take his turn. Danny was every bit as good a skier as anyone our age, probably from the fact his family had the boat for about four years and he skied every chance he got. In fact, he taught me to ski when we were nine.

Willie, on the other hand, had never been in a ski boat in his life. He seemed a little disappointed when we told him he would have to ski on two skis at first, until he got the hang of it. Two skis offered better balance and required less technique, and was the usual manner in which people learned the sport.

In all of my short life, I had never seen anyone successfully get up on one ski, or a pair of skis, the very first attempt. After receiving pointers from Danny and me, Willie astounded us and kept his balance, actually surfacing on the pair of skis on his first try. He looked uncomfortable but he stayed up, until he tried to cross the boat's wake the first time and wiped out like a true neophyte. We instructed him to bend his knees a little as he passed over the bumps and on his second attempt, he was able to ski back and forth, gaining confidence with every pass. After a few minutes, he dropped off and we circled back to him, expecting him to get into the boat. Instead he floated us one of his skis and announced, "I'm going to slalom."

I tried not to laugh, since I had witnessed amazing feats by Willie in the past several months and wanted to give him the benefit of the doubt. Anything he tried, he seemed to master, but slalom skiing is a lot tougher to learn than it appears. As I leaned down to pick up the discarded ski, I looked Willie in the eye and said, "You are one crazy Colored boy."

"Maybe. Seems if I could get up on two, I ought to be able to ski on one. What do I do with the rope?" Willie asked.

Danny spoke up first, "Put it on the opposite side of your front foot."

"Which foot should I put forward?"

"Put your best leg in the front," I answered.

Willie arranged his feet in the slalom ski and Thad coasted forward to pull the ski rope taut. Willie gave the thumbs up and Thad punched the throttle, which launched Willie immediately over and out of his ski. He made another critical mistake when he fell. He forgot to let go of the rope and was dragged for twenty feet before he came to his senses and let go. Thad brought the boat around as Willie shrugged and said, "What did I do wrong?"

"Everything," I said. "You have to be ready for the lunge of the boat. Keep your knees bent a little, keep your weight back, and try to stay on top of the ski. Let the boat do the work and pull you up."

"Take out the slack, Thad," Willie shouted. "I'm getting up this time for sure."

Lo and behold, he did just that. On his second try, Willie not only surfaced on his ski, but stayed up for a couple of minutes. It was remarkable. My blood brother never stopped astounding me, through both his physical prowess and spiritual tenacity.

We returned to the boat dock at the lake house and Thad and Danny took out the next kids waiting to ski. Mary, Willie and I swam over to the island and relaxed on the deck.

While I was continuing to be enamored with the beautiful, brown-eyed Mary, Willie turned to me and whispered, "Man, have you thought about what you're gonna do about your Kitty?"

I immediately felt a sense of pain in my chest. I was ashamed that Kitty hadn't entered my psyche since the moment Mary jumped out of the truck. I said to Willie, "I guess I'll talk to her when she gets back from New Mexico. I think it may be time to move on."

"I think you already have," Willie said with a grin. "Mary is a terrific girl and she told me she really likes you. Good luck, my blood brother."

"I sure hate hurting Kitty on the first day of junior high," I said, "but something's happened here and I can't fight it."

Thad returned the boat to the dock after everyone had gotten their fills of water fun, and Danny's mother rang a triangle iron to signal that food was on the table. While we chowed down on ribs, chicken, and brisket, we reminisced about our glorious summer of baseball. Eventually, the conversation evolved to our anxieties concerning the start of junior high. No matter what elementary school we had attended, all of us would be going to O. Henry. Willie and I were looking forward to playing football and basketball together, alongside Danny and Jack. We all felt junior high was not going to be dull. Attending a school named after a world famous author gave us the realization it was going to be an education.

William Sydney Porter, behind Mark Twain and Edgar Allan Poe, is the third most widely read American author throughout the world. Dedicated to his surprise-ending style, he became known as the father of the American short story. He wrote, of course, under the pen name of O. Henry. During the late 1890's, while in his early twenties, O. Henry lived in Austin and worked at First National Bank as a teller. However, this particular job in Austin led to federal charges of bank fraud. After O. Henry had been on

197

the lam for a couple of years in New Orleans, he returned to Texas to face his fate and was sentenced to five years in a federal penitentiary in Ohio. He wrote many of the early works in prison, which were based on his Central Texas and North Carolina experiences that were to earn him a reputation as a master of coincidence. So, despite the fact that his two years in Austin were criminally-laden, the city showed respect for his works by naming a junior high school after him.

O. Henry Junior High was built in 1953 on the Westside, and for several years was segregated from the black teenagers of nearby Clarksville, though the school was located less than six blocks away. That had all changed a few years before, when Willie's older cousin, Don Baylor, and a couple of Clarksville friends integrated the junior high. The three black pioneers were accepted, for the most part, by all of the whites that went to O. Henry, as well as most of the teachers and administration. Of course, there had been rumblings in the community and Mr. Prentice, not surprisingly, had organized protests, but to no avail, as O. Henry Junior High was never segregated again.

Willie and I met at a pre-determined spot on the playground before our first day of O. Henry so that we could walk in together to demonstrate our bond of brotherhood. I told him I was going to have my talk with Kitty while walking her home after school, since she had called me the night before and made the date. We spotted Mary being dropped off by her sister at the back entrance to the school and Willie yelled for her to wait for us. After a brief conversation about how truly great the picnic had been the day before, we entered the building we were certain would be our home for the next few years.

As we walked into the cafeteria laughing, I immediately ran into Kitty just inside the door. There was an awkward moment as we came face-to-face with one another because Mary was arm in arm with both of us. I self-consciously jerked away from Mary out of guilt and gave Kitty a hug. Kitty smiled and cordially said hello to Willie and Mary. We joined a lot of our friends at a table in the center of the room as the principal, Mr. Wiley, approached the lectern set up on the center of the stage overlooking the new students.

He welcomed everyone to O. Henry and encouraged us to look him up personally, if we had any problems with our adjustment. He wanted us to enjoy junior high and be active in as many extracurricular activities as possible. He reminded us that we were at O. Henry primarily to learn, gain wisdom, enhance our knowledge, and to further our education in preparation for the higher levels to follow. Mr. Wiley concluded by challenging us to dedicate ourselves to our school, and all it had to offer, and that in so doing, we improved the chances that we would accomplish our ultimate goals.

We left the cafeteria and located our homerooms where we received our class schedules. The rest of the day went okay, though I did get lost a few times in the hallways searching for my next period class. The school had four wings and several annexes but I was never tardy -- we had about ten minutes between classes. Even with all the stops to talk to friends, there was plenty of time.

After the final bell rang at 3:00, I met Kitty at her locker where she was putting away her books. She reached down and grabbed my hand, led me down the crowded hallway, weaving through the many taller, older students, until we reached the back exit of the school. As we walked down the sidewalk along Exposition Boulevard, I tried to figure out what I was going to say to my soon to be ex-girlfriend. We walked in silence for a block or two before Kitty looked at me and said, "Mickey, I think we should break up."

"What?" I said, taken back by the surprise disclosure. "Why?"

"You don't have that special feeling for me anymore. You met someone else. Look, I have nothing against Mary. In fact, I really like her and I really like you. Anyway, I think you two want to be together, so I'm stepping out of the way."

"But, Kitty --"

"Mickey, it's over. I hope we can still be friends. Deal?"

"Are you sure," I said, hesitantly taking her hand, "this is what you want?"

"I'm sure," she said, as she wiped at some tears. She reached into her purse and retrieved the bracelet I had given her as a pledge of my affections six months before. She handed it to me and said, "I'll see you later, Mickey." Kitty turned down Enfield Road and started for her house a few blocks away. I watched her grow small in the distance, trying to realize what had just happened and why I felt so horrible. I walked down Exposition toward my house, confused and bewildered even though the end result was what I wanted. I was actually shocked that Kitty had beaten me to the punch.

As I cut through Jack's yard toward my house, I spotted Napoleon stopping another car in the middle of the street and attacking the bumper. I yelled out to the driver, "Floor it, you'll never hit him." The car lunged forward in uncertain lurches, then stopped. The driver screamed something about not wanting to kill the dog. I grabbed Napoleon's collar and drug him toward my driveway, enabling the lady to motor on down our street. "Napy, what are we going to do with you?" I asked, somewhat rhetorically.

As I opened the door to our house, my mother was preparing dinner in the kitchen. She looked up and asked, "How was your first day at O. Henry?"

"Very interesting," I said, not really wanting to talk at the moment because of my heavy heart.

"Do you like your teachers?" she asked.

"They're okay. All of them mentioned they taught my older brothers and expected great things from me."

"You do have some big shoes to fill. But, Mickey, you'll have to find your own way. Your brothers' reputations as school leaders can't make you one. You have to apply yourself and dedicate yourself and challenge yourself. Do you understand, son?"

"Yes m'am."

"I'm sure you will. Do you have any homework?"

"A little."

"Why don't you get it out of the way before dinner. Oh, and by the way, a letter came for you today. I left it on your desk."

I walked to my room, set down my textbooks on the bed, and opened my notebook. I looked at my notes from the teachers' assignments for the next day: read the first chapter of Texas History, complete the first lessons in the English and Algebra handbooks. Seemed like a lot of homework, to me. I looked for the letter my mother had mentioned, as it was rare that one ever had my name on it. I spotted the envelope and saw that it was very officially addressed to me from Major League Baseball. I tore open the envelope, opened the letter, and began to read:

COMMISSIONER FORD C. FRICK
MAJOR LEAGUE BASEBALL
4600 AVENUE OF THE AMERICAS
NEW YORK CITY, NEW YORK 10012

September 5, 1962

Mr. Mickey Charles
2904 Greenlee Avenue
Austin, Texas 78703

Re: World Series

Dear Mickey,

In honor of the accomplishments of the West Austin Little League All-Star team, it is my pleasure to invite you, your teammates, and the team's coaches to the fourth game of this year's Major League World Series. It will be played on or around, October 10, 1962. Of course, I do not know which teams will be competing at this time -- however I look forward to your attendance. You will have a chance to meet some of the players, be treated to an exclusive tour of the stadium, and enjoy prime seats for the fall classic. We will fly your team, coaches, and three additional chaperones to the host city, where all of you will be provided with suitable hotel accommodations for two nights.

I look forward to meeting you in person at a banquet honoring all the American Little League teams that were represented at Williamsport, which will be held the night before the game. Details will follow.

Congratulations on your success this season and best of luck in the future. Maybe someday I will see you playing at the professional level.

Sincerely Yours,

Ford C Frick

Ford C. Frick
Commissioner of Baseball

"Well, I'll be a monkey's uncle!" I shouted. I ran toward the kitchen, yelling for my mom at the top of my lungs, "I'm going to the World Series -- I'm going to the World Series -- I'm going to the World Series!"

CHAPTER NINETEEN

With the anticipation of attending a World Series game constantly on my mind, the next month went by slower than any other thirty days ever had in my short twelve years of living. I was consumed with the pennant races -- calculating who might win and what city our All-Star team would be visiting to attend Game Four of the Fall Classic. During the second week of September, the New York Yankees had a one-game lead on Detroit in the American League; in the elder circuit, the Los Angeles Dodgers had a three game lead on the San Francisco Giants. Willie and I were rooting for our favorite teams from the Big Apple and the City by the Bay, hoping we would get to see our namesake heroes play against one another.

We both tried out for, and made, the O. Henry seventh grade flag football team along with most of our fellow All-Stars. Eighth grade was the start of organized tackle football, but I made the decision not to participate at that level, especially after both my brothers suffered knee injuries during scrimmages in practice. I decided I would concentrate on basketball and baseball in the later grades. During seventh grade at O. Henry, the flag game was a gentler version of the contact sport and I was enjoying playing wide receiver and safety. Willie was our running back and Danny the QB. Jack, Stan and Ras anchored the defense. We had a bunch of talented athletes and figured to do well.

The load of homework at O. Henry was brutal. Many an evening after football practice, I would have to read two or three chapters in various subjects, maybe write a paper, do notebook exercises, and cram for tests. Another new twist was the "pop" quiz. Some teachers loved to pop one on you when you weren't expecting it, as he or she would proclaim, "Answer these question from the chapter you read last night." That's usually when I wished I hadn't fallen asleep before I finished that particular chapter. Yet, to discredit the "pop" quiz, most teachers gave enough hints the day before that only the idiots weren't ready for it.

I did have three very interesting teachers. The first was Mrs. Ward, my math teacher. She was a legend at the school having taught there since it opened and twenty years before that. All the while she never lost her tremendous sense of humor. Even though she was one who would surprise you with a legitimate "pop" quiz, it was a pleasure learning algebra and geometry from Mrs. Ward.

The real character of the teaching staff, Mrs. Henslee, was my speech and drama teacher. She used to sneak off to the teachers' lounge to smoke an occasional cigarette. To mask that fact from the students, Mrs. Henslee would douse her body with the strongest, most nose-shattering perfume. If Mrs. Henslee had recently passed down a hall of one of the wings, you knew it -- the aura of her scent permeated the area. However, she was one of the best teachers in the school, so everyone tolerated her idiosyncrasies.

Finally, there was Mr. Gober, whom all of the students called 'Chrome Dome' because of his completely bald head. He taught I.A., short for industrial arts, but all the kids just called it 'shop'. In addition to teaching us about tools and woodworking, he also coached the seventh grade flag-football team. He was a great guy and frequently smiled and joked with his students. Some of the kids at O. Henry, who had no proclivity for craftworks, took shop just to have Chrome Dome as their teacher.

One bright spot occurred a couple of weeks after Kitty and I broke up. I asked Mary to go steady and she accepted. We spent a lot of time with one another between classes and after school, until I had to report to football practice. We had lunch together every day at the same table with Willie, Jack, Stan, Ras, Danny, and Kitty, who were now an item. In fact, to my complete surprise, Kitty had rebounded and was going steady with Danny before I had even asked Mary. I was learning firsthand about the fickle hearts of adolescent heartthrobs. During the first weeks at O. Henry, Kitty and Mary were elected to the cheerleading squad. To my surprise and delight, their relationship developed into a budding friendship.

Mary wasn't quite as keen on the sports world as Kitty had been, but that wasn't why I was attracted to her. This became most evident one Monday at lunch when I was bragging to my friends about the Yankees winning the pennant during the previous weekend. Mary, sitting next to me as always, leaned over and whispered, "So, if they've already won, I don't understand what game your All-Star team will be watching?"

"Mary, that's the World Series," I said. "It starts next week. The Yankees won the American League. It's called a pennant, and they get to play the pennant winner from the National League. It'll probably be the Los Angeles Dodgers."

"Oh -- I see," she said softly.

"I heard that, Bro. Don't go countin' your L.A. chickens," warned Willie. "The Giants were four and a half games out with ten to play, but now, they're only one back. If they win tonight and the Dodgers lose, we have a playoff. I'm not counting out Buck and the boys."

The next morning I woke up and looked at the newspaper. Willie Mays had hit his forty-ninth home run of the season to lead the Giants to a 2-1 victory over the Houston Colt 45's. Meanwhile, the St. Louis Cardinals beat the Dodgers. During the next three days, the two teams would play a very competitive best of three playoff.

We followed each game like our lives depended on the outcomes. In the end, the Giants came out on top and earned the right to face the mighty Yankees in the 1962 World Series. To our great delight, we would get to watch our favorite Major Leaguers, Willie Mays and Mickey Mantle, face each other in a World Series. Willie was finally going to get to see his hero play in historic Yankee Stadium.

But in the interim, junior high life continued on in spite of our growing anticipation about the trip. Our O. Henry Mustangs played their first flag football game on the second Friday in October, against the cross-town rival, Lamar Junior High Scotties. The first time I heard "On O. Henry" before the game, I thought it was such an original and uplifting fight song, before

I discovered it was a direct rip off of "On Wisconsin." Our team dominated the game from the opening kickoff when Willie received the ball around the ten-yard line and weaved and darted his way ninety yards for a touchdown. Danny took over the game by completing his first ten passes, which happily led to two more scores. It started raining in the second half but didn't dampen our resolve, or slow us down, because we scored two more times on our way to a 33 to 6 victory. We didn't get to celebrate for very long because our time had finally arrived and our All-Stars had to rush home and pack for our six p.m. airplane flight to New York City.

Jack and Ras were experienced flyers having traveled extensively with their parents on vacations throughout the years. However, this was the first commercial flight for the rest of us and that fact was almost as exciting as the prospect of attending a World Series game. I gripped the seat with white knuckles as we took off in the Braniff 707 El Dorado Super Jet from Austin's Mueller Airport. I was fascinated as I watched my hometown shrink in size as we soared into the dense cumulus clouds that were still dropping rain on the River City.

When we reached our cruising speed of 600 miles per hour, at an altitude of 21,000 feet, the plane leveled off. Willie, Danny, and I were discussing what had already happened in the World Series, which had started a few days before in San Francisco. In Game One, Clete Boyer, the Yankees' third baseman, broke a 2-2 tie with an eighth inning homer to win the game. Whitey Ford earned his tenth World Series victory and extended his record setting scoreless streak to thirty-three and two-thirds innings, before Willie Mays knocked in a run in the fourth.

Game Two exposed the kind of up-and-down series it was going to be when San Francisco rebounded, led by Jack Sanford's three-hit shutout. Willie Mays was on second after a double to the gap in left center, when Willie McCovey provided the only runs Sanford would need, with a massive home run in front of 43,900 delirious Giants' fans.

Game Three was played at the same time we were beating the Lamar Scotties in flag football. It was played at Yankee Stadium in front of 71,434 fanatics. Mickey Mantle got two hits, including a double, and scored a couple of runs. Roger Maris had two hits as well, and knocked in the game-winning run in the seventh inning. The Yanks led the series two games to one, and there was a day off before the fourth game on Sunday in New York -- where we would be watching.

My first glimpse of New York City was one I'll never forget. I had recently filled an air-sick bag due to a little nausea from my adjustment to air travel and was feeling a little peaked. The sight of the massive skyscrapers covering the island of Manhattan brought on a speedy recovery from my condition. The tall buildings, lit up like jewels in the night, were beyond anything I had ever expected. As we made our final approach to Idyllwild International Airport in Queens, Travis pointed out Yankee Stadium in the Bronx off to the left side of the airplane. Knowing we would be attending a game at the historic ballpark, our collective blood pressures started to rise exponentially.

Our team along with Travis and Coach T, as well as our chaperones, Tildy, Jack's mother, and my mom, boarded a chartered bus for the trip from the airport to the city. As we crossed the East River on the Queensboro Bridge, we all marveled at the majesty of the city's illuminated skyscrapers. We were extremely impressed by the tallest building in the world, at the time, the Empire State building, rising out of the center of Manhattan to incredible heights as if it was watching over the other massive structures of the city.

We arrived at the New York Hilton Hotel on Avenue of the America's, which was located only several blocks north of the famous Broadway theater district. Willie, Danny, Ras and I shared a room with twin beds and two roll-aways. Our view from the tenth floor looked down on Broadway and 42nd Street and the massive billboards that advertised plays on The Great White Way. It was nearly midnight and the number of people on the streets astounded us -- we were in a city that truly never slept.

Saturday morning came awfully early. We were worn out from our first flight's late arrival and the building anxiety about game four. But, we were all soon revived after a mid-morning breakfast in the hotel's restaurant. Everyone was jazzed again as we boarded our bus for a trip to the Bronx and a preview tour of historic Yankee Stadium.

Our first stop was the New York locker room where we met the "Keeper of the Pin Stripes," Pete Sheehy, the only equipment manager for the Yankees since their Murderer's Row years of the 1920's. During his tenure, Pete witnessed nineteen world championships. He was happy to share stories with us about various events, that happened over the years while he revealed where Babe Ruth, Lou Gehrig, Joe DiMaggio, and other Yankee greats had dressed. Pete told us that many of the Hall of Fame Yankees from the past would talk to the current players before important games, like the one taking place the next day. He said he wouldn't be surprised if DiMaggio, Bill Dickey, or Johnny Mize was in attendance for Game Four. Showing us a typical locker with the cleaned uniform on a hanger, Pete explained that the famous Yankee pin stripes first appeared on April 11, 1912, when the team, then known as the New York Highlanders, played in Harlem at Hilltop Park. It was that same year when local sportswriters coined the term 'Yankees' when describing the team. The nickname stuck and it was officially made the moniker for the team several years before they settled into their new home at Yankee Stadium in 1923. Pete said the interlocking NY insignia on the caps had come from a design originally created by Louis B. Tiffany, the famous jeweler on Fifth Avenue, to honor the death of the first NYC policeman killed in the line of duty in 1877. The Yankees adopted the insignia and placed the interlocking NY on their caps prior to the 1922 season.

Pete introduced us to our tour guide, Mr. Matson, who led us down a long tunnel to the Yankee dugout. I sat in the exact spot where I'd seen The Mick sit during the Saturday Game of the Week. Looking out on the field for the first time from the perspective of the bench was a numbing experience. I sat frozen, trying to picture myself on the mound in front of all those cheering fans. I could almost hear the roar.

My fantasies were interrupted when Mr. Matson took us to the press box area, where we sat in the seats of some famous sports journalists and looked out on the colossal 'House that Ruth built'. One after another, we watched as our names flashed across the country's first electronic scoreboard. I smiled like a circus clown when it flashed:

NOW PITCHING FOR THE NEW YORK YANKEES
MICKEY CHARLES

My mother snapped a picture of it. I would proudly display the framed photograph, as well as other souvenirs from the World Series trip, on the walls of my bedroom throughout my teenage years.

We watched the maintenance crew fire up their mowers and cut the Kentucky blue grass to the exact length of 1-1/2 inches, in a checkerboard design. Our tour guide informed us that the Yankees' red, white, and blue logo painted on the field behind home plate, was created in 1946 to honor the patriotism of all the baseball players who participated in World War II.

Next, we followed our guide down to the field and around the warning track to the deepest part of the stadium in left centerfield. Coined by the New York sportswriters as "Death Valley," the fence was 461 feet from home plate. In front of the fence, the Yankee's organization and New York sportswriters had erected three stone and bronze monuments honoring the lives of Lou Gehrig, Babe Ruth and Miller Huggins. We took turns reading them:

Miller James Huggins
Manager of the New York Yankees, 1918-1929
Pennant Winners 1921-22-23-26-27-28
World Champions 1923, 1927, 1928
As a tribute to a splendid character who made
priceless contributions to baseball and on this
field brought glory to the New York Club of the
American League. This memorial, erected by
Col. Jacob Ruppert and the baseball writers of New York
May 30, 1937

Henry Louis Gehrig
June 19, 1903 – June 2, 1941
A Man, a gentleman and a great ball player whose
amazing Record of 2,130 consecutive games should
stand for all time. This memorial is a tribute
from the Yankee Players to their beloved
captain and teammate.
July 4, 1941

George Herman "Babe" Ruth

1895 – 1948
A great ball player, A Great Man, A Great American
Erected by the Yankees and The New York Baseball Writers
April 19, 1949

I surveyed the stadium from the depths of Death Valley and marveled once more at the sheer size of the ballpark. I was standing there, in the presence of the ghosts of greatness, and I still couldn't believe we were going to watch a World Series game in this Taj Mahal of baseball diamonds. My mother took a picture of Willie and me, standing in centerfield, arms around each other's shoulders with the stadium as the backdrop. After snapping the picture, she said, "Well, boys, what do you think?"

"Mrs. Lilly," Willie said with a smile, "I think I know what Heaven looks like."

"Yeah, but for your Giants, I'm afraid it's going to look a bit more like a big field in Hell."

"Oh, Mickey," my mother growled. "Why did you go and say that?"

"I was bustin' his chops, Mom. He's a Giants' fan."

"You still shouldn't be so rude."

"It was no offense, Mrs. Lilly," Willie said. "Besides, I'll bet my Giants shut him up tomorrow by winning Game Four."

"How much, Willie? Name your price," I responded.

"How about a hot dog and a bag of peanuts?"

"Throw in a cotton candy and you've got a bet."

Willie stuck out his hand and we shook to seal the deal. My mother looked at us and said, "I don't know what I'm going to do with you two."

Mr. Matson called everyone together and led us down the warning track toward left field and under the grandstands. We followed him down a tunnel and found ourselves outside the stadium where our bus was waiting. We all thanked the guide and boarded the charter to set off on a tour of the sights of Manhattan.

We stopped at Rockefeller Center and were amazed by the size of Radio City Music Hall with its 7,000 seats. We walked across Fifth Avenue, away from the seventy-story-tall RCA building, the home of NBC TV, to St. Patrick's Cathedral. Even as a twelve-year-old, I recognized that the collection of stained glass windows, with their stories of the Bible adorning all sides of the immense place of worship, was truly beautiful and quite awe-inspiring.

We re-boarded the tour bus and were driven to the Fulton Street Fish Market. We disembarked and walked past the hundreds of fishmongers, toward a restaurant underneath one of the two great towers of Maine granite that supported the magnificent Brooklyn Bridge. The one hundred and forty-year-old Sweets, at number two Fulton Street, was as Trudy described to all of us, "the best place to eat fresh fish in the world." Entering through two twenty-foot aged glass and wood doors, we walked up twenty steps to the second floor restaurant. We were led past huge tanks of future meals swimming in salt water, waiting to be chosen by the customers lined up for lunch. Our group was led to a couple of long tables set up at the end of the room and we chose our seats.

Willie, sitting across from me, faced the window and gazed out at the magnificent steel and stone structure stretching over the East River connecting Brooklyn to Manhattan. He looked a little in awe and said, "Would you look at that bridge."

"It's really something," I said.

"Never seen nothing like that in Texas."

When our meals arrived, I looked down on a fish, larger than the plate it was served on, with its head intact. It seemed as if the fish was staring at me and it put me a little off eating it. Willie looked up at me and said, "Never seen nothing like that in Texas."

I looked up from the fish I thought was looking at me and focused on my buddy across the table. I spotted two customers behind him, a Negro man and a Caucasian woman, walking hand-in-hand, following the maître d' leading them to their table. The interracial couple remained affectionate as they sat down across from each other. I leaned into Willie, indicating for him to look around, and whispered, "Never seen nothing like that in Texas."

Willie slowly turned and glanced at the couple, then turned to me and said, "Texas ain't ready for that."

After a moment, we reluctantly took a fork to the evil-eyed fish. After the first bite of the sea bass dissolved in my mouth, I had no problem devouring the delicious fish as fast as I could. None of the others had any trouble, either.

After the unique lunch, we were back on the bus for a ride to the American Museum of History, on the West side of Central Park, where we would be treated to a unique experience at the Hayden Planetarium. In 1935, Charles Hayden had donated $150,000 to aid in the construction of a facility to display the heavens. A plaque at the entrance, dedicated to the philanthropist, stated that he hoped the planetarium would "provide the public a more lively and sincere appreciation of the magnitude of the universe -- everyone should have the experience of feeling the immensity of the sky and one's own littleness."

After we settled into our reclining seats and leaned back to look at the brilliant white domed ceiling, the room went dark and we suddenly found ourselves traveling through the planets of our solar system and the mammoth Milky Way galaxy. I was thrilled and exhilarated by tripping through the light fantastic of stars and planets in our infinite Universe. For the first time in my life, I was able to comprehend a fleeting sense of something beyond our collective imaginations. In fact, I was amazed how much I had learned from our one-day journey through the past, present, and future, in New York City.

We left the planetarium and returned to our hotel for a quick shower and change of clothes before we went down to the Art Deco lobby of the Hilton and waited for everyone to gather. When the rest of our group arrived, we walked a block south and two blocks west to Gallagher's Steak House on 52nd Street. We were to attend a banquet honoring all of the American teams recently represented at Williamsport.

The famous eatery was established as a speakeasy in 1927 when mobster Jack Solomon's moll, Helen Gallagher, an ex-show girl, requested a place to host a party every night. Solomon found a site in the present location, opening it to conduct his bookie business while his mistress played host to her many friends and their drinking demands during Prohibition. Since 1933,

Gallagher's had evolved into an old-fashioned, manly steakhouse, catering to the sports, entertainment, and political stars of the day.

We were ushered into the elegant banquet hall known as the Trophy Room. The All-Star squads we'd seen from Hilo, Kankakee, Manchester, and San Juan greeted us, as we were the last team to arrive for the banquet. After exchanging pleasantries with our fellow Little Leaguers in the sumptuous Trophy Room, we were escorted to circular tables where we took seats with our names printed on placards that added a personal touch to the elegant designer china and shining sets of silverware. Signed photographs of Broadway, movie, and sports stars of the past four decades adorned the walls. The tables were covered with red and white checkerboard cloths and chandeliers shimmered from several positions illuminating the grand dining hall. Sitting on each china plate was a 1962 World Series cap, in our size, as commemoration of our accomplishments. I tried mine on and it was a perfect fit.

At one end of the room was a platform with a table looming over us that had a lectern and seats for seven people. After a few minutes, the Commissioner of Baseball, Ford C. Frick, walked up to the dais and approached the microphone, where he blew in to it to see if it was working properly.

I overheard Trudy, sitting at the next table, talking to Travis.

"If that had been me," she said, "there would have been feedback or a small explosion." Travis shared a laugh with her.

"My name is Ford Frick," the Commissioner said, "and I would like to welcome all of the Little League All-Star teams represented here this evening. Major League Baseball is proud to host you young ballplayers in honor of your deeds on the Little League diamonds this past summer. I would especially like to congratulate the team from Kankakee for winning the World Championship last month in Williamsport."

We all applauded the Illinois team.

"But I want all of you kids to know, you are all winners. Congratulations to all of you for a great season. Give yourselves a round of applause for your conduct on and off the field, which ultimately earned you this honor."

Another round of hoots and hollers went up from the crowd.

"We have a treat for you players tonight," he continued. "Here to honor your accomplishments as Little Leaguers, we have three representatives from each team playing in the World Series this year, and I would like to introduce them to you at this time. First of all, from the San Francisco Giants, we have Jack Sanford, Willie McCovey, and Willie Mays."

As the three Greats appeared from a door behind the dais, they waved at the crowd and took seats at the front table. Willie, who was sitting next to me, punched me in the ribs, saying in total awe, "Willie Mays."

After the applause ended, Mr. Frick said, "And, from the world champion New York Yankees, we have Bobby Richardson, Whitey Ford, and Mickey Mantle."

One-by-one the great Yankees appeared on the platform. The last to appear was The Mick, dressed in a suit and tie, sporting his classic smile while holding a cocktail in his hand. I immediately rose to my feet and applauded my favorite player of all time.

After the commotion had settled, Mr. Frick said, "Major League Baseball would like to congratulate all of you young ballplayers."

The six big league ballplayers rose, and, with Mr. Frick, applauded our efforts. Mickey Mantle was clapping for *me*. Wow, that moment was really huge, something beyond all comparison to anything I'd ever felt before. I hoped before the evening was over that I would get to meet him.

"In conclusion," Frick continued, "I would like all of you to enjoy this evening and tomorrow's Game Four. After dinner, these six great Major Leaguers will be available for a short autograph and meet session."

Willie and I looked at each other and simultaneously said, "Neat!"

Frick concluded, "All right everyone, let's dig in."

The eating frenzy that followed was a blur of jumbo shrimp cocktail, horseradish sauce, lobster, and pork chops. Then came a new delight -- New York Cheese Cake. It melted almost before it hit my mouth, however, the strawberries and whipped cream piled high on top kept it all in perfect balance. Texas Barbecue was a distant memory -- I had experienced feedlot nirvana in the Big Apple.

After dinner, the teams lined up behind their managers and filed by the Major Leaguers like a reception line for a wedding. One by one, kids shook hands with the greats, some talked for a while and almost all had their commemorative World Series caps signed by the star players.

Willie was in front of me in line and when he reached Willie Mays, the great centerfielder looked him in the eye and said, "You're Willie Veils, right?"

"Yes sir!" Willie almost shouted, as he was stunned that his hero knew his name.

"I have heard some stories about you, young man. Your coach told me you handled some tough racial situations back home with courage, dignity, and ability. Congratulations, son."

"Thank you, Mr. Mays," chirped Willie. "I'm glad you think so. You're my favorite player, ever."

"Then let me give you a couple of pointers, son. Back in 1950, after I signed with the Giants, they sent me to a minor league team in Hagerstown, Maryland. The people in the stadium hadn't seen no black folk playing on the field, ever. The first game -- well, you can't imagine all the ugly, mean, rotten words they shouted out at me that day. Some were downright hurtful. I'm sure you know what I'm talking about, don't you, son?"

"Yes sir, I've heard a earful."

"You see. Like you, I never lost my cool. I had two doubles and a homer, and by the end of that first game, some of those same people who were shouting hate from the grandstands, were actually cheering me on. From time to time, even after I joined the Big Show, I suffered the ignorance of prejudice. But, I never got in a fight over racism. I always kept my cool. You understand what I'm saying, son?"

"I should let my playing shut them up."

"That's it, Willie. In order to be the best person you can be, you have to be completely dedicated. You have to work hard and be willing to accept constructive criticism. If you can't do that, you won't be able to do this. But, if you work hard and stay cool, who knows, maybe you could make a living as a ballplayer, too -- and trust me on this, son, it's the greatest job in the world."

"Thank you, Mr. Mays," Willie whispered. "Thank you so much. Wait 'til my folks hear about this. Could you sign my cap?"

"Sure thing, kid," Mays said and signed the bill on Willie's cap. "But, call me Buck."

"Thanks, Buck."

"You're welcome, son. Remember, Willie, stay cool and always work harder than the others." Mays winked and extended his hand to Willie.

"Yes, sir. I will."

After shaking hands with his idol, Willie slowly moved on to McCovey sitting to Mays' right and I stepped up to the Giants captain.

I offered my cap to the Say Hey Kid, he took it, and signed the bill. "Thank you, Mr. Mays," I said as I shook his hand.

Next, we approached the Yankees' table. I felt a surge of energy throughout my body as I stuck out my hand to Mickey Mantle. He took it firmly, looked me in the eye, and smiled, "What's your name, young fella?"

"Mickey Charles," I said, mesmerized by my proximity to my hero.

"Really? I like the name, kid."

"You were my dad's favorite ball player. He named me after you."

"You know, my father taught me the game. Is that how you learned to play?"

"No. My brothers taught me," I said. "My dad died when I was four."

"Sorry to hear about that, Mickey. I lost my father, too." Mantle took my cap and prepared to sign it, which put me into a virtual state of grace.

"What position do you play, Mickey?" he asked.

"Pitcher," I said.

He signed the inside bill of my cap and handed it to me. I read it immediately.

To Mickey Charles
Keep throwing strikes
Mickey Mantle

"Thanks Mr. Mantle," I said. "Good luck tomorrow, I've got a big bet on the Yankees."

The Mick took a sip of his cocktail and smiled. "Remember three things, son. Stay away from excessive gambling, drinking, and loose women and you'll be okay."

"Yes, sir," I said taking his advice as Gospel. He shook my hand again and gave me a wink in the process.

Goose bumps returned to my arms and legs, and the line of guys behind me sort of pushed me along, and I suppose I stumbled on down the line, but as far as I could tell, I was floating.

CHAPTER TWENTY

Walking in New York City is very stimulating. It is similar to strolling through a valley surrounded by mountains covered with snow, while being serenaded by the constant noise of traffic. In place of the ridges and peaks are the skyscrapers rising toward the sky like monoliths dedicated to corporate America. As we strolled toward the subway station at eleven in the morning, I couldn't stop staring at the massive structures, continually amazed by their dimensions.

At Columbus Circle on 59th and Central Park West, we descended the stairs to the subway and, using tokens given out by Trudy at the bottom of the steps, we entered the station through metal turnstiles. We walked up some stairs, over the tracks and down, and waited on the Uptown platform for a B or D train to arrive. The smells and sounds of the subway stations in NYC were extremely distinctive.

There was a lone saxophone player blowing his horn on the Downtown platform across the tracks. The eerie rhythms from the instrument lilted through the rafters of the station giving the place a ghostly sense. In the distance, I could hear squealing brakes and screeching train wheels rolling across the metal tracks. Lights from a train could be seen from a long distance as it approached. The beam of light was hypnotic, yet, appearing in the darkness, an illuminated "A" could be seen in the engineer's front window of the train. Travis reminded everyone we were looking for a B or D -- that the A train would take us to Duke Ellington's Harlem rather than the

Bronx. So, we waited a few more minutes before a B train lumbered noisily to a stop in front of us. We all found seats spread around the compartment. Everyone else on the subway was wearing Yankee caps, so I assumed they all were attending the game with us.

A swift eight minutes later, after passing under the Harlem River, the train surfaced above ground and arrived at Yankee Stadium in the Bronx. Looking out the window to our right, we were able to see the Mecca of baseball from the right centerfield fence. We could see the Giants taking batting practice and running in the outfield. From this great distance they looked just like a Little League team warming up before a game. We walked down the platform steps to River Avenue and, following Travis and Trudy, we crossed the street to an entrance below a huge Coca-Cola sign.

Trudy then led us to our section situated high above left field in the upper deck. Our seats were on the bottom three rows of the elevated grandstands. We were directly behind left field, just inside the foul pole. Perfect, I thought, if The Mick pulls one of his tape measure homers from the right side of the plate, one of us might get another chance for a souvenir of the trip.

It didn't take long before my desires were met, when the Yankees took the field for batting practice. Mickey batted from the left side of the plate because he would be facing Juan Marichal. The right-handed Marichal would be making his first start of the series in Game Four. The Giants' ace pitched the victorious last game of the pennant playoff with the Dodgers, and he required a necessary four days of rest between starts. During an impressive batting practice power display, Mick deposited six balls in the right field bleachers in his first ten swings -- a couple of which reached the upper deck, over 400 feet from home plate. Then, the Yankees brought in a left-handed batting practice pitcher. Mick switched to the right side of the plate and we all stood and waited in silent anticipation of a few massive missiles from the bat of the great slugger. He didn't disappoint us -- on the first two pitches he hit mighty shots that headed for our section. The first fell short of the third deck, and my extended glove, but by only a few feet. The second, Don was lucky enough to grab with his bare hands. Naturally, I was filled with envy and the remainder of the warm-up period was a blur until game time arrived.

"Ladies and Gentlemen," Yankee announcer, Bob Sheppard barked, "to throw out the ceremonial first pitch, please welcome the Attorney General of the United States, Robert Fitzgerald Kennedy."

The younger brother of the President strolled to the rubber, made his awkward wind up, and threw a perfect strike to Elston Howard. The first black Yankee, who replaced the legendary Yogi as catcher the year before, returned the ball to "Bobby" and they shook hands and posed for photos by home plate.

"Ladies and Gentlemen," the announcer reported, "to sing the national anthem, RCA recording star, Tony Bennett." The suave singer approached a microphone on the field and belted "The Star-Spangled Banner" while 70,000 fans and the players on the field joined him.

At exactly 3:10 p.m., Eastern Standard Time, the New York Yankees took the field and the feeling in the stadium was nothing less than electric. Whitey Ford strolled to the mound for his second start of the Series. He already had the record for most wins in World Series games and had been practically invincible in October, so I was feeling pretty good about my bet with Willie. We were sitting next to one another as Mickey Mantle took his position in centerfield and started throwing warm-up tosses with left fielder, Tommy Tresh. As my team warmed up and prepared for the first pitch, I took in the view and listened to the various chants from the crowd. I soon learned the typical New York fan was very vocal and might say anything. And, that was only a small part of the fun.

The stadium was decorated with red, white, and blue bunting that hung from all of the decks around the field. A light breeze was lifting the flags of the American League teams and Old Glory, which were perched on top of the facades. The temperature was perfect; the sky was clear blue. It was a beautiful day for baseball.

The first four innings were fairly routine for the two aces on the field, both shutting down their opponents. During the same span, Willie and I consumed two hot dogs and shared a bag of peanuts and, since they didn't sell cotton candy, we each ate another hot dog. I remember thinking Willie might've been right with his divine reference about the stadium, for it felt like I was experiencing Heaven on Earth.

In the top of the fifth, Marichal led off. Ford accidentally threw too far inside and hit the Puerto Rican on his pitching hand. When a pitched ball racing at ninety miles per hour hits a finger wrapped tightly around a bat, broken bones are usually a result. We didn't know if this was the case with the Giant ace, but the injury was enough to force Alvin Dark to replace him with a pinch runner.

"It's over, buddy," I said somberly. "Without Marichal, you can stick a fork in it; the Giants are done!"

"You should know by now, it ain't over till it's over," Willie responded, quoting the famous Yogism. "We thought it was over against Mexico, didn't we?"

I couldn't respond to the stinging reminder.

The next inning, Clete Boyer knocked in two runs, so Houk decided to bat Yogi for Whitey in an effort to create a big inning. With Whitey lifted for a pinch hitter, neither of the starting aces were around for the ultimate outcome. Don Larsen, an ex-Yankee hero, was now a Giant, and Alvin Dark brought him out of the bullpen to face his old battery mate. The usually free-swinging Yogi showed patience and worked Larsen for a walk, which loaded the bases. Tony Kubek stepped into the box and sent a slow roller down the first base line. Cepeda scooped it up and tossed to Larsen, who was covering the bag, to end the rally. The game went to the seventh inning with the score tied two all. After gorging ourselves for the first six innings, Willie and I were finally full and had settled into our seats expecting a barnburning finish.

The top of the seventh, however, took all of the drama away. Ralph Houk brought in several relievers during the inning to try and stop the tide, but the Giants were able to load the bases on a walk, a double, and another base on balls. The San Francisco second baseman, Chuck Hiller, strode to the plate with a modest .154 Series batting average. It is not unusual in World Series games for the weaker hitting players to step-up and provide something special in a crucial moment. That's the beauty of baseball. On a given at bat, or with a given pitch, historical data can fall victim to the uncertainties of a round ball colliding violently with the rounded surface of a bat. Anything can happen.

And in this case, it did, with the bases loaded. In front of my disbelieving eyes, Chuck Hiller hit the first pitch from the Yankee left-handed reliever, Marshall Bridges, and deposited it over the short porch in right field for a grand slam home run. In the history of the World Series, there had only been eight Grand Slams, six of which were by Yankees. Hiller's was the first ever by a National League player giving Larsen, and the Giants, a six to two lead going into the bottom of the seventh. On the sixth anniversary of his legendary World Series perfect game, Larsen's strong relief appearance proved up to the task, and he held the Yankees to only one more run. The game ended with a surprising score: Giants 7 -- Yankees 3.

I slowly, perhaps even dramatically dragged out a loose dollar bill from my pocket and gave it to Willie to pay off our bet, but I couldn't really feel disappointed about the overall experience. Those few days were so mesmerizing, that despite my momentary unhappiness with the Yankees' loss, I was still living a fantasy.

After all the anticipation of watching our heroes, it was ironic that both Willie Mays and Mickey Mantle had been relatively quiet at the plate during the game. However, both contributed with long running catches in Death Valley to quell rallies. Willie and I found special meaning as we watched them play in the Fall Classic. From that day on, we no longer watched distant images of our heroes. We watched men we knew, savored the words of wisdom they shared with us, and could still feel the strength of their grips as we shook their hands. Willie and I had lived a dream bigger than any twelve-year-old had a right to expect.

CHAPTER TWENTY-ONE

For the sports fanatic, October is arguably the best month of the year. You have the World Series at center stage, pro football has started, pro hockey and pro basketball are in pre-season, and the pageantry that is college football is in full swing. One of the perks of attending junior high in Austin was the ability to obtain a seat in the end zone for Texas Longhorn football games at Memorial Stadium. For a grand total of fifty cents, a student at any junior high in the city could purchase a ticket for even the most popular games. The seats, set-aside for the teenagers, were located in the horseshoe part of the stadium that was affectionately known as the "Knothole" section.

On an absolutely perfect fall day for football, Willie, Danny, Kitty, David, Stephanie, Mary, and I were sitting together in the Knothole section at the Longhorn/Arkansas Razorback game. It was the first Saturday after our All-Star team had returned from our exciting New York journey. We were all enjoying the stunning October afternoon, and we laughed and joked among ourselves during the pre-game entertainment on the field. When the team appeared from under the stadium, the crowd went bananas, and everyone in our group exchanged high fives. We all raised our hands and flashed the 'Hook 'em Horns' sign while we sang "Texas Fight" like mad fanatics. Our frenzy mixed with the greater chaos of 60,000 alumni and UT students in the fully packed stadium. Mary leaned over and gave me a hug and kiss on the cheek and said, "This is so much fun."

"How could it miss?" I said.

"I know, I know -- number one in the nation, against number seven."

"Very good. You're reading the sports pages now?"

"Hardly. Willie gave me some background on the teams while we rode the bus to meet y'all," she replied and then giggled. I was completely caught in the vortex of her aura when Willie elbowed me in the ribs.

"This is going to be a great game!" he said as he held up his hand for another high five.

I couldn't have been any happier than I was in that moment. My Yankees were playing in the World Series, my Longhorns were number one in the country, my seventh grade flag football team was undefeated, and I was totally infatuated with my new girlfriend. In addition, I had developed what I thought would be lifetime friendships with my fellow All-Stars from our time together during our incredible summer winning streak. The experience of traveling around the country with my mates had enlightened and matured me. I was feeling on top of the world.

A field goal by Arkansas on the opening drive of the game was the only score at halftime. Since then, the top ranked defenses in the country shut down the offenses completely. Willie and I walked down under the stands to get some soft drinks. Standing in line, surrounded by the crazed Texas football fans, we were creatures of narrow habit and were still thinking about baseball and discussing the present situation going on in the City by the Bay.

The World Series should have been over by now but unrelenting rain in San Francisco had delayed game five by a day. When the game was played the previous Tuesday, Tommy Tresh and pitcher Ralph Terry led the Yankees to a 5 to 3 victory. Game six was delayed several more days because of torrential downpours on the West Coast. After two postponements, the Giants' management hired three helicopters to hover over the field six feet above the ground in an attempt to dry it off enough for the game to be played. After an hour, the umpires and coaches met at home plate and decided the field was in reasonably good condition and they would continue the series. Willie tried to convince me that it was all in their plan.

The sixth game was decided on a rare throwing error by the normally steady fielding Yankee ace, Whitey Ford. When he tried to pick-off Mays at first in the sixth inning, the lefty threw wild and the ball traveled all the way to the corner in right field where Maris had to retrieve the ball. The Giants scored two unearned runs and with left-hander Billy Pierce throwing a three hitter, the Bay Area team evened the series at three apiece with a 5 to 2 victory. Game seven would be played on the following Monday and Willie and I were hoping our teachers would let us watch the deciding game on television at school. With our hearts saturated temporarily with World Series updates, Willie and I decided to return to our seats for the football game. Both of us were sure the remainder of the game would be different.

The second half continued to be a nail-biter. With the score still 3 to 0, the Longhorns got the ball with six minutes left in the fourth quarter, after an Arkansas punt went out of bounds on the Texas ten-yard line. Duke Carlisle, UT's quarterback, led the Horns on their first sustained drive of the afternoon. Coming right at us in the Knothole section, we watched as the Horns ran nineteen plays, covered 87 yards, and arrived at the Arkansas three-yard line with thirty-six seconds left in the game. On the next play, Tommy Ford plunged through the line for the winning touchdown, setting off a melee in the stands. Everyone went bonkers. It was as if the stadium lifted off the ground from the explosion of elation for the dramatic, last-second, come-from-behind victory.

After the game, our group headed for Dirty Martin's, a famous hamburger hangout on the Drag. That famous section of Austin included a stretch of stores, bars, and restaurants that were located along Guadalupe Street on the West side of the UT campus. To our right, the top of the twenty-six-story library tower was lit up bright orange, which was the University's way of announcing another pigskin victory for the Longhorns. On the Drag, Mary and I walked hand in hand alongside Willie. We had started to refer to ourselves as "The Three Musketeers," as we had become inseparable during the first months of junior high school. "All for one and one for all" had become our rallying cry, just like the famous swordsmen from the Alexander Dumas' story.

At Dirty's, we ordered cheeseburger combinations and cokes at the outdoor picnic tables by the entrance. While we waited for our food, we watched the college co-ed carhops float back and forth between the many vehicles, as they served the parked customers. We were all a little spent, emotionally, from the super-charged gridiron classic we had just witnessed. When our food arrived, no more conversation took place until all burgers, fries, and onion rings had been consumed. As soon as we were finished, my brother showed up to give me a ride home. I asked if he could drop Willie and Mary by their homes as well, and he agreed. We piled into his throaty 444 Sports Fury and were in Clarksville in a flash. As Willie was unloading, we reaffirmed our plans to watch the World Series finale together at O. Henry on Monday. David drove Mary and I to her house, which was a couple of blocks away on the other side of the tracks from Clarksville. I walked her to the front door of the house, and looking back to make sure my brother wasn't watching, I leaned in and gave Mary a quick kiss.

She grabbed my arm, "You better call me later."

Suddenly she pulled me to her and planted a passionate kiss on my lips. I forgot, momentarily, about my brother and fell into the kiss.

As we parted lips, I smiled and said somewhat breathlessly, "I'll -- call you later."

I turned toward my brother's car, but I was dazed, and walking on air. I did call Mary later, and the rest of the weekend went by in a series of bits, pieces, and blurs.

Some teachers are sports fans and some aren't. I was lucky. When Monday came, my afternoon teachers approved my absence from their classes so I could go to the gym to watch Game Seven between the Yankees and the Giants. I was not surprised by the number of kids in that gym, since most of our teachers were compassionate. As the game started, I was sitting with Mary and Danny, and we were transfixed on the three television sets brought in for the occasion by Chrome Dome and the other coaches. I was a little concerned because Willie was a no-show at game time. Mary figured one of his teachers wouldn't let him out and he would probably join us after the class period ended.

The game turned into a pitcher's duel between Jack Sanford and Ralph Terry. The Yankees scored a run in the fifth on a double play RBI by Tony Kubek. As the game went into the sixth inning, Willie was still conspicuous in his absence. It pained me that he had teachers who wouldn't allow him to watch this ultimate contest of the baseball season.

When the eighth inning ended, the score was still 1 to 0, in favor of the World Champion Yankees. Suddenly, the doors to the gym opened, and Willie entered. He looked around and I waved at him to join us. As he made his way into the stands to our position, I noticed he was in a sullen, almost angry mood. He gave a heavy sigh as he plopped down beside me on the wooden bench.

"What's wrong?" I asked.

"I don't want to talk about it now. Is it still one to nothing?"

"Yeah, and the ninth is coming up. What's wrong?" I asked. "What the heck happened to you?"

"I'll tell you later," he said, stopping my inquiry. It seemed like his eyes were puffy from crying. I decided not to pursue the matter any further, knowing he would tell me when he was good and ready. We never hid anything from each other -- for us, that's what best friends were all about.

The Yankees went down one, two, three in the top of the ninth, setting the stage for a classic finish to a classic series. Matty Alou, pinch-hitting for the pitcher, led off with a bunt single. Ralph Terry then struck out the next two Giants, bringing Willie Mays to the plate representing the winning run. The crowd barely had time to get excited before the Say Hey Kid came through in the clutch with a smash down the third base line for a double. Tom Tresh retrieved the ball and fired it to Kubek in the cutoff position, which forced the Giants third base coach to hold Alou at third.

With two outs, the tying run ninety feet away, and Mays representing the winning run on second base, the power-hitting lefty, Willie McCovey, stepped up to the plate. Ralph Houk asked for time and approached the mound. Surprisingly, he not only chose to leave Terry in the game, but also decided to pitch to McCovey. Everyone knew trying to pitch to McCovey was dangerous. But even more so, Orlando Cepeda, who was on deck, had been killing the Yankee pitchers during the entire series. On Terry's third pitch to the slugger, McCovey hit the hardest ball of the seven games, smashing a screaming line drive that second baseman, Bobby Richardson, was barely able to grab out of the sky. Instead of the double that scored a victory for the Giants, it became the third out, ended the series, and gave the Yankees their 20th World Series title. Sudden drama is the trademark of baseball, whether one is describing Little League, or the pros who play in the World Series. But, it was over, and I knew the Yankee win wouldn't help Willie's mood.

The game ended at exactly the same time the final school bell rang. We had fifteen minutes before we had to report for football practice and I needed to know what was bothering Willie earlier. I excused myself from Mary with a promise to call her in the evening. Willie and I walked out the back of the gymnasium and sat down on a bench by the tetherball poles. After I set my textbooks on the bench between us, I gently placed a hand on Willie's shoulder.

"You must have some pretty rotten teachers," I suggested, "if they wouldn't let you out of class for the seventh game of the World Series."

"That wasn't it."

"It can't be that bad," I said with a nudge. "What is it, buddy?"

He looked me in the eye with the countenance of death. A single tear ran down his cheek, and his lips quivered as he prepared to speak.

"We're moving to Texarkana."

"WHAT!" I blurted out. "No way."

"Pop's work takes him up there all of the time, so my folks decided to move there so we could spend more time together."

I was stunned. Beyond stunned. I'd heard the words, but their exact meaning didn't compute. This was the last thing I ever expected and I simply couldn't fathom my best friend and blood brother moving away.

"When do you have to leave?" I asked.

"My mother took me out of school today," Willie mumbled, in the saddest voice I ever heard. "We move on Wednesday."

"That's not fair. We were going to play basketball together," I said with waves of emotion tugging at my voice. "This can't be happening."

"My folks have known for a while, but didn't know how to tell me."

"This ain't right. What about 'all for one and one for --'"

I was suddenly interrupted by a nasty voice behind us.

"How's your dog, nigger-lover?" Noah Parkes growled at the back of my neck.

Willie stood up and unflinchingly faced Noah, "How's your car, Cracker?"

228

"Did you have something to do with my car, Nigger?"

I stood up, joined Willie, and faced the brute. "Noah, you're an ignorant asshole!"

Without thinking, or blinking, I snapped my leg and viciously kicked Noah in the groin as hard as I could. He doubled over in obvious pain, but to my surprise, he didn't fall.

"And you always will be!" shouted Willie as he grabbed my textbook from the bench and raised it above his head.

He slammed that book like a hammer on the back of Noah's head. The bully stumbled forward three quick steps and violently rammed his head into the tetherball pole, whereupon his knees buckled and he collapsed, unconscious, into the dirt like a big sack of laundry.

Willie and I looked at each other like we just turned a triple play, busting at the seams with an adrenaline rush. We smiled, lifted our arms, and gave each other a high five as we simultaneously shouted, "Yes!"

****

The distant, shrill whistle of the Southern Pacific freight train passing between Clarksville and Tarrytown brought me back from my childhood and deposited me into the present with an almost brutal abruptness. Standing on the worn mound in the overgrown Clearing of my youth, I smiled at the image of Noah Parkes receiving his comeuppance. Luckily for me, when Noah regained consciousness, he had total amnesia from two blows to the head and never remembered his confrontation with Willie and me. Soon after the incident by the tetherball pole, Noah's mother remarried and the family moved to the East side of town where Noah was forced to attend the predominantly black Kealing Junior High. The bigot was sentenced to his own private hell, and the irony was not lost on me.

The undulating months of 1962 represented the high watermark year in the growth of my character and the loss of my innocence. I saw racism and found the best reason to stand against it. I experienced the bliss of love, betrayed it, and then found it again. I discovered the ultimate sensation

229

of winning and found balance in the emotional thunderbolt of losing. I experienced new worlds and new cultures that existed outside of Texas as I toured the countryside of America with my teammates on our unforgettable journey to Williamsport.

Somehow, through some magical adolescent transformation, the world beyond my neighborhood was closer, and the largest impediments to my growing up, faded. Visiting New York City had opened my eyes to the universe of possibilities that existed for each and every one of us in this land of opportunity. Meeting my hero, Mickey Mantle, was the whipped cream on top of the pudding. And, perhaps most importantly, all of those experiences were woven into, or wrapped around, my groundbreaking friendship with Willie Veils.

I met him in The Clearing when I beaned him on the side of the head and as fast as our friendship had budded, the vicious wheels of fate ploughed it under. Two days after our tag-team knockout of Noah Parkes, I stood in Willie's driveway and waved goodbye to my friend as Walter and Teresa's truck motored down the rutted streets of Clarksville. Willie and I, in a tearful goodbye a few moments before, had promised to stay in touch. How were we to know that the world around us would change so suddenly, and darken that which had blossomed in the light.

On the very night Willie left Austin for Texarkana, our President appeared on television to inform us that we were on the brink of nuclear war. The Russians were shipping planes and bombs to Cuba, which he contended, could reduce the Southern United States to nothing but radioactive ash. Paranoia began to creep into the consciousness of everyone I knew. Fear became a constant. The pursuit of happiness had to take a back seat until the crisis ended some eleven days later. Unfortunately, the paranoia didn't. That's about when people in mid-America started digging bomb shelters in their back yards.

We were all scared, but like most Americans, it was many years later that I learned just how close to disaster we had come. Sadly, wars and rumors of wars continued. Assassinations occurred. Scandals ripped at the fabric of people's beliefs. Dark powers were striking in the shadows and innocence was only one of the victims in the decades that followed. It certainly died in the white kid from West Austin and the jet-legged black kid from Clarksville.

About ten days after the Cuban Missile Crises became a footnote in the history of the Cold War, I received a letter from Willie. He wrote how much he missed Austin and everyone he had met during the summer our dreams came true. He despised his life in Texarkana, and felt more isolated and oppressed than in the worst days in his homey confines back in Clarksville. He wrote that his family was living in some temporary projects until they could move into an apartment or a house. Ever the optimist as a kid, Willie offered a final perspective when he finished his letter with the thought, "No matter how bad it gets, I plan to work hard and stay cool."

I immediately sat down and wrote a reply, filling him in on the progress of our flag football team and my relationship with Mary. I thanked him again for introducing us that fateful day at Barton Springs. I invited him to come visit me during Christmas break, if he could. I finished the letter and sailed it off into the U.S. Postal ether and anxiously awaited the next report.

Two weeks later, my letter came back unopened. The post office stamped the explanation:

Return to Sender – NOT AT THIS ADDRESS

I tried to find a way to locate my friend, but it was not to be. For whatever reason, he never wrote me again, and we subsequently lost touch. I tried to locate Willie many times over the years, but was unsuccessful. I always wondered what happened to him. It struck me as funny almost, how somebody you only knew for a very short time could stick in your mind as long as Willie had stuck in mine.

Looking back, my relationship with Willie had taught me several valuable lessons. Knowing him taught me that compassion and tolerance were essential to peace. I strove to live my life, after our brief but vital companionship, with a non-judgmental attitude. I came to understand that people may be either stubbornly opinionated or open to change, flawed or solid as a rock, of every different color and style or a carbon copy of the neighbors, and almost all of us are prejudiced in one way or another. I came to believe that God conceived the essence of everyone walking this planet, no matter where we happened to be from or what color of skin or religion we might have been born into. And that was a dump truck load to learn as I transitioned into a teen.

I glanced at my watch and was amazed at how long I had been daydreaming. I only had about thirty minutes to shower and dress before I attended our 35th high school reunion at the Zilker Park Clubhouse. I was suddenly excited about seeing all of my old teammates, but there was a special curiosity about seeing Kitty and Mary again, after so many years.

Unfortunately, for me, Mary had moved on to an older boy from another school by the time we were in ninth grade, but I remember fondly the two years we were boyfriend and girlfriend at O. Henry. The last time I saw Mary was at our twenty-year high school reunion. When I met her husband and daughter at the picnic that year, we briefly talked about those seventh grade days when we were experiencing the throes of puppy love. We talked about Willie, and speculated about the fact he had disappeared from the face of the earth. We all agreed how unfortunate it was that we lost touch with him. Mary said she was going to try to locate him, but I got a letter from her a few months later saying she had run into dead ends. The pangs of that left me even more anxious to see everyone else.

After a quick shower back at my parent's townhouse, I dressed casually chic in some brand new clothes purchased for the occasion. On the way to the reunion, I decided to drive by my old childhood residence and was astounded by the construction of a massive new house, dwarfing the size of the home of my youth. It completely obliterated the great yard in which we used to play. Then, taking a small detour on the way to the party, I passed through Clarksville, wondering what Willie's old yellow house looked like, and I found another surprise. The developers had moved in and purchased all the houses in Clarksville and turned the old black village of Willie and his kin into a neighborhood of white upper-middle class condos and trendy restaurants. "Hum, nothing stays the same," I mumbled to myself. "I wonder where all the Black families went?"

After a short five-minute drive from Clarksville, I pulled into the packed parking lot of the Zilker Club House. It was located on a hill overlooking the lake with a stunning view of the growing skyline of downtown Austin. On the outdoor patio a band was entertaining the crowd, and to my additional surprise, it was made up of some of my classmates. Standing just inside the gate, beers in hand, I found Jack, Stan, and Danny.

We exchanged high fives and hugs. Danny said, "We followed Ben today at the Seniors' tournament at Lakeway. He shot a three-under."

We had all followed Ben Crenshaw's golfing career. He was from Tarrytown and had been a teammate of mine on Rylanders when I was ten and eleven.

I smiled at my old friends and sardonically queried, "Can you believe, we are considered senior citizens?"

Suddenly, hands covered my eyes from behind. I heard, "Guess who?"

It could have only been one person, "Kitty, I know it's you." As she released her hands, I turned and gazed into the eyes of my first crush. "You look great."

We hugged and kissed each other on the cheek.

"So do you," she said. "How's Hollyweird?"

"I'm staying busy. Just finished work on a Rob Reiner film that's pretty funny."

"You won't believe this! My daughter, Kelly, wants to be an actress. She's moving to L.A. in a couple of months to pursue her dream."

"Have her call me after she's settled in, and I'll try to give her some pointers. It's a tough nut to crack out there, but I wish her the best."

Kitty took my hand and whispered in my ear, "Did I hear you were recently divorced?"

"Bad news travels fast."

"Well, let's see -- who is single? There's been a few split-ups here in Austin, you know," Kitty whispered with a glint in her eye.

"Are you still married to number two husband?"

"Yes. Happily, I might add," Kitty said with emphasis. Then, she lit up like a candle. "But, you know who is recently available?"

"Who?" I asked.

"Mary."

"Mary is single!" I stated, perking up noticeably. "Where is she?"

"She had to do something with her daughter. But, her divorce was final last week, so she'll be here to celebrate her new found freedom."

"I'm thirsty. Where's the beer?" I asked, suddenly parched from the thought of seeing Mary again -- single.

"This way," Kitty said. Still holding onto my hand she led me through the throng and inside to the bar.

As I was about to ask Kitty what she would like to drink, she spotted someone and excused herself. I ordered a beer from the bartender and placed a buck in the tip jar. I scanned the room as I took a long cold drink of the suds. Suddenly, there she was, in the doorway -- the object of more than one teenage fantasy, and a ghost that lingered still.

Mary waved at me and indicated she wanted me to join her. I moved toward her and she looked more beautiful with every step I took. I gave her a hug that she was very slow to release, and I melted when she looked in my eyes, just like I did that first day at Barton Springs.

"It's good to see you, Mickey," Mary said with sparkling eyes.

"You look great, Mary," I said, trying desperately not to drool. "How do you manage to get prettier with time?"

"Thanks, you're so kind."

"It's the truth."

She smiled for a moment, then she looked me over, "I heard you were recently single again."

"I heard the same thing about you. We must be sharing the same spies."

"Before we do anything about that, I have a surprise for you," Mary said. "Close your eyes until I tell you to look. No peeking."

I closed my eyes for a moment or two before she said, "Okay, open."

Standing in front of me was a middle-aged black man, smiling like the Cheshire cat. Despite the gray hair, and years of aging etched on his face, he was instantly recognizable.

"I'll be a son of a bitch," I mumbled.

"Hello, my blood brother," Willie said as he stepped toward me.

We embraced one another in the magic of the moment. Releasing my grip from around my old buddy, I turned to Mary.

"How did you find him?"

"I tried a number I found on the Internet and Willie answered. I invited him to the party. Doesn't he look great?" Mary placed her arms around both of our shoulders.

"How's that lump on your head?" I asked with as straight a face as I could muster. "Swellin's almost down," he replied, with a slight tilt of his head.

"I can't believe this. It is really great to see you. I was reminiscing about our trip to Williamsport just today."

"We had a great run, didn't we?"

"We sure did. Can we all sit down and bring each other up to speed?"

"Let me get a Dr Pepper first," Willie stated, accompanied by the belly laugh that I remembered from the past.

After Willie got his soda and brought Mary a beer, we all sat down at a table overlooking the city lights. As the band played old favorites in the background, we caught up with each other. Ironically, it became evident that all of the events of our youth had a significant influence on each of us.

Willie never got my letter because his father had died suddenly, from a heart attack shortly after they had arrived in Texarkana. Another change followed when his mother decided to move in with her sister in Corsicana, Texas. He said he was in a dark mood for a while after the sudden loss and didn't feel like communicating with anyone. After a second move, Willie told us that the memory of his Austin days dimmed. To get past the anguish, Willie said he had continued to play baseball. In fact, he bragged a little about becoming a three-sport star at Corsicana Jackson High School in the all black Prairie View Interscholastic League.

The segregated Texas High School football program had been incorporated into the previously all white University Interscholastic League after 1968, which had been our senior year. So, it made sense, I had never heard of Willie's exploits, as the Austin American-Statesman didn't cover the Prairie View League. I asked if he had tried to go to college or play professionally in any of the sports. He said in their 1968 state football championship 31-

6 victory over Gladewater Weldon, he tore up his knee on a run late in the game. It had been pretty bad and never really healed properly. He lost his jets, but not his desire. So, after four years at a community college in Houston, he landed a job as an assistant baseball coach. Eventually, he had become the head coach at Yates High School where he had been enlightening the kids who played for him for the past 19 years. His bright self-confidence and faith in overcoming hardships that I had witnessed so many years ago, had obviously served him well in his adult life.

Mary had recovered from the recent loss of her first marriage and was successfully raising her daughter and working for an uncle in his floral business. It seemed fitting, as she was beautiful and had a knack for dealing with people. Listening to her talk about her daughter exposed something that didn't surprise anybody. She appeared to be a stand-up parent and mother, and she was raising a fine daughter with a lot of love.

As for myself, I found a form of confirmation about friendships and memories of days gone by. I discovered that which was previously lost to me, could be found in the endless loops that life affords. It's funny. I also learned that the past could come walking through the door in the present.

The band started playing "The Twist," and all of our classmates started toward the dance floor. Mary looked at us and said, "Shall we join 'em?"

Willie and I nodded and stood up, and in a flash we were arm in arm with Mary and walking across the patio.

"Wow, guys," she said. "This is too familiar. Just like the old days again."

THE END

ACKNOWLEDGMENTS

In the writing of this book, I am indebted to a great many people and sources, but particularly to the following:

Genie Callahan, a true friend, for getting me started, listening and motivation.

My father, Stuart Benson, for his coaching, proof reading and support.

Amy Heinlen for her editorial suggestions and helping me finish.

And, finally, Max Swafford of Tradewinds Publications for all of his hard work copy editing my manuscript.

Thanks to David Dulak at Red Sky Creative for cover photography and photo shop editing.

I would like to acknowledge Baseball- Almanac (www.baseball-almanac.com) for providing the background image of the classic Yankees Stadium on the front cover.

Made in the USA
Lexington, KY
20 June 2014